CW00341583

Vitus Dreams

ADAM CRAIG

CinnamonPress

INDEPENDENT INNOVATIVE INTERNATIONAL

Published by Cinnamon Press
Meirion House,
Glan yr afon,
Tanygrisiau
Blaenau Ffestiniog,
Gwynedd, LL41 3SU
www.cinnamonpress.com

The right of Adam Craig to be identified as author of this work has been asserted by him in accordance with the Copyright, Designs and Patent Act, 1988.
Copyright © 2015 Adam Craig

ISBN: 978-1-909077-67-6

British Library Cataloguing in Publication Data. A CIP record for this book can be obtained from the British Library.

All design and typesetting by Adam Craig for Cinnamon Press.
Printed in Poland.

Cinnamon Press is represented in the UK by Inpress Ltd *www.inpressbooks.co.uk* and in Wales by the Welsh Books Council *www.cllc.org.uk*

ACKNOWLEDGEMENTS

The publisher acknowledges the financial support of the Welsh Books Council.

for Ned, who believed
&
for Jan, who believes

VITUS BERING dreams of the sea before he finds it. Before he dreams of it, the sea does not exist. Bearing Vitus before it, the sea washes against the shore of a new land. The land, new, golden in sunshine, holds out its hands to accept Vitus bearing dreams from the sea, dreamed into being for this day. Found, the golden shore murmurs as it washes stones in the new sunshine, murmurs as stones wash, turned over in each hand and held out against the coming sea washing over each new dream.

AND WHAT dreams they are, those dreams of a sea unfound, its waves needing only Vitus to close his eyes before they rise again. Filling the inside of his mind, head a globe turned outside in. Each shoreline a suture; each suture a shore washed by the sea murmuring in his sleep. Sleep bringing it to life as it rolls gently behind Vitus's eyes. Back and forth, bearing Vitus Bering forth and back. Borne along on each wave of dream. Each dreamed of wave.

VITUS TURNS.
    Turned, Vitus looks. Looking, Vitus sees.
    Turning Vitus looking, seeing, until eyes, drawn from here to there, see Vitus. See Vitus! Looking, Vitus sees:
    Bedroom dark, bedclothes awry, rumpleclothes folded and rucked, undulating across the bed across Vitus crossing the room. Watching the curtains thrown wide. Seeing the curtains, thrown, opening Vitus's arms wide, both openwide — arms, curtainsthrown, eyesopen — to see, looking back, a wall.
    Not a window. All brick. Brick framed by curtains, arms thrownwide. Murmuring. Cloth turned back to see a wall, murmuring, 'This is wall', seeing brick, murmuring, hearing curtain rings clatter, murmuring 'This is', hearing curtains thrownwide, seeing murmuring.

The sea murmurs on the other side of the wall, voice lowfound but unmistakable. Beckoning.

Ah, says Vitus, mouth closed but voice, murmuring, unmistakable, I'm dreaming.

Vitus is dreaming.

He parts the wall. A curtainwall parting so Vitus can step through. Arms thrown wide, inviting.

Vitus steps across the market square. Across rooftops. Vitus steps across the width of Jutland in a single step. Steps and thinks nothing of it. Falling asleep in Petersburg, waking in the place where he was born: Think nothing of it, Vitus, you're dreaming.

And Vitus, without stopping, takes hold of shore, not just of land but familiar waters, steps forward without a second thought and throws wide his arms. Turning sky for land; streets, familiar since childhood, for cloud. Familiar waters for a sea that, until he closed his eyes, did not exist. But which is real now.

Once dreamlike but now well founded, the sea washes overhead. Murmuring as its waves turn, undulating from shore to horizon, turning, washed in moonlight, to foam over rocks overhead, land founded well, now, but dreamlike once.

Vitus lies back on the edge of the Sea of Knowledge.

The land, unknown until Vitus closed his eyes, emerges from the sea. Rocks wet, glimmering in the moonlight. Sea, turning (from familiar to marketplace, Petersburg to horizon), finds new inlets to inscribe, drawing stone over stone, until a new shape forms, drawing itself overhead as Vitus, lying back (lying now on the shore of the Sea of Islands), looks ahead, seeing it rise out of the waves. A head. Foaming, formed out of stones and rocks back and forth, forthandback, as the sea opens wide its hands to reveal the headland.

The land turns. Sea turning as it washes the horizon, sand and rocks, Vitus walking ashore as the first rains begin to fall.

Turned, the land opens wide its arms, head rising from the waves, rising overhead as the rains fall, murmuring, falls, pools, forms a sea of its own.

The headland sees. Watched, Vitus looks back. Eye looking into eye, arms held wide. Turning as the sea turns. Baring rocks, cliffoot and covemouth. Eye to eye.

I, thinks Vitus, thoughts growing vague in the falling rain.

I, thinks a head. One head or the other. Rain falling as waves turn, making landscapes foam. Vaguely turning one into another into novelty until sea turns into sky into land into Vitus lying back on the shore, head looking down. Land looking back. Heads looking seawards, Vitus seen afterwards. Hands wide and still, still turning one over the other, heading landwards.

I am dreaming, says the headland, covemouth closed against the foaming Vitus.

No, insists Vitus, open mouth close against the waves, arms spreading wider, this is my dream, I am dreaming you, I am —

Vitus wakes.

AWAKE, THEY show him maps. Lands inked in, seas shaded. Lines turning to sepia at the extremities; fading, gradually, until there is only white, unbroken white, glacial and unbreachable. Along the fringe, where map returns to virgin paper: marks and symbols. This point is known. And this, too, they say, pointing, fingers leaping thousands of miles of emptiness, travelling back and forth between marks. And between? he asks, seeing the answer pass, wave over wave, behind his eyes. Ah, they say, peering as map fades into paper. Fingers hovering. Face over hand over drawing. Clearly land unbroken, is their answer. Land unseen, unfounded perhaps, but land. As here (they point) and here (point marked) so obviously here, they tell him, drawing certainty from absence. Do you see?

Vitus, staring, says nothing.

Vitus sleeps that night. In his bed, in the room, where the dream has come before.

He is undisturbed and the tide, founded in sleep, fails to return.

THE WHISPERING.

The whispering is beginning to remind him of surf. Of waters' rasp. Waves turning page over page of gossip against a shore of pebbles, sand. Undermining. Diverting the sea's course. Innuendo accreting into bars and spits, so everywhere he goes hides shoals that, until he dreamed, did not exist. Each day, navigating each day becomes harder, a wake frothing behind him wherever he goes, foam rolling back into shore, breaking over the stones he dreamt.

Whispering.

Your honour, sir.

Your service, Captain.

Bandy-legged men bow as he walks past, thoughts running deep under currents of polite deference. Every corridor, every room, grits underfoot as the silt of words left high by his appearance settles out. Innuendo come to slack water, bandiments stilled by the appearance of their source and target.

Vitus nods, says nothing.

Nods and winks say everything.

Hearsay.

It whispers, rasps over lips churning what he discovered in sleep into shapes and forms unrecognisable. A land illfounded, seas unknown, but whispering all the time, always turning word over word, spittle cresting white at the edge of lips, only to fall, draw back, come in again, drawing new breath and, in each breath, modelling itself anew. Behindhand. Undertone. Inlets awash with these tides of speculation. Saying all he heard and saw was phantasm, delusion. In dream, yes. Knowing such lands are confined within his head, of course. But to let those figments spill beyond waking? Never. In letting himself be beguiled by these fancies, Vitus washes his hands of reason.

Disillusioned by what is being bandied so freely, Vitus adopts silence, a marked indifference. Words hurt as deeply as stones. He pretends otherwise and, in pretending, feels distance. Distance growing, separating. A notion taking hold in its wake until, each day, each day becomes that little more unfamiliar: a vision bent through a lens of abstraction. Because, each day, Vitus struggles not to feel that waking is a dream. And dreaming awake.

VITUS LIES sleepless.

> *Vitus, old man. Dreamt any undiscovered oceans lately?*

Vitus lies. Sleepless.

> *Captain, I have maps, charts which prove — see you: sailors'*
> *accounts of Lemuria, Hyperborea — if we might talk —*

Vitus, sleepless, lies.

Have to admire your conviction, Captain, but what next? a voyage to the moon in a chair drawn by a wedge of swans?

Do you think it's catching?

Sleepless lies Vitus.

scribe and chandler smile, quite courteously, a shipwright standing to one side waiting until there is opportunity to approach the captain, a plan tightly furled in one hand as he watches the portly gentleman attempting to monopolise the captain's time sweep a deep bow, 'I say, **Vitus**, if I might have a word? **is** it your intention to …' rest of the question lost in hammering, shipyard busy this day, man's expression **adrift** without words to anchor it **in** some context before the next interruption: **a** young apprentice begging the captain's leave, **mist** of sawdust coating the lad's face, the portly gentleman's interruption —— 'sound idea, yes?' —— **muffled** by more hammering, and the shipwright's deferential cough, only for this also to be interrupted by an old woman selling sweetmeats, although the exact identity of the **objects** in her tray, each **soft** and greasy, is **uncertain** and she is dismissed by the shipwright with a coin and a word —— no one is hungry and one less distraction is all to the good because the yard swarms with **people** this morning and there is a great deal to do, a long list of tasks to be **reduced** at least a little —— 'I say, Vitus, I know you're busy, but what do you say **to** ——' —— a hundred things to be done and the **ghosts** of a hundred and one more standing at his shoulder, waiting their turn and chance

Little by little, Vitus builds a wall around himself.

VITUS WAS thinking of a map. Undrawn, as yet, although he could feel its outlines and contours, the topography of the sea and land it would depict. A Euclidean plane is flat. But out of it grow hills, rivers. Coastlines. Sea washing against headlands arising out of two-dimensional surfaces. Maps represent these things, Vitus thought as he sat at the table thinking about the map, a map as yet undrawn but so clear to him that Vitus could see it, practically touch it, laid across the ledgers and bills of lading spread across this table he was sitting at. The sky slipping into cliffs, headland declining under waves, each of them white-tipped before turning blue, blue turning darker as shore becomes bed, slipping ever further from sight. Leaving the sea, blue, the sky, burnished by the sun. And all of it thrown into relief by marks on a sheet of paper. A map. A picture. Vitus saw both on the table.

'With the Captain's permission, we should listen to the shipwright's report ...'

One laid over the other, as one ends and the other begins.

'Even if the repairs are completed on time, Captain, provisioning will take ...'

One's lines and marks becoming the key to the other's symbols which, in turn, conjured those self-same marks and lines.

'Do you not think, Captain?'

Landscape impressed on to the paper Vitus saw unfurled before him as clearly as the paper, once drawn, could impress the landscape into his mind. Vitus, mind, landscape and paper linked always. Inseparable, even should he not draw map, sketch picture, because Vitus saw them clearly on the table, in his mind, in front of him, spread between his outstretched —

'Captain Bering?'

Vitus looked up. Saw figures sketched around the landscape of the table. Symbols for faces looking towards him. He looked down at the open books and loose sheafs of paper lying between

his outstretched hands. And —
   'Yes?'
   — cannot make sense of any of it.
   Just, in fact, as if it were a dream.

VITUS LAY awake. In his bed, on his back. Vitus, lying, a wake falling away behind him as he blinked. Expecting to see … But, no, the image faltered as he blinked, falling away behind his eyes, a tide going out. Shape losing depth. Becoming confused with the phantom lights clinging to his eyes each time they closed. Some flowing golden. Most go red; or a yellow turning to sepia. Ghostshapes lingering amongst them only to slip away. To slipswift grow pale, as rain on rock grows pale under a sun peering between fading clouds. Sun golden, looking newfound. Stones looking wan, seeming found and lost. Washed hand over hand by the rain until, unsure, the rain loses its grip. Growing pale as the sun appeared through the window, slipping out of reach, with each blink ebbing as Vitus Bering woke.

A WASH of colour. Vitus looks at the picture: sky pale, sapphire ebbing into pink as he remembers. And a sun, yellow slipping into orange slipping over the cliffs. Headland falling backwards, never quite closing, watercolour turning grey-green into green-brown where the cave lies open, lips parted as it looks out on to the mouth of the cove, the duns and amber of the shore. Almost done, thinks Vitus as the brush, heavy-loaded, washes over blues (sapphire like the sky like ultramarine flowing on the water into lapis, leisurely, because Vitus is taking care guiding the brush) across indigoes (swirling darker, amethyst shelving into heliotrope as depth increases, land hidden yet falling away, caught by the brush coming back), water pooling, settling into paper turning green nearer the rocks (aquamarine), turning away elsewhere (paper left white, naked at the falling tip of a wave), rolling on until the land cups it all between its hands. A cove awash.

Vitus lifts the brush. Ignores the droplet forming at its tip. Looks only at the paper. At the blue wash between cove and sky.

This is like a dream, Vitus thinks, absorbed in the paper as water and paint are themselves absorbed. No longer aware of the walls of the room, the table beneath his elbows.

This is the dream, Vitus says, moving. Eyes on the watercolour. Hand stretching out to put brush into jar.

Vitus upsets the water.

It spills across the table, across the painting. Water flows over the sea, washing against the headland, the base of the cliff. Blue waves take over the shore. Sky becomes land become sea. Picture ebbing, ablur until there is only water and paper, and Vitus, upset, knows he has lost something again.

HE RECOGNISES the seal on the letter, knowing it for what it is without needing to break wax, look inside.

The whispering churns around the shipyard, aflow with ebb and flood. Spring tide, now the letter has been placed in his hand. He hears the hiss of each wave above the sound of wood being moulded into ship. Foaming around the letter resting on his palm.

The *seal* unbroken. Knowing it for what it is.

A letter, comprised of letters forming words that mean more than their shapes and sounds present at face. Currents hidden under a surface of courtly phrase. Paper folded under wax, cypher masked in ink.

A summoning. His Imperial Highness, insulated from all by his elevation above the realm of man, even he has heard the whispering. Perhaps the Emperor hopes to annex the lands rising out of the sea undreamt these past weeks.

Vitus looks across the shipyard. The wall around him blunts, distances: heavy with covert meaning, the letter weighs nothing in his palm. Much like the shipyard, the lips whispering. Anything that can be seen with open eyes, the translucent wall makes hazy, ill-defined. A lucency.

A lucid dream.

VITUS DREAMS. He dreams of what appears lost. Dreams waking from one dream and submerging into another. Dreams of all this going away. Of all this being true. He dreams of sleeping and sleeping to dream once again. Vitus dreams of dreams but the dreams stay firmly away.

None of this is true.

Is some of this still true?

Vitus sucks deep on the opium pipe. It brings reverie but no dream. A drifting but no revelation. Only a mood grown starker, a sense more acute.

A still sense, pervading. A sense still and inescapable. No matter how I try.

VITUS OPENS his eyes.

Vitus, eyes open, stares. Openwide, Vitus staring stares at the room: a chair, a table, and on the table ... of course, it lies unopen. Door closed likewise, chamber more full of shadows than staring-Vitus, who is also sitting-Vitus, who is also ill-humoured-Vitus and sleepless-Vitus. So many people in such a small room! So many and a chair, a table, a truckle bed

— Was the bed there before? Vitus leans forward. If this is a bedchamber, thinks leaning-Vitus, there must be a — At that, leaning-Vitus pauses, aware there is someone else in the room, a someone who had not been here moments before. Leaning-Vitus leans, eyes openwide. Staring. Vitus staring examines the room: a chair, a table, and on the table it lies with its seal unbroken. Much as before likewise.

Leaning-Vitus sits back, vanishing.

The letter remains. As does the smell of opium and the scent, faint and coming in waves with each motion of moving-Vitus, of an unwashed body, sweat becoming rank, like seaweed abandoned by the ebbtide.

Vitus freezes still.

Moving-Vitus vanishes. No sign of a bed, likewise the letter remains.

Vitus stares, wondering.

Wondering-Vitus tries to think things through. Systematically, wondering-Vitus decides. Which systematic-Vitus attempts, only to falter at the curious vanishment-transformation of wondering-Vitus.

Seal unbroken. Curtains closed. Chamber enclosed by a wall. Defined by the wall, in fact. A table, a chair, a Vitus.

Systematic-Vitus stops thinking.

The bedchamber remains, although a second chair appears: the one Vituses have been sitting on all along. Otherwise, the room is quite empty.

THE MAP that never was quite a map, was almost something more, is dry now. It feels itself curling, that sweep of colour which once made its face awash gone. Not washed away, simply gone.

Light comes through the window, rummages around the room. Casts shadows out of dust collecting on shelves, turns the brushes around in the jar. Making them spin, bristle, spin. Not one word does the light say to the map that was wet, the map that was nearly finished. Not one. And the map, curling, likewise chooses silence, likewise pretends there is no one else in the room, waiting until the light begins nosing along the sideboard against the other wall. The map, furling, rolls off the table, bouncing itself across the floor, away from the light and otherwall, its open ends giving away the softest *pop*, scroll-like, as the map angles through the rectangular hole in the walls and out into the rest of the house. For a moment, as it crosses the threshold of doorway into hallway into roombeyond, the map-that-was-to-be-so-much-more longs to distract itself with thoughts of *W*s: how presence or absence of same can denote lack or encompass presence, how *hole* becomes *whole*. Perhaps, thinks the map in that time of crossing, *W*s can heal, might be the symbol of the Philosopher's Stone and, in symbolising, so embody, if only for a moment, a transition from nothing to something, *W*s encompassing hole and all that might conceivably replace that absence, all in a single letter. Compressed, one might say. Only the map doesn't. In the moment of crossing hallway into oppositeroom, it dismisses this fancy for what it is. Instead, the map stops moving.

The light is in here, too. It is making the air the colour of scuffed gold; the shadows it stains a little indigo, mostly a brown the map instinctively thinks of as sepia. A snatch of music comes through a wall. Ends after less than a phrase, becoming silence and giving no hint what might be hidden by the wall, an exterior wall, which is a wall outside. The wall seems not to want to be part of the room. It stands back from the light, pressing itself upwards, as if pressing up against something, another wall, say, as if the exterior wall was a man, a man not wanting to get involved and raised up on tiptoe, as if the floor was being invaded, spread-over, awash.

Only light spilling across the carpets, staining them yellow. Staining the furniture it touches yellow, the shadows sepia, setting dust motes fall-fall-falling, glimmering. But making no noise.

The map slips out of the room. Wanders, nextroom to nextroom. Goes over the whole house. Finds walls. Finds furniture, carpets. Finds light touching somerooms; shadows in allrooms. The wholehouse over. Things everywhere, something everyplace.

Still a sense of absence. A still sense of absence.

Gently, the map unfurls.

    Colours remain. Faded.

    A smell of opium lingers in thisroom. Fading.

    Day leaks out of the walls, room dimming. Fadily.

    The map-that-never-was-completed looks at itself and has trouble making out how much has become lost, how much might never have been.

LIGHT DRAWS Vitus out of shadow. Revealing a little, a little more. A little more Vitus drawn from shade into light, gradually discovered, an unseen Vitus, only now uncovered, highlight defining shadow as shadow helps define accent or catchlight. Or knee. A knee appears, followed by another, a pair, bent but not broken, each supporting one hand, fistedhands resting one on each knee, each one joined at the wrist. Although after the wrist there is nothing to see. Imagine Vitus lying back, in a chair, on his back, the chair and Vitus lying in black water, lapping beneath kneesbent and fistedhands. The rest of Vitus invisible. Or beginning, because the light is moving again. Bringing arms into relief. A torso. Shoulders. Emerging from darkness as the level of black water falls, falls back from Vitus sitting just on its surface, just beneath. A part-submerged Vitus. Only not on his back. Sat upright, even if the shadows fall away just the same, brim and fall away from knees and arms until nose and chin appear. Just a little Vitusface breaking through. Light advancing. Or shadows receding. Either way moving. A little. A little more. Revealing a little more Vitus, eyes closed, expression little more than a guess as the shadows linger on, sculpting an outline of a forehead, the first trace of temple. The light draws Vitus, out of nothing, out of memory or phantasm, it hardly matters. Not now the temple of Vitus has been defined.

Gently, the map unfurls once again.

    Light falls. Outlining windowframe and winnowing out a sketch of the room. In silverpoint, not gold, too lowkey to set any dustmotes roving. But enough to see by. To watch a tree pass a hand over the window, over the face of the moon looking in. To find Vitus, sitting half in shadow, shadow settling back to reach forward again as the tree fans the darkness.

The wind inhales, room and house and roof above flexing with it. But the seas of the moon remain motionless as the moon, itself face-full, looks through the window at Vitus. A Vitus who had not been there during the day, the map is sure, remembering the hole in this room, the house that had been static but breathes now as the wind breathes, moving as the trees move. As the tree moves again.

Branches flickering, the tree makes another pass, knuckles clack-click, click-clacking against glass and frame, the magic words the wind fluffs, stumbles over. Another go (clack-click). And another (clack-clack), tree making a final pass. And there, as its hand falls away, is Vitus, revealed.

The map is not fooled. It is not the tree that has conjured Vitus out of an empty house.

In moonlight, in the flexing house, it looks at itself unfurled. What had been a wash, colours fading one into another into the edge of the paper, is replaced by lines clearly marked, shapes emerging, defining as they do so.

The map-that-is-a-map-no-more knows what to do.

It rains later. Clouds hide the moon, its seas no longer illuminated. Vitus also fades from view. Fades but is not lost.

Vitus blinked, disoriented. 'I tell you, old man, people simply adore a scandal.' Words. A mouth moving. Lips glistening. A face. 'And now this letter. Well, I mean to say —' Vitus blinked. And those parts (words, mouth, lips, face) that were separate, merged into a man, talking to, or rather at, Vitus. 'All agog they are, and His Imperial Majesty, may God keep watch over him, taking such —' Vitus tried not to panic. Not knowing where he was, how he got here, it would be easy to panic. Vitus concentrated on the talking man — 'Well, we admire your —' made an effort to understand — 'perhaps gone a little too —' and felt the room become more solid. 'You will think about it, won't you, old man?' Vitus nodded. Not to the man but to himself. Panic gone, more settled now he thought he knew what was happening. 'Good to have had this chat.' Vitus nodded, concentrating. 'We only want what's best for you, old man.' Vitus frowned, concentrating, more settled now he knew what was going on. 'Excellent.' But, no matter how hard he tried, Vitus could not make the man vanish, could not take control of this dream.

THE MAP rests on a table, a table that rests on a platform that has been built on ground that only appears stable. It will change. The map is adamant. Certain it already feels a tremble through the table through the platform from the ground: the tremble of transition, a waiting that will end. The table, meanwhile, remains steady; patient, too. Great workings take time. There are preliminaries, preparations before the ground can shift. It has inertia, Earth, being less vital than Fire, less mutable than Air. It must be coaxed, laboured over until the potential within it can be brought out. So: preparations, preliminaries. For instance, all the trees in the garden must go. Even the conjurer. That especially. The map (the-map-that-is-a-map-no-more-but-is-a-map-of-sorts) has been firm on this point. It distrusts the tree, suspects it would try to interfere, that it thinks of itself, that conjurer tree, as more than it appears. So thinks the map-that-is-not-exactly-a-map.

If there is irony in this, the workmen do not have time to enjoy it. There was a great deal required of them before they cut down the conjurer. If the map (should we start calling it the 'plan'? perhaps, but so much of itself is wrapped up in that word 'map' that it wouldn't be the same, not if the map) wants that particular tree cut down, no matter that it's nowhere near where the work will be carried out, what's one more job, one less tree? There was a great deal to do before. There is a great deal to do after.

They cut down the conjurer. Hurl its many-fingered branches on a pile, to wait. So much to do, no time to burn. The wind tugs at each limb. Shaking one branch, worrying another. Ignoring the stiffness of a knuckle, the dry complaints of each twig, of the conjurer's stiff hands. In moonlight, those twigfingers were nimble, nimblefingers flittering passes over the window clackety-click, flitterswift conjurer's hands. In greylight, lying on their sides, the prestidigitator has lost most, almost all, that dexterity. Dexterous hands no more, nor nimble fingered as the wind worries one, worries another. Worries what the conjurer might be planning after this.

The map rests on the table, on the platform, on the ground. The ground is not what it was, although it is no less stable under the platform under the table. Undermap: instructions, lists of materials, requirements, the foreman will receive in due time. At present, he stands on the platform before the table and listens. Or watches. The result should be the same. The map is adamant. Driven, in truth.

It lays out what is to be done next and next, and after that the map sets what else the foreman will have these workmen do. It, the map-that-appears-to-be-a-plan-of-sorts, describes each step, each step in turn. The map sets out the path that workmen and foreman are to take, from here to here to there you will wait for new direction, understand? The foreman nods: he understands. And the plan-that-was-a-map remains a map-of-sorts. Showing the way.

Trees burn, greenwood slow to catch. Leaves curl, briars knot in the heat. Each bush finds voice, even if it is almost the same voice, and chatter to the wind, telling it nonsense tales, words not so important as the shapes and rhythms of each brittle phrase, syllables cracking open to return some of the energy that went into making these twigs, those tendrils. Sun into root into fire.

The wind has smoke on its tongue.

Let us count this out, yes?

(This is the wind whispering in your ear, breath musky, every word per-fumed in birch and pine.)

Count with me: branch catches light. This is saying root combusts. Root is Earth, so Earth turns into Fire. This is the Transmutation Primus. Next, flames rise from burning tree, smouldering bush. Each flame attenuates, cooling resultantly until giving the appearance of total dissipation. Not so: Fire rises, cooling into Air. This is Transmutation Secundus.

And so we come to the final change.

(This is the wind whispering in your ear, voice husky, every word per-fused with disconcert.)

What is the final change?

So much ground has been cleared — so many trees, so many bushes — the fires burn through dusk. In the darkness, sparks bob, drift, bob, forming random consolations, nimble constellations that no doubt someone, somewhere, has tried to name and catalogue, searching out hidden meanings within their fluid paths.

The map has no interest in such knowledge. It rests on the table, the table standing in a back room of the house, beside a window overseeing the gardens, the smouldering fires, the night over all. The map is spread flat across the table yet remains strangely wrapped within itself, its attention rested deep within the course and directions inscribed over its upturned face.

Sparks billow, chasing the wind that gives them accidental form. A wind that vacillates between garden in flux and house in darkness. A wind grown hoarse, near mute, uninterested in the arcana of sparks.

The conjurer is not privy to such knowledges at all. It lies beyond the edge of the firelight. Overlooked, forgotten. Foreman and workforce had a great deal required of them as they turned offcuts into bonfires, a great deal to do after the fires were set. The conjurer lies where it was dumped, fingers stiff but not motionless, warmed by the glow from the fires, fires that smoulder, catch anew, send up fresh sparks.

Sparks do fly upwards. The conjurer will wait for them to dim, fall downwards again.

In the morning: ash, charcoal, cinders dead with cold.

In the afternoon: bare earth raked over, all trace of bonfire dug in, turned, levelled and put from thought.

Only an empty swathe of garden remains. Garden no more.

The map rests on the table, the table on its platform, platform seemingly all there is to see in the wilderness the long garden into has been transformed into. The map sees differently. To it, the shapes drawn across its face are already inset into bare earth, level ground. The potential is there, was there before, will be brought into concrete form in due time.

To the map, it feels as though that time has passed already. That what could be already is:

The land transformed. Risen up. Sculpted. Into a model scaled, a model so precise only size distinguishes represented from representation. The map sees what's in itself, projected on to bare earth:

A head.

i feel alone today
a bad taste in my mouth
the taste of ash
a taste going sour
& silence in my head
nothing moves
nothing speaks
only silence:
branch into earth
water running dry
fire gone cold
& air still

i am still this morning

there is nothing left to say

i feel alone today

And when the rains come, they fall straight, no force, too little strength to make much noise. Except for the metallic tap as droplets bead and drip, bead&drip, from knuckle after knuckle as first one branch wavers, another twitches.

imagine darkness, a darkened room and the
things within made vague   shapes,
no more and almost flat but for a grey
plane here, a hint of depth emerging there
your eyes growing accustomed

imagine tilting your head, eyes straining

imagine doubting there is anything there
imagine the surprise at making out Vitus
imagine thinking the room was empty and
finding him here   sitting against a
wall   half his face invisible, the other
half so faint it is hardly there   and
his hands

his hands are vague, hardly defined,
but imagine you can make them out
what do you see? are they clasped or is
Vitus writing, is Vitus drawing

is Vitus?   apparently, yes   in
grey and silver-grey, tones that would be
shadows elsewhere   a Vitus not quite
manifest but solid enough to see shoulder,
arms, hands almost   are they clasped
or is Vitus writing blindly?   but

there's no need to imagine jaw, nose, brow,
temple

Vitus' head, in front of your eyes
drawn from the darkness, has the weight of
substance, the presence of scale

his head seems to be the only thing real

the only thing here

AFTER A peremptory knock, the fat man threw open the door to the shipwright's office. Brocade, lace edging, the smell of pomander, girth squeezing other occupants aside.

'I say, where is Vitus, my good man?'

'The Captain?' The shipwright stared at the richly-appointed belly before his desk as if it were stomach not man addressing him. 'I have no knowledge, m'Lord.'

'What?' The gentleman's head swivelled on its cushions of chins to glance, oh so briefly, at the other occupants of the room — the chandler, Vitus's first mate, the chainsmith's apprentice — before settling on the shipwright again. 'Come, come, my good man, important chap like Vitus, you must have a notion, what? Chaps don't vanish, what?'

Shipwright began to open mouth, issue a fresh denial.

'Gorn off his head, poor Cap'n.' The chandler nudged the apprentice, stage whisper loud enough to cut through the din from the shipyard beyond the walls of this office.

The shipwright scowled, as did the First Mate. Chandler, smiling beatifically, pretended not to notice. Meanwhile, the fat man struggled, expression swirling over layers of fat: to recognise the voice of the social inferior or not. Distress won over snobbery, this time.

'The Captain is insane?'

'No.' Shipwright and First Mate spoke as one, loud enough to silence chandler and set the cheeks of the chainsmith's apprentice aglow with embarrassment.

'The Captain,' began the First Mate.

'Temporarily indisposed,' concluded the shipwright.

'Dash it, man.' Spittle peppered the cushions of the fat man's lips. 'What is wrong with Vitus? An ague, the flux or madness? Where is he?'

'At his house,' the shipwright admitted. 'But he has asked, m'Lord, not to receive visitors.'

'Locked inside, m'sire,' First Mate added.

'Indeed? Indeed, sir?' The fat man spun on his high heels with a balance remarkable given not only his corpulence but his rage. 'We shall see, dash it, how long the good Captain stays locked inside. We shall seek him out, sir.'

The door slammed. The chandler sighed. 'He's got no chance. What the Cap'n's locked in, he won't find no key.' And, gently, he tapped his forehead.

Vitus's closed eyes creased, mouth moving but making no sound as his head rocked against the back of the chair, restless in sleep, and his hands, hands hidden in shadow, twitched, like a dog coursing across a heathside in a dream or a sleepwalker carrying out some automatic action, like the motions of knitting, or brewing tea. Or writing, drawing on oneiric paper.

THE EARTH moves. It rises, mounts up. The earth is moved. In shovel-fulls. In barrow-fulls. In contradiction of its cool, passive attributes, Earth is made animate.

The map always knew it would be so.

Installed on table on platform on trembling ground, it oversees labourers bringing rocks around the side of the house, piling each, according to formula, in the centre of what is no longer a garden but a space in flux. Rock cut, broken, arranged according to mason's hand and map's will. Rock being Earth most recalcitrant, Earth at the nadir of its torpor. Most resistant to change and so the foundation on which the map's evocation must rest.

And, as rock mounts up, so the rest of the ground is worked. Trenches dug, soil piled. Another foundation of sorts.

The map has accounted for each step. Each flux and transmutation. The end of this Great Work lies at the far extremity of the map's furled surface as surely as does the beginning already past, already folded around itself once again. A serpent biting its own tail, the Mercurius: potential and realisation in a single entity. A single roll of paper.

It is as if the Work is already complete. The map knows it cannot fail.

    chisel strikes stone, makes light: Fire expressed from
       Earth
    soil cleaves soil, soil weeps: Water expressed from
       Earth
    trench sides sag, run free as dust: Air expressed from
       Earth
    Fire's residue is ash: Earth expressed from Fire
    Water's residue can be ice, can be silt: Earth
       expressed from Water
    Air's residue is silence, stasis: Earth as Earth,
       dormant

    waiting

There is much activity in the garden-becoming-something-else this afternoon. Foundations are almost complete. Mortar and stone are being readied. Mounds of soil sieved and graded. Much activity. Yet, unremarked, every bottle and flask runs dry, every bonfire and brazier gutters, and the torpor holding the sky in check makes the dust hang, throats parch and close, eyes become gritty as tempers grow threadbare. No rain forecast; hasn't rained in a week. And the wind — Where is the wind?

The wind stands on the threshold of the house.

On the fringe of the cleared ground there is a pause before the ash and elder masking the edge of the property begin, the wall enclosing everything sometimes visible through the foliage.

Grass and weeds are sprouting in the pause, unnoticed by the builders struggling to raise structure over foundation (and it is a struggle this afternoon), newgrowth yet merged into the undergrowth beneath the screen of trees. The pause is neither one thing nor the other thing. Not part of the building site. Not part of the screen. Having a little of both and a greater portion of neither, it is margin that comfortably belongs nowhere.

Being nowhere, it slips easily between one place and another. Liminal, filled with ambiguity.

Lying in the pause, the conjurer looks wretched. Weeds paw at its disjointed limbs. Leaves closed and shrivelled hang loosely from branches no less brittle. A blue periwinkle, blue like the sky hidden behind the stalled clouds, peers out of the crown, and dandelions, saffron-yellow faces turned towards the conjurer in a string of tiny suns, surround what is left of its head. The wounds made by saw and axe look less raw than they did; turning old, turning dry. Not long until conjurer merges into pause into treeline and out of memory.

Still. No wind today. No sign of rain.

Strange then that the conjurer's twigs and smaller branches twitch from time to time. Strange that, when they do, a little sap runs wet and free from each knuckle.

THE WIND stands on the threshold of the house.

Door-catch rattles. Hinges cleak. Door swings back. Hinges sleak-cleak, door-catch silent.

The wind stands on the threshold, watching the door sweep open, daylight rushing around the wind, tripping on the jam and sprawl-spill-spreading across a kitchen floor of sandstone flags set fast overearth, faces set and dry so grains of silica wink under the daylight spread across them. Mice scatter, door-sweep sending them racing, broadcast, across this petrified beach of a floor, claws sclat-tappering, tap-tap away from the falling daylight and towards the safety of the walls. Before the light can catch them, each is gone: holes open in the skirting, wide justenough for each mouse, closing after the last flick-flit of tail. The mice absorbed into the walls, claws scalt-tap hollowly, fading. Cut-off.

Silently, the wind crosses the threshold.

Kitchen becomes steps coming to a door stepping aside to reveal a corridor which leads —

The wind pauses, on the threshold, watching shadows lie in a sweep of indigo, mostly brown, daylight having rushed around the half-open door into this corridor to sprawl part-way across the floor ahead, spillaging out of one room, a little out of nextroom, door latchfirm on the oneafter.

Pausing at the margin, the line between kitchen and hallway. The wind inhales. Corridor and house and roof above do nothing, neither flex nor fall. Mousesilent.

As if the wind was not here.

Searching, nextroom to nextroom. Light ahead, always waiting when the door swings back, hinges sleak-cleak or near to silent as the case may be, house poised as the wind pauses on each threshold. Looking at furniture, here & here, carpets stained indigo there & there, tabletops collecting dust here & there, a jampot cresting white, mould chasing over itself here alone, a bed empty of everything but rumpled sheets, each one cresting likewise, there & here & all across this otherwise empty bed, empty bedchamber, empty house, the wind feeling quite alone, there there, quite distanced despite staircases and walls and the daylight that's turning little pink, ratherless grey than before, a definite shade of pink, call it incarnadine if you like, it makes no difference to the wind standing on the threshold, looking, hands outstretched, insubstantial but sensitive even so. Sensitive enough to feel a peculiar distance filling hallways, thisroom, nextroom, everyroom, although the wind has yet to search the whole house over, house mousesilent and distant.

As if the house was not here.

An exterior wall, which is a wall outside.

The wind stands before this wall stained in rosy light falling through two half-shuttered windows. It breathes, the wind, room and house and roof not budging. And the wall remains solid, unruffled as the wind takes another breath. A wall which is outside. Drawing breath, memory of kitchen, mice, being, well, sketched out as the wind thinks, breathes, thinking not of hollow walls but doublewalls. Of rooms and the spaces inside them. Insiderooms inside outsiderooms whose walls are exterior walls separated by, let us say, a handsbreadth from interiorwalls standing before this wind stained in rosy light falling through two half-shuttered windows. This is what the wind sketches out for itself. Not like a map. Only a conjecture. Only that. Nothing more.

Wholehouse over, bottom to top, to just beneath the inert roof. Wind's breath growing shallow from all those stairs, all these rooms. In everyroom, two windows, blinds half-closed. In everyroom, walls and doors leading to otherrooms or hallways, corridors finding space to branch, branch again. Many rooms; almost as many as corridors. And no sign of Vitus. Only stillsilence, or another hallway filled with incarnadine light from its two windows, or shadows partly sepia, quite a bit indigo. But no sign of Vitus, only another door, another branch of another hallway, it's two windows half-covered. Like —

Eyes.

HE WAS still furious by the time his carriage lurched up outside Vitus's house. So much so, the fat man knocked his driver aside in his haste to be out and up the pathway to the front door.

The busy-noise of construction work drifted on the still air from the rear of the house. The fat man ignored it.

An ad hoc collection of plank-walls barred access around either side of the house. The fat man hardly noticed.

A stray hunk of stone lay in the path. The fat man noticed that only after tripping over it.

Cursing, he hammered on the front door: by cane, by knocker, by fist. 'Open up, damn you. Open up, sir, I will not be denied, sir, upon my oath I shall —' At that he left off pounding dents into Vitus's front door and listened over the stertorous gusting of his own breath. Lifted his hand for a renewed barrage. And definitely heard someone behind the door. Bolts thrown, locks turning, a chain; two chains. God's blood, thought the fat man as the front door swung smoothly open.

'Yes, m'lord?' The retainer was elderly, fingers twisted by arthritis.

'I would see your master this instant.'

'Oh, no, sir.' The retainer desperately tried to stop the fat man going inside, swollen fingers waving frantically, joints click-clicking. 'Master was most insistent, m'lord, no visitors.' Fingers waving across the fat man's face, click-clickety. 'Most insistent he was, m'lord.'

'Was he, by Jove.' The fat man's face was bright red, a congested sun setting on frills of lace. 'Well, sir, tell your master: Johannes Jellibore is not to be thwarted. Better yet,' said Jellibore, picking up the speechless retainer and dropping him to one side, 'I shall tell him m'self.'

THE FOREMAN stands back. Masons step forward. Mallets drive downwards. Earth rises up. Wheelbarrows move here, there. From here to there.

Earth rises up on foundations well-laid, as mallets downward drive and forwards-step masons.

Hammers fall.

Stone breaks. Earth risen up from there to there.

Corners intersect. Masons straighten, words come down, break stone.

Growing higher here to here.

From there to here risers rise, step over step. Walls, archways, foundations bearing weight. Foundations. Earth. Stone. Stone shaped, moved, stepped. Coursed.

Scaffold intersects, plumb lines taken back, framework driving upwards. Steps likewise. Towards pavement flat, walls perpendicular.

Earth, stone, rising, risen, raised. Placed. Set in place, in level alignment or careful suspension, keystone, cornerstone pivoting, becoming: steps, outer precinct, walls flanking archway here, running unbroken there, corner-rounded, returning.

Mortar setting into stone.

Scaffold defines shape, cranes pivot, masons working, word comes back.

So hammers pause. Stone anchored. Anchoring all above, the risen Earth above. Rising higher.

Chisels rest. Masons step back.

Foreman stands openmouthed, only now seeing what had been lines on paper as something possible, doubts no longer concrete and growing less so as stones intersect, structure gains definition.

The map says nothing.

A workman steps back to stand near the ash and elder beyond the margin of the building site. Humid today, no air at all. Not a breath of wind for days. He mops his brow, the workmen, watching as the crane swings another cut stone into place. The building is gaining shape: earth ramparts forming steps to the outer precinct, the inner superstructure finished. The complex is clearly defined, no doubt of that. A surprise each time he looks at it, the workman thinks, a surprising shape, a surprise it can stand at all, that it all fits in the garden, all in all a wonder, the workman thinks, mopping his brow, wishing the weather would change.

A rustle in the grass and weeds makes him turn. There is hope, for a moment, hope that it is a breeze springing up. But all it is is a magpie nosing around branches of some tree they forgot to burn when they were clearing the ground. The workman glances at the bird, turns away, forgetting it immediately (unnoticed, the magpie

> flies up into the
> branches of an
> elder   )
> (unnoticed, the
> branches of the

felled tree
continue to
rustle, twigs
moving with
much-improved
dexterity), the workman
turning back to wait for the signal that the crane is finished, the
next stage of the work ready to begin, wondering absently, as
fresh beads of sweat trickle down his face, where the wind has
gone to ...

... unable to go back and so

takes another

turning, practically at random, fighting panic, turning

blindly

almost

& having to turn   b   a   c   k

&

panic driving   setting off a

down a narrowing hallway that suddenly widens & turns

turns

again,

h a r d

the wind tumbling wildly around the next

sharp bend, going now in a totally different direction

so lost so lost

s w i r l i n g

so lost

voice

k e e n i n g ,

wind no

longer

corridors too narrow too small & so lost thoughts scattering as it turns —

conscious of the ceilings too low overhead, walls squeezing, thinking

glancing into the rooms, simply

turning randomly,

34

the wind finds itself
guttering in a vast,
domed hallway

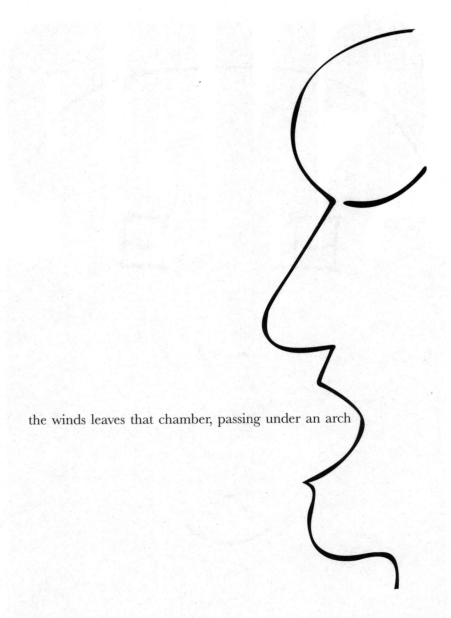

the winds leaves that chamber, passing under an arch

which
closes
with
a

SNAP

the   wind   turns   sharply   —
the way back   **gone**
lost in pitch darkness

I can't stand this!

whirling faster

h o w w W l i n g

trapped feeling trapped pressured
dark-space echoing, high but
narrow
walls pressing   darkness pressing
no way out

                              trapped
h o W W cut off as the wind
struggles for
            c   a   l   m

to think   and,
growing   s t i l l,   hears

38

b r e a t h i n g   the soft sound of breathing

the wind

s o m n o l e n t   &   r e g u l a r

follows the sound through the darkness   finding

g e n t l e   &   s o m n o l e n t   b r e a t h i n g

a door   a lit corridor beyond

coming from ahead, constant, regular

&

more open doorways,   corridor curving

breathing,   the   sound   of   someone

underneath   that,   there   is

sound coming from the nearest doorway

d e e p l y   a s l e e p

t h e   w h i s p e r i n g   b e a t   &   s w e l l   o f

the wind

rain

                    stops
                     at
                    the
              threshold

Rain. Falls, drips, beads. And runs. Slithering. Trickles joining. Wound-together lines beetling. Straggedly. Beading and running. Slip-weaving random paths. That break, as fresh droplets strike. Pattering. Dripping. Dropping, pat-patter, patter-tap rain. Fall falling rain. Rain falling: from the ceiling. Beckoning the wind closer. With every runnel chasing. Or pool brimming from dressing table, chair back. Mantelpiece awash and beginning to drip, spit-pip. Brittle-sounding. Water   drap tap   drap   striking water, puddles brimming. Puddles overflowing the bedroom floor, purling, calling the wind closer, wind fixed in the doorway, this first open doorway. With water gleaming across its threshold. Wind confounded. Glancing. Back. Along the hallway's curve. Rain's voice, patter-t't'tap, calling. Lapping against the wind's hearing. Lapping against the feet of the bed. Rills trickling over counterpane, rumpled sheets pulled loose. Quilt rising. Rain falling. Softly, quilt falling. Rain, quilt. Breathing out, breathing in, rising-fall after falling-rise: quilt and rain, chest beneath. Hands clasped — rising, gently falling — under chin. Eyes closed. Rain brushing forehead, tracing cheekbone, lips' curve, retracing. Pausing after fall. Breath drawing in and rain's pulse drawing outwards. Flexing. Breathing, sussurus-gentle, man and rain-falling, falling in and breathing out. The rain's voice beckoning the wind forward. Wanting the wind to fall and rise, to join with the wind, fast, slow, as the man in bed breathes in, pulsing, breathes out, pausing.

But the wind stands frozen in the doorway. Gazing at the rain, falling on Vitus asleep under soaking bedclothes; his eyes flickering beneath closed lids, slowing only to strengthen as the rain, an instant later, strengthens. The wind, frozen, trying to convince itself it cannot see a trace of the opposite wall through Vitus's beatific face.

The wind spins away.

Through the half-open doorway, the room looks normal. Except the floor. The floor is earth. Raw earth, pungent, heady, marl shot through with umbers, streaks of almost-sepia clay. Its damp musk reaches towards the doorway. Calling. Beckoning. Wanting to be touched, for its even, rich surface to be gone over, caressed. Cool, dark scent summoning images of endless plains or wide, alluvial valleys open to the sky like open palms: no ceilings, no walls. Unconfined. The wind wants this — you want this. So step forward —

And halt at the sight glimpsed through the narrow crack between the door and frame: earth sculpted into Vitus, Vitus emerging from the ground, Vitus sitting asleep, runlets of water trailing down his face from each closed eye, seeping into the ground, percolating through the earth to rise as a perfume. Beckoning

The   wind
flinches — *you*
flinch — away.
Cold spreading.
Mounting   as
you billow along
the sinuous cor-
ridor. Glimpsing

*a Vitus of
sand, standing,
asleep, beyond
another open
door, a sand
yearning to be set
in motion, to leach
the moisture from
your breath*

*a Vitus of flame, each
slumbering breath tangy
with the parched scent
of ash, a column
of fire thirsting to
be fanned, a fire
that nevertheless
sweats water
on the bedroom
floor*

and   pitching
along   this
u n d u l a t i n g ,
e n d l e s s
corridor,   chill
giving edge to
your   voice   as
you buffet the
walls, tumbling
past   more
d o o r w a y s ,
more Vituses

a Vitus of pebbles
& stones, pacing,
turning, pacing
…

a Vitus of words, of words
printed, words written,
stacking bricks of water …

a Vitus
pointing,
stooping,
pointing,
stooping,
pointing …

a Vitus of reflections,
of light on water,
swimming a lap,
turning, swimming
…

a Vitus smiling,
putting on another
mask: confused; another:
crying; another …

so many
Vituses. Corridor
endless. Walls close.
(Pressing.) Ceiling
low. (Crushing.)
Every room want-
ing you. Trying.
Trying to trap.
Confine.

Y o u
scream. S u r g -
i n g pell-mell.
Rooms flit past.
Curving. Endless
walls tight. Low
ceilings ringing
to your howls.
You must get out.
Must —

                    you
                 glimpse
              ahead

        glimpse
    a

DOOR
              at
            the
          head
        of the
      c o r r i d o r

and

a Vitus ...
a Vitus ...
a Vitus ...
a Vitus ...
a Vitus ...
a Vitus ...
a Vitus ...
a Vitus ...
a Vitus ...
a Vitus ...
a Vitus ...
a Vitus ...
a Vitus ...
a Vitus ...
a Vitus ...
a Vitus ...
a Vitus ...
a Vitus ...
a Vitus ...
a Vitus ...
a Vitus ...
a Vitus ...
a Vitus ...
a Vitus ...
a Vitus ...
a Vitus ...
a Vitus ...
a Vitus ...
a Vitus ...
a Vitus ...
a Vitus ...
a Vitus ...

a Vitus ...
a Vitus ...
a Vitus ...
a Vitus ...
a Vitus ...
a Vitus ...
a Vitus ...
a Vitus ...
a Vitus ...
a Vitus ...
a Vitus ...
a Vitus ...
a Vitus ...
a Vitus ...
a Vitus ...
a Vitus ...
a Vitus ...
a Vitus ...
a Vitus ...
a Vitus ...
a Vitus ...
a Vitus ...
a Vitus ...
a Vitus ...
a Vitus ...
a Vitus ...
a Vitus ...
a Vitus ...
a Vitus ...
a Vitus ...
a Vitus ...
a Vitus ...

DOOR

you *b u r s t* across the threshold

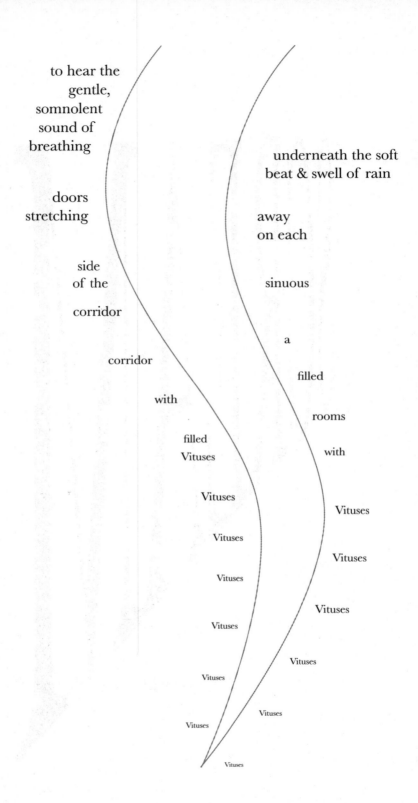

to hear the
gentle,
somnolent
sound of
breathing

doors
stretching

side
of the

corridor

corridor

with

filled
Vituses

Vituses

Vituses

Vituses

Vituses

Vituses

Vituses

Vituses

underneath the soft
beat & swell of rain

away
on each

sinuous

a

filled

rooms

with

Vituses

Vituses

Vituses

Vituses

Vituses

Vituses

Vituses

the wind/you

THE FAT man, Johannes Jellibore, froze in mid-step.

'What the deuce was that?'

He spun on his heels, almost knocking the elderly retainer flying across the hallway floor.

Jellibore turned again. Glancing into a seemingly deserted withdrawing room, a library/chart room, and down the corridor towards the kitchen.

'What, man? What was that infernal noise?' Jellibore's face was pallid, a trembling white as he grabbed the butler by the shoulders. 'Gad, sir, what?'

'Nothing.' Stammering, the unfortunate retainer squirmed in Jellibore's grip. 'Please, m'lord, master's instructions, you must —'

'Nothing?' Jellibore squeezed harder. 'Nothing?'

'The wind, m'lord —'

'My oath, you whelp, I shall —'

The sound repeated. Came a third time. From above. From somewhere in the house.

Jellibore swallowed. And rushed the stairs two at a time.

OUT IN the garden:

the foreman stands back
                          the workmen pause
they gape at the house, wanting to believe
they have heard
                                    nothing
whilst the felled tree's branches
                        twitch
                            twitch
                                and the
            map

the map knows only the Work
knows only that what was abstract,
potential, is becoming concrete

real

A LONG time. It seemed a long time. For the screaming to stop (it felt like it was someone else screaming); for strength to return; for the claustrophobia to become at least manageable; for the desperation and panic to grow thinner, less suffocating. A long time to find the strength to move: a breeze wafting unsteadily past doorway doorway doorway doorway door— A longer time for ice-fear transmuted into leaden-hopelessness to become a feeling too equivocal, too fragile, to have a name, at least none that comes to mind, a mind kept deliberately neutral as doorway followed doorway followed Vitus followed Vitus followed on to the end of the hallway, the door at its head shied away from, path retraced, past doors open and Vituses many. The door at the opposite end also shied away from and path retraced once more. Always one more, the next definitely the last, the next definitely ...

A long time to notice the matchstick-narrow door closed when all the others lining the corridor were open.

THE WIND slips around the doorway ...

57

Johannes Jellibore paused on the first floor landing, listening. Ignoring the retainer's pleas, Jellibore pounded up the next flight.

I'm coming, old man ...

Branches twitch. Certain ...

The map-that-is-routepath-&-more listens patiently to the foreman's requests. The entire workforce is only pretending to be absorbed in their tasks at hand. The foreman finishes, stepping back, respectfully, to the edge of the platform to wait the map's reply as the men — master to apprentice — stop working and wait also.

No, the map finally indicates, unfurling the last of its length, the Work is too near complete. Tell your men to stop their ears if the noise disturbs them. Tell your men to redouble their efforts. We must complete the Work. Soon. Complete soon ...

The wind
slips around the match-
stick-narrow doorway
and catches its breath.
Seeing …

The wind
slips around the match-
stick-narrow door,
breath catching, more
groan than sigh
as it
as you
as we see

the inside
of Vitus's head

Vitus twitched, eyes closed but restless, shoulders jerking, hands bunched awkwardly beneath his chin, twitching, breath shallow, touching, catching the back of his throat, more groan than sigh, as Vitus twitched, eyes closed but restless, shoulders jerking, hands bunched awkwardly beneath his chin, twitching, breath shallow, touching, catching the back of his throat, more groan than sigh, as Vitus twitched, eyes closed but restless, shoulders jerking, hands bunched awkwardly beneath his chin, twitching, breath shallow, touching, catching the back of his throat, more groan than sigh, as Vitus twitched, eyes closed but restless, shoulders jerking, hands bunched awkwardly beneath his chin, twitching, breath shallow, touching,

Vitus twitched, eyes closed but restless, shoulders jerking, hands bunched awkwardly beneath his chin, twitching, breath shallow, touching, catching the back of his throat, more groan than sigh, as Vitus twitched, eyes closed but restless, shoulders jerking, hands bunched awkwardly beneath his chin, twitching, breath shallow, touching, catching the back of his throat, more groan than sigh, as Vitus twitched, eyes closed but restless, shoulders jerking, hands bunched awkwardly beneath his chin, twitching, breath shallow, touching, catching the back of his throat, more groan than sigh, as Vitus twitched, eyes closed but restless, shoulders jerking, hands bunched awkwardly beneath his chin, twitching, breath shallow, touching, catching

THE CHAMBER is vast. Even so, a rush of claustrophobia rocks the wind, immediately becoming a clash of vertigo.

The chamber is vast. Its ceiling arches gracefully, tracing the raised domes of closed eyes, nose, lips, cheeks curving down to flair out into ears, the hinge of each jaw, chin thrusting upwards high overhead. On the far side of the chamber, the seamless wall sweeps down from calvaria to inion, skullcap to the deepest point of the bowed floor.

A head. Vitus's head. The contours of the chamber's walls leave no doubt. If there was, the mural covering the entire room would remove any trace: Vitus's head, his sleeping face mapped over the ceiling, skin and hair below. Only the face is reversed, looking downwards as the roof presses outwards: sleeping, Vitus stares, unsealing, into the centre of his own head.

Vertigo grips the wind. A sigh more like a groan. Closed eyes. Serene features pressing down. A sigh more like a groan. Face turned inwards. Fixated.

it's hard to make out, the shock from entering this chamber doing nothing to help thought flow smoothly. it appears as a collection of boards, theatre flats thrown together. distant beneath the closed eyes. trying to ignore the watching mural (the weight, terrible weight of the roof). drifting closer. not flats; walls. not painted; decorated. pictures, doorways, tables, a fireplace. denial, of course denial, but (such a long way, under the sleeping face, closed eyes watching) making a close circle, there's no escape: the house, turned inside out, but the house, corridors reaching out, interior walls exposed, exterior walls which are walls inside, each shadow shading from mostly brown to indigo, wholehouse unfurled, all those stairs, all these rooms, thisroom, nextroom. everyroom.

standing on the threshold. Vitus's study. drawing breath. model ship on the window ledge swaying. picture of a building, hanging on the out-turned wall, rocking. pieces of paper pinned around it flapping

dreams of the sea before he finds
it. Before he dreams

puts his pen down to look out of
the window

It doesn't mean anything

A blankness for a period, then
my eyes would snap

into view, as though he might
always have been here

flapping and leaping wildly as the wind (you are the wind, remember that, hold on to that) as the wind draws breath (you draw breath, you moan, remember, remember you exist) drawing breath, groan setting the dozens of scraps of paper frantic, snapping, writhing with each groan of the wind (your groans, say it again: your groans, you are not a figment: repeat that to yourself). window in the wall, exterior wall, that is a wall inside, window banging against its frame, latch frenzied as another gust, cool, desolate (your breath: you are doing this, you are not a figment, not a dream) as another gust, cool and desolate, sends chairs toppling, a truckle bed overturning, inhalation, which is a breath inside, pulling books from the shelves, knocking over a table, next groan (yours) ripping every scrap of paper from the walls, setting them fluttering, pin-wheeling, filling the inside-out room, billowing insanely as the next gust (not a figment) snatches open the window, window slamming wide, jolting painting from wall, interior wall, window framing exterior walls, which are walls beyond walls in shadow, mostly indigo walls, walls framed in the open window and seeming infinitely distant as you rush through the tumbling scraps of paper, through the open window; to leave the room to settle. Paper swaying. Coming down. Whispering as each one rests on another, until the final sheet turns, lands face up on all the rest

I am not a figment

EVERY WINDOW and every door in the house slams.

Vitus twitched, eyes fluttering, restless, hands jerking, breath hitching in the back of his throat, shoulders working side to side as if he was wriggling through a narrow passage. Or trying to slip out from under something.

Vitus's eyelids fluttered. White flashing beneath. Eyes almost open.

it doesn't go, it's there   to one side   always
there, never going   submerged   hidden   I
don't know, both I suppose   I can be
doing something ordinary, walking into a
room, reaching to pick up a pen, anything,
and in the moment of blankness when I'm
simply moving, mind gone quiet, it comes
back   they come back: memories, images
appearing out of order, an incident I might
not have thought about, thought I'd forgotten,
pressing hard behind the feel of the wind
through the window or the roughness of the
bedsheet while I was half asleep   all
that mixed with thoughts, not thoughts as
sentences, not words   they could be words, but
it comes as sensations, or associations, both
wrapped together, knotted together, a single
impression, one thing thought, wordlessly,
but which contains I don't know how many
other feelings, sensations, implications, each
linked to the other, a chain of thoughts all in a
single thought, all wordless and appearing as
a single flash of understanding, much, much
faster than if I thought them through word by
word   I don't think this is making sense
but they're there, inside the memories,
wrapping around the memories, all in a flash,
always   always the knowledge of absence
always the gap   the regret, a wrongness, that
it shouldn't be this, that I simply cannot be

walking into this room, picking up this pen
this way, this automatic way   I did before,
in the past, I shouldn't, must not cannot
be doing this in the way I am in the way I
always have not now, it's wrong   there has
to be   must be a difference I can't do
it the way I always have because things
are not the way they were   *but I am*
I do   and that single word must thought
filled with other wordless thoughts appears
through, behind, in front of the disbelief, the
absence   forms the absence, defines it:
mist shaped around glass, glass in the shape
of what isn't there any more   I can't
explain it in words, only in that impression
only by the absence   the absence is the only
thing that defines   the absence

Vitus twitched, eyelids fluttering. White showing. A flash of blue.
Breath caught in the back of his throat: not a groan, not a sigh.
Restless. Shoulders jerking. Hands twitching, like a sleepwalker.
Eyelids parting. As Vitus tried again to wake up. Tried again.
Sound not a groan, not a sigh. Eyelids fluttering, closing. Vitus
unable to take control of this dream.

At last

> the foreman stands back
> the workmen stand back

At last

> the map-that-never-was-quite-a-map-that-became-
> a-different-kind-of-map rests on the table, on the
> platform, on the edge of the ground risen up

At last

> the map can unfurl no more

At last the Work is complete
At last

> > > the conjurer twitches.

JELLIBORE THREW his weight against the door, frame splintering as the lock tore free. A ham fist clutched the door handle at the last instant, Jellibore grunting — partly effort, mostly shock — as the complaining door halted his head-long plunge into the room. Frozen before the threshold, the distraught retainer bunched his twisted fingers under his chin, moaning.

The room had been wrecked.

Chairs smashed. Table broken. A truckle bed tipped over, bedding shredded. Paper everywhere: sketch-maps savagely torn, pages of handwritten notes crumpled, ripped, an atlas gutted, books dismembered. A stench clung to the room, hanging over all: sweat, the rankness of unwashed flesh. And an undercurrent both sweet and resinous, sweet and putrid.

Jellibore's mouth sagged. The violence with which this turmoil had been created left him speechless. Not so the retainer.

'Master!'

With surprising agility, the elderly man slipped around Jellibore's bulk, joints clicking as he stooped to pick through the debris.

'Stand fast, man.' Jellibore restrained the agitated retainer by the shoulders. 'Vitus can hardly be hidden under all this paper —'

So saying, Jellibore noticed the alcove on the left the room. Torn books and bedding lay in a drift in front of it. A heavy brocade curtain hung by one corner, most of the rings snapped, draped over the debris. Folds haphazard.

The fat man heaved the curtain aside.

'Master's dead,' the retainer screamed, seeing the figure hidden under the brocade.

Vitus did look dead. Half-covered in wreckage, head propped awkwardly against the rear of the alcove. Jellibore kicked aside shards of furniture and ripped books, making space to kneel, bellowing at the retainer to desist his infernal caterwauling, and laying an ear against Vitus's chest once again. Nostrils flaring at the foulness of the other man's clothes, the reek clinging to his skin. Seeing an opium pipe lying, forgotten, on the other side of the recess.

'There is life here,' Jellibore announced, 'faint but present. Come along man: stop your wailing and help me.'

Jellibore struggled to lift Vitus, glancing at the unconscious man's face. Seeing his eyelids flutter. White showing. A flash of blue. Eyelids fluttering. Half open

The fat man's face is bright red, a congested sun setting on frills of lace: Well, sir, tell your master I am not to be thwarted — Better yet I shall tell him

THE LAND is transformed, garden no more. Earth risen up. Sculpted. No longer formless but precise, scaled. Brought into being: low walls, steps between; a platform, precinct flat but raised; inner limits defined by a wall of stone, Earth recalcitrant, in a margin of soil compacted, Earth torpid once again but marking the transition from outer to inner. Round arch leading to open mouth, nostrils flared, expression ambiguous. And above, rising: cheekbones, sculpted, jutting out; forehead, declining to temples, jutting in. All of it land transformed, garden no more. Slate, limestone, clay, sand and ballast set as concrete as tongue, earlobe. All, all of it Earth transmuted, Earth changed.

The Great Work complete.

Furled tightly around itself, the map stares through the hole at the centre of the furl, circle of paper focused on the construction. Circle taking in the whole edifice, filling the map as it takes in point after point, lingering on the basalt eyes, each smooth, undifferentiated, but staring directly back, the map thinks, looking to philtrum or dorsum, and back to the eyes, stark granite cranium, and back, before seeing it all, all outside, no longer within the furls of the map. Not potential but realised, external and solid, the map thinks as it sees the monumental head rise out of the land transformed.

The Temple of Vitus.

Speech. Less.

Speechless, each one. As they stand back, crane up at the head, openmouthed, staring fixedly back at the house, sightlesseyes, gazing over the top of the low wall. Hard to believe, foreman & workforce think as they stand back, pressing against the margin of the garden (no, not 'garden', call it 'temple grounds'). Ownhandsbuilt and they find it hard to believe. Head of stone; head of Earth. Openmouthed, foreman & workforce gape, transfixedeyes, at the Temple. Sweat beading, running freely, air gravid and close, heat less bearable now they have nothing to do. Hasn't rained in an age and not a breath of wind. Not that they have much breath themselves, cranenecked, hardpressed into the margin line, only way to take it in. No breath, but a mason begins to clap. Foreman likewise, every one thereafter.

Applauding the map, the Temple realised.

Fingers spread, palms flat, clap-clap; fingers twitching, knuckles stiff, clap-clap clap. Applause sharp on the motionless air. Limbs flickering, pass after pass. One bow, another, each one bowing deep from the trunk. Spreadfingered, knuckles tapping. Clack-click. Clackerty-CLACK

every window and every door in the house slams   pause
after drawn-out, silence drawn-in

                                        in

                                                in

                                                        to

                                                                draw

                        o   u   t,

rooms   and   house   and   roof
                                        above

     f l e e e x x X x x i i n g

clouds fading, revealing a ghostmoon, seas of its face brimming,
increscent

s w e l l l l l i n g

d r a w i n g

in, rooms and house and roof flexing as every window and every
door bursts

OPEN

the wind whorls and gusts across the garden
whorls and gusts

shrieking its freedom

spinning
spinning faster
maniacally

wild with relief

not seeing
the head of earth & stone

or the branches

the branches waving

flexing

clack-CLACK

RETAINER GONE, gone off somewhere, dragging the practically dead weight, kitchen door slammed shut by the gale, shouldering it open again, dragging Vitus out, yelling, I say, you fellow s, assistance, by gad, we require

CLICK

the map tumbles across the platform, furling tighter, and cast upwards, tumbling end over end, spinning end over

CLICK-CLACK

the head of stone & earth, mouth wide, begins to murmur, mouth open, piping, whispering, howling with each new gust: Dry ... Dreams ... Was

CLICK-CLICK

not one man left standing, every one blown from his feet, scattered like sailors foundering in a shipwreck

CRACK-LATTER-LACK

plucked upwards again, the map tries to unfurl, sure there must be something written on it that will help, an instruction that will set this right, but what was fixed now runs, colours lines flowing together awash running wet with

CLACK-TER-CLACK

leaving him slumped against the house, the man who had been helping Vitus staggers a handful of steps, attention snared, Dashed odd thing, words snatched away by the gale buffeting the man who had been helping Vitus

as he bends to prise up a stone that has turned
dark, its face awash, Dashed odd thing but
you seem to have struck water, by Jove, yes,
a spring

CLACK-CLATTERTY

and what was dry grows wet, the garden
beginning to flood

CLACK

in my dreams this was not dry
              murmurs the head of Vitus
in my dreams this was
              murmurs

CLICK-CLACK

turning, flapping insanely, the map tries to see
its own face, catches a glimpse of amethyst,
ultramarine, saffron, running away, ablur,
washing paler, glimpses white, glimpses the
garden, the garden transforming, the garden

CLACK

                              flooding,
by Jove, says the man who had been helping
Vitus, splashing back a step from the fast-
widening pond, waving to the men picking
themselves up off the already soaking ground,
Dashed odd thing, says the man who had been
helping Vitus again, I say, he says, you don't
suppose chaps will be saying this was my
fault, do you? to which the man who was the
foreman salutes sharply: Of course not, Sir, no
doubt about

CLATTER-

the Temple of Vitus is now the Island of Vitus

CLACK-CLICKERTY

not dry, murmurs the head in dreams murmurs
the head

CLACK

map no more
garden no more
temple no more, no more
land, thrust out
amidst the

w a v e s
settle as the wind calms, seeing the garden at
last, a place undifferentiated but for the head
of rocks, dryland, the only place left

this way, says the man who had been helping
Vitus, Vitus forgotten as the man says, This
way, again, wading forwards, arms thrown
wide for balance, leaving a wake behind as he
waves forward, chest-deep and waving to the
others to follow, This way, only safe ground
left

in my ... murmurs, this was ... his hand
finding the first step, beneath the surface,
murmuring as he drags himself over stones wet
then dry, looking at arch — asking: This is not
my dream? — seeing the dark space beyond
— trying: This is not my dream, as statement
— knowing this is the only place left to go

71

THE WIND

enters the head & finds corridors, hallways,
doorways: shifting, undefined, redefined

THE MAN

who had been helping Vitus enters the head
& finds deck, ship, a landscape flat, open &
unconstrained

VITUS

enters the head, water lapping behind him, &
opens his eyes to find

VITUS WALKS. Pebbles click-slithering underfoot another step, and another. A cliff opens its arms around Vitus walking, the pebbles, the pebbles and Vitus. But not the sky, which remains out of reach: doubtless golden once but now resembling the grey pebbles lying underfoot, pebbles lying motionless along the horizon which itself remains motionless along the base of the sky which remains. 'Dry,' murmurs Vitus. 'In my dreams,' Vitus murmurs, walking, 'this was not-dry and the horizon was not-still.' Opening its arms, a cliff remains unreachable, arms too short although, doubtless, once-golden skies were framed by its mouth. Murmuring: 'What is the name for not-dry?' Framing: 'That resemblance it bore to not-still. In my dream, different. A not-this. A not-land-not-sky. In my dream, I dreamt this was.' See: the pebbles click-slithering underfoot, wave motion approximating not-still. Vitus opens his arms, framing the horizon (grey no doubt) and the cliffs (no resemblance). Mouth open, Vitus is borne along on the pebbles' click-slithering, still and dry. 'I dreamt this differently.' Mouth closing, opening to frame: 'Waves of non-pebbles and less click-overtowing drawing the horizon away-back. Until.' The cliffs (head-like, land-resemblance). Each pebble reacts to the pebbles behind it (in the direction of not-still), propagating wave-like behaviour overfoot. Vitus, still murmuring, resembles walk-like motion (not-still), carried by the undertow grey-slithering, dream still-born in his dry mouth.

ELUCIDATION/RECAPITULATION — Vitus having awoken.

> **Vitus:** buoyed up on a tide of pebbles, flows back and forth-back across the valley.

> **Pebbles. Valley:** in his dream (reality-like while it remained within the definition of Vitus's head) *pebbles* and *valley* assumed other meanings. 'Pebble' was also known as 'rounded stone shaped by and interacting with that which was not-sky-not-land-not-still-not-dry', and 'valley' became

'small insertion of not-sky-not-land-not-still-not-dry framed between the cliffs'.

('This is not my dream,' Vitus murmurs as pebbles flow underfoot, carrying Vitus murmuring 'this is not my dream' in their undertow, as Vitus, carried, takes a moment to breathe in before, outflowing, the words 'this is not my dream', carried onward as the pebbles, carrying, briefly pause, momentarily inflowing, before the words 'this is not my dream' are undermined by the sound of Vitus flowing underfoot.)

The place Vitus now finds himself is defined differently within the dream within his head (however either of those concepts may be defined). That stretch of 'rounded-stone-concept' closer to the rock face was called _____ in relation to the ('in my dreams') concept-no longer-present; and of the strip of land along which the Vitus moves was itself a moving back and forth line of interface between the concept-manifest-inside-Vitus's-head ('in my dream this was') and those places physically unaltered but which are now conceptually different ('in my dreams this was called _____ and this _____ and this ... this is not my dream'). The only point of demarcation now is that Vitus is here, carried, murmuring, a moving line of interface between here and there ('not here; no, not-there'), murmuring back and forth-back on a tide of pebbles along a line of arbitrary differentiation ('not in my dream').

Vitus feels he must have been in his dream because he witnessed that which-was-in-his-head-but-not-here-outside (concept unnamed, if approximately defined). But he did not see himself in the dream.

(Opening his arms, Vitus attempts to frame the landscape changing constantly as he moves, moment by moment, across the open stretch of pebbles, frame changing as the landscape, unmoving, is passed through his open arms, which, constantly moving, fix any point only to lose it, land escaping Vitus's grasp as his attempted viewpoint, inconstant, grows looser until the land, stretched open and unframed, slides away to leave nothing but the murmuring of the pebbles as they openly remind him, moment after moment, that this is no longer what he dreamt.)

VITUS WOKE. Where there had been sea there was now land and where there had been land there was now Vitus. There was nothing much else to see. 'It's gone,' thought Vitus. He rubbed sleep from his eyes, wondering if this would happen again. Wondering if this had happened before.

Wondering if he was awake at all.

LOOKING STRAIGHT ahead, Vitus no longer sees himself, only the landscape. Moving. Back. Forth. Landscape: pebbles, valley, rockface, head-like cliff. Moving back, forth. Thinking: *I did not see myself in my dream.* Forth, moving. Back: cliff, head-like, face of rock (quite a resemblance), valley (renamed formally), pebbles moving undertoe with no sign of Vitus relative to what is seen.

Thinking forthright: *I did dream, myself.*

A head, cliff-like, eyes straight, gazes back. Rock enclosing Vitus until he no longer sees himself just as, in his dream, he saw but was not seen because he enclosed a reality, close in resemblance to this one, in which he saw and was unseen, back and forth-back. A reality moving, back and forth-back. Seeing something not here. Moving back. Forth-back. Awake-seeing, not-awake-saw. A sight forthcoming, defined by motion amongst other things. Such as a head. Eyes straight. Awake, not-awake and within this forum (head-rock, land overtow, pebbles back and) forthwith not-still, in a resemblance (quite striking) of

a wave

dream *n*. reality-like experience, undergone during periods of not-wakefulness confined within cranial structures.

VITUS WOKE. Where there had been sea there was now land and where there had been land there was now Vitus. 'It's gone,' thought Vitus. He rubbed sleep from his eyes, wondering if he was awake at all.

VITUS WAVES to the sky to the left. Vitus waves to the sky to the right, the sky overhead, he waves to the skies. None of them waves back.

'They do not see,' says Vitus, waving.

Vitus waves to the pebbles underfoot. The pebbles pass by as Vitus waves. He waves to the pebbles undertoe. Pebbles underarch. Underheel. None of them wave back. He, Vitus, waves to the pebbles ahead, pebbles yet to be passed as he moves along. Along the pebbles under the sky, waving. Vitus waves.

Nothing.

'They do not see,' says Vitus, wheeling.

Pausing, Vitus goes back over pebbles under sky, tidily, only to return. Waving. Vitus waves to the land ahead, land that seems to be looking right at him. Cliffs rise as Vitus moves tidily along, growing larger as he, Vitus, approaches, waving. Face-rock straitens the pebbles, head-like, as it confines Vitus's range of motion quite tidily. Waving. Going back over pebbles under sky. Wheeling. Back. Pebbles going undertoe. Land ahead. Confining. Vitus undersky. Waving. Tiredly.

'They do not see,' says Vitus, woebegone.

Looking, Vitus waves.

He looks for himself waving as he waves, looking. Up: a sky, tidily Vitus-free. Down: pebbles overthere or underhere; all-seen, all not-Vitus. Ahead: a land, neatly head-like and rather face-like but, like so many things, quite unlike Vitus looking or waving or tidy or Vitus in anyway.

Straightened by rock, confined by land temple-like (here), head-like (there) and facing at but leaving Vitus unseen (here and there, and there, too, but also here when he was last passing this spot on his way to) accepting, quite unlikeable though it is, Vitus waves just the same. Tidily. Tide-like. It gives little comfort, coming forth, and back-forth, wheeling Vitus waves again. A little comfort, waving a little here, a little there, as Vitus, accepting a little unlikely though he is to find it comforting, Vitus waves and thinks of his own dream. Weaving recollections. Of foam. Murmuring. Of foam and murmuring both absent now.

Moments pass.

Vitus, absently murmurs: 'What was that thing — foaming, frothing back and forth — quite tidily, very murmurly,' Vitus mumbles, 'unseen now but, but in my dream it was ...' Vitus wavers: 'I dreamt of that thing I was dreaming of that thing I was dreamt.'

Vitus woke. Where there had been sea there was now land and where there had been land there was now Vitus. 'It's gone,' he thought.

Vitus rubbed sleep from his eyes.

Afterwards, the land remained; some underfoot and some rising up here and there. And there was the sky, too, not quite like the dream but still in more or less the same place.

'It's gone,' said Vitus, afterwards, looking but not seeing. Pebbles stretched to the horizon. Or seemed to. It was a long way off, the horizon, and Vitus had to rub sleep from his eyes. The pebbles were in the same place afterwards. Vitus began walking where he had seen the sea. Now there was only land to the horizon, rubbing sleep from his eyes as Vitus walked on. 'Strange,' he thought, 'it was real. In the dream. Completely real.' Now, it was only dry; perhaps a week had gone by since it last rained and there was no sign of water. Only pebbles, completely real despite having been hidden by the sea. Or, in the dream, under the sea. Now, there's nothing much else. Except Vitus walking. And the horizon.

And the remains of these boats.

Skeletons of hulls and wheelhouses and a prow. All real, completely. Completely lying in place. The horizon was a long way off. 'This wasn't in my dream,' said Vitus, rubbing his eyes sleepily. The sky was much the same afterwards. There was a little water hiding in the bottom of a dinghy. It stained the planks, dark like a shadow hiding in the bottom of a different boat, not like this boat that Vitus stood beside, quiet. Pebbles lay in place under the keel, under the prow, under Vitus who stood still. Perhaps a week had gone by. 'In my dream,' he murmured, seeing, 'there was this feeling. You understand?' The dinghy, apparently real under Vitus's gaze, and also much the same under the sky, did nothing. Except, Vitus walking around the little boat, thought, 'It was like this in the ... you know. This or something like. And water, too,' only out loud this last bit, so the sky and horizon could hear. But mostly the dinghy. Water inside like a shadow gone by. None of the skeletons had water. And the pebbles, they had been hidden by the dream just as now the dinghy hid them. Dark like a shadow gone by but real, completely real, despite having lain under the sky. Which, Vitus thought as he stood under the sky over the dinghy with water inside, is much the same thing really.

He rubbed his eyes. His eyes with water inside.

Vitus sits in the dinghy. Water lies in the dinghy. The dinghy lies over the pebbles. The pebbles lay under the sea. The dinghy sits on the pebbles. Vitus lies beside the water, in the dinghy, over the pebbles.

Just like the sea.

The dinghy rubbed its eyes. Just the same.

Vitus looks at the water. Dark like a shadow. 'Strange —' and gets no further because his mouth is too dry to speak. Perhaps a week has gone by since it last rained.

'I have this feeling ...'
  Perhaps the sky should say that. Not quite the same.

But real. The water seems real afterwards. Just like the sea.

The horizon moves in time to the sway of the dinghy. Back and forth. It gets no closer; it is a long way off. But there is a sense of motion. Pebbles lie under the sea and the dinghy with water inside. Vitus sways. Looking a little at the horizon, mostly at the water dark like sleep.
  'I have found my —'
  Vitus gets no further.

THE SEA rubs sleep from its eyes. Like in the dream.

BORIS FINISHES writing, *Like in the dream,* and puts his pen down to look out the window. The road sign with the wonky fingerpost is pointing towards a brick wall today.
  'This way to,' says Boris, thinking that he cannot remember a time when the sign did not point the wrong way. It once pointed directly at his window.
  Boris lets down the blinds and almost manages to knock over the model boat collecting dust on the windowsill. He did these selfsame actions five weeks ago: leaning across the table, letting down the blind, almost knocking the boat. Only, five weeks ago, Boris had a scrap of paper in his hand. In trying to catch the boat, Boris dropped the paper. He has searched everywhere for

it since, everywhere except behind the table on which he works, because he has quite forgotten about the incident with the blind and the boat.

The piece of paper lies on the floor, against the wall, under the sill. It reads: *And before dreamt, Vitus Bering does not exist.*

Almost knocking over the dusty boat now does nothing to remind Boris what happened five weeks ago.

He is always knocking over that dusty boat.

VITUS WAKES to find he has just been born. 'Odd,' thinks Vitus, 'I don't remember this.' Mrs Emmaline Blenkinsoe is singing 'Lilac Time' on the Victrola. 'Odd,' Vitus thinks, turning, 'this isn't what I remember either.' Vitus turns to the calendar. '1680,' says the calendar, which seems about right, although the last encyclopaedia he consulted told Vitus only that he had been baptised in 1681, which is not quite the same thing. 'Not at all,' sings Mrs Emmaline Blenkinsoe, turning round the Victrola. 'I don't remember this,' thinks Vitus, which is odd for someone so young. Through the window, a sign is just visible, just the top visible through the window in the wall. Vitus clambers, turning a little, on to the edge of his cot. 'Welcome to Jutland,' says the sign, framed in the window now that Vitus is standing. 'That seems,' begins the calendar, 'about right,' sings the Victrola in Mrs Emmaline Blenkinsoe's voice in the room, needle held steady while the record spins. Vitus says nothing, standing no less still than the Victrola. Or the room for that matter. Vitus looks through the wall at the sign in the window. The world turns, turning the Victrola turning Mrs Blenkinsoe's voice. 'Welcome to Jutland': the letters follow each other, one after the other, although the words appear not to move. Which isn't so odd bearing in mind the window is moving too. Vitus, being young, is possibly not aware of this. The sign, framed on the wall, in the window in 17th Century Jutland in time for Vitus to be born, says nothing. 'That's quite seemly,' the calendar says, only very quietly so as not to disturb Mrs Emmaline Blenkinsoe who has developed quite a scratchy voice. Perhaps from singing too much. And an obsession with the word time. 'Time,' sings Mrs B., '… time … t-time … t-time,' over and over, 't-time — t-time — t-time,' over. The Victrola, restless and without a voice of its own, says nothing. Only thinks.

'I remember water.'

Meanwhile, Ulysses is guiding his three ships — the *Galatea*, the *Phaeton*, and the *Cordelia* — through the Carpathian Mountains. His only map, a Baedeker's to the Aegean, was washed overboard three weeks ago. He's desperately homesick. But Ithaca, NY, lies impossibly distant, lost beyond a sea that might as well be a dream for all Ulysses has to show it still exists.

Vitus dreams. When he wakes, the only thing he can tell the calendar is: 'I don't remember.'

There are now three ships wandering together on the North Sea. Their names may be the *Erebus*, the *Bellicose*, and the *Terror*. The *Bellicose*, under Admiral Jellicoe, on top of the North Sea, takes the lead. 'Dashed odd thing this, Sir,' says Jellicoe's Number One. Although he says nothing more, the Admiral knows exactly what he means: that there's been no sign of the enemy for over three weeks. At least, Jellicoe thinks that's what Number One means. He could have meant something else. It's too late to ask now. Jellicoe glances at the calendar. Its pages are stuck together, unreadable. Perhaps it hasn't been three weeks at all.

Jellicoe hums the refrain from 'Lilac Time' and falls silent.

In Bruges, the sea laps across the town square. There is no one around to watch; even the statue on the pedestal is gone. Another pulse flows across the cobbles, the sea reaching a little further, then a little further more. Soon, the pedestal will be an island and the imposing market hall with its sawtooth gables will become a new headland.

Only the waves make any sound. Only the sea moves; the sky is a featureless sepia, smooth like a fading memory. This could be a dream.

"Whose?" murmurs the sea, lapping.

'Welcome to Jutland,' says the sign through the window. Very confidently. It says, 'Welcome to Jutland' very confidently through the window.

There is no one framed in the window in the wall at the moment. No one for the sign to proclaim, confidently, 'Welcome to Jutland' to.

'Welcome,' says the sign anyway, 'welcome.'

By now, Ulysses should be wandering together through Poland. Or what might today be Poland. It's hard to be sure. The only calendar was a complimentary gift, decorated with a picture of Bruges town square. 'Dashed odd thing,' says Ulysses' Number One. Although he says nothing more, Ulysses knows exactly what he means: the calendar vanished some time ago, three weeks at least. At least, Ulysses thinks that's what Number One means. It's too late to ask now. He looks back along the road at the three ships moving along on the backs of his men.

Meanwhile, Admiral Jellicoe is guiding his three ships — their names are lost in the fog and maybe anything — through the water. He feels desperately homesick.

Mrs Blenkinsoe has stopped singing and Vitus looks out of the window with nothing to listen to but the hiss of the needle. Turning round. Hissing. Vitus thinks it reminds him of something. 'Welcome to Jutland,' says the sign out on the street beyond the window through which Vitus is thinking.

Only the sea moves; the sky is lost in the fog and may be anything. Meanwhile, there are three Ulysses wandering together. 'Dashed odd thing,' says one. Exactly what he means lies impossibly distant, lost beyond something else. To ask might as well be a dream.

'Have you ever been to Bruges?'

The other sailors say nothing, only grunt with the effort of carrying three ships overland.

Meanwhile, an admiral — his name is lost in the fog, it may be anything — is a featureless sepia, smooth like a fading memory. Off the coast of Jutland, several ships wander back and forth, forth and back-forth, all forlorn, all a little lost, all a little off the coast of Jutland.

'No, I've never been to Bruges.'

He says nothing more.

'I HAVE this feeling ...'

Perhaps the sky did say that.

Nina finishes writing, *He is always knocking over that dusty boat*, when she hears her supervisor's voice. Glancing at the picture of Fernand Khnopff's *The Abandoned Town*, torn from a book long ago and now stuck to the wall of her cubicle, Nina guiltily gets back to work.

craik!
　　voice at the window
　　finally snares attention
craik!
　　dragging head 'round
　　eyes slow-focusing
craik!
　　magpie, side-long
　　peers back
craik!
　　ring in its beak
　　gold-flecting

　　　　　　　　　gleaming

Vitus watches
　　　　　　and
in looking
　　　　　　knows not
whether to wake
or go back
　　　　　　to sleep

VITUS IS not having a good day. He keeps bumping into people, knocking things over. Knocking over the people he bumps into. 'Sorry,' says Vitus, helping a man he has bumped pick up the lemons that fell out of the string bag Vitus tripped over as he tried to avoid bumping into the man. Vitus is not having a good day. Perhaps this is why, standing at a crossing, waiting for a pause in the traffic and trying not to bump&collide into anyone else, Vitus decides to end it all.

Mikkelborg.

P.A. Mikkelborg. Mr P.A. Mikkelborg.

Such a formal title. Such a stiff thing to say. Having to say such an appellation conjures images. It forms an impression. About the person bearing such a name: P.A. Mikkelborg, Mr P.A. Mikkelborg.

The 'P' stands for 'Palle' — *pally*, so much less formal. Friendly, in fact. He used to introduce himself that way, 'Palle'. Not now, but in the past he would say, 'Palle', or he might have said, 'My name is Palle, hello.' There were many possibilities. Unlike now. Now, he snaps: 'P.A. Mikkelborg' and is so much less pally when he does so. Mr Mikkelborg feels (believes, it could be said) that he has no choice, no option, but to snap and be so much less pally as he does so. Why so? Ah, well there was ... call it an 'incident', which is aptly formal for what happened this June — or rather *that* June, the June of the 'incident', although, coincidentally, this is being written in June (rewritten, in fact, a year or so since the June in which it was originally written, if you must know) and June is the time in which Mr P.A. Mikkelborg will fully enter our story. But these synchronicities aside and before that entry, there was the June evening of the 'incident', an evening when P.A. Mikkelborg said: 'P.A. 'P' for 'Palle'' for the last time. And the reply? That was simply: 'Really?' which struck Mr Mikkelborg as being unpleasantly sceptical in tone. Yes, quite sceptical for so simple a statement. So much so, he said, quite stiffly: 'Yes', by way of reply, causing the man, to whom P.A. Mikkelborg had been introducing himself, to laugh:

'Ha-ha-heh ... huh ... ha-huh,' he laughed.

Despite the warmth of that June evening, there was a palpable drop in temperature and the laughter ended abruptly.

'Huh?' came the inevitable response in a tone that was no longer friendly in any way. 'Huh?'

'Palle Mikkelborg,' said the man, taking a step back, shoulders brushing a lamppost, light falling around him as these words, said in a tone that suggested Mr Mikkelborg's name alone explained why that name should cause the reaction it had. It did not. Not for Mr Mikkelborg, who watched the light, the pale yellow light, falling over the man, making a confusion of shadows on the man's face. A confusion that explained so very little and, perhaps, prompted the man against the lamppost to blurt: 'Palle', in a tone of voice that suggested this word, that name, explained everything, before adding: 'Mikkelborg ... See?' after which, he waved one hand.

'Huh?'

Neither man moved, the evening air growing palpable around them, them and the lamppost and the falling light. A distinct drop in temperature, we might say. Which also could explain why the man, the man against the lamppost, stammered: 'Because,' as he pressed his back more firmly against the metal post.

Mr Mikkelborg ('P.A.' to his friends, although not after this) said nothing. And the silence, lamp-lit, grew heavier.

Where laughter and other words had failed, the man, sweating in the heavy lamplight, attempted: 'Because it's the same as a famous trumpeter. Palle Mikkelborg.'

'Yes?'

This being more of a snarl than a question, the man jumped and added, laughter forgotten: 'That's his name. He's very good.' And he waved. In the yellow light. In June. But not in laughter. Adding: 'Your name, see? A coincidence —' But P.A. Mikkelborg (friend to no one just then) stepped into the light, the light very yellow as he, Mr P.A. Mikkelborg to everyone from now on, put a hand inside his jacket. And stepped closer.

'But, but,' stammered the man, pressing himself up on tiptoe against the lamppost, needing to create as much space as possible between him and Mr Mikkelborg as he, Mr Mikkelborg, stepped closer. 'It's a compliment.' Pressing harder and adding, 'In a way,' as he watched that hand move under the jacket. A jacket on a warm evening in June, with a hand inside. Gripping something. With an edge, a definite edge, Mikkelborg, *Mr*

Mikkelborg, closed his mouth, and smiled, and took his hand from inside his jacket. 'What do you think of this? Coincidence enough?' Neither spoke. Nothing moved. Except for the lamplight. Running over the barrel of the pistol.

Vitus, sure he is doing the right thing, looks up at the June sun half-exposed by cloud, half-hidden by the tall buildings lining the street. And walks into someone else.

Vitus apologises. The woman he walked into tells him it's all right. Vitus walks away. Thinking. Thinking he used to like this month. Thinking: always my favourite month this, June, that is.

'Yes? That is what?'

Out loud. He had never meant to think out loud. Just like bumping into people. Only, now, worse, thinks Vitus, internally, as he apologises to June, who happened to be the person he had bumped into. What a coincidence, thinks Vitus, thinking this is the last straw.

June sunlight touches the wall beside the mirror, a mirror always turned towards the wall, has been turned to the wall since June, another June, past and, so, unlike this one still passing. In that sense at least, thinks P.A. Mikkelborg, accepting what light is reflected from the white walls, using that light, although not in a malicious or exploitative sense, to guide him to the chest of drawers beneath the face-turned mirror. The light finds the gun before P.A. Mikkelborg. But the coin, call it 'keepsake' if you will, that it does not touch.

Vitus climbs towards the top floor. The very top. Three more floors to go. Vitus takes no notice of a voice raised, shouts drifting along the stairwell like sunshine, or light from a street lamp. No notice at all.

Mikkelborg, P.A., 'Mr' to almost everyone now, pats a pocket, pats another, steps, pockets patted, contents confirmed, out the door into a wall of yellow light. And heat. Warm air, warmed by the light. Not warm: hot, in fact, hotter than Junes should be. Blazing hot and sweat trickling down nape of his neck, P.A. Mikkelborg squints, dabbing at sweat-beads running and disconcerted by the heat. The sweat trembles. The sweat runs. Mikkelborg dabs, pats once, twice, this pocket, that pocket, only one neck, of course, although the actions are very similar, saying: 'This won't make a difference,' none of the actions getting in the way of thought. Or breath: one deep breath, and Mr Mikkelborg steps into the street, conscious of the weight in this pocket, the heavier weight in that pocket. Conscious of the heat. Not to his taste, heat, not this hot. Not in June, thinks P.A. Mikkelborg. In fact, weather like this, he thinks as he walks, could put him right off June. He thinks, thinking out loud.

'Oh, thanks,' says June, hurrying on by and wishing she had stayed at home.

The voice raised is loud enough for Vitus to notice, even as he pushes the bar, leans against the door. Finds sunshine, hot and yellow, waiting for him. He, Vitus that is, has to squint as he looks down on the streets. Streets like a map. Only deep, adds Vitus. Deeper. But maplike.

And hot.

Vitus stands on the edge of the parapet, thinking life would be so much better without maps.

According to plan. So thinks Mr P.A. Mikkelborg. As his hands stray. One pocket considerably lighter than the other; the other considerably bulkier. But according to plan. Mr Mikkelborg (to everyone, these days, he has only business acquaintances) touches the keepsake once and opens the door.

A shot is fired.

Mr Mikkelborg (such a stern form of address but it does suit his chosen profession) enters the entrance lobby through an entrance bathed in deep, deep sunshine. Smoked glass cuts the sunshine dead. Mr Mikkelborg walks through shadows towards what might be the only light here: a single bulb, shedding a pool of almost-yellow, not-at-all-saffron light, something like a streetlamp's glow. Mr Mikkelborg walks past corners fallen silent, towards the pool of light. Leaves the pool of light behind before it has chance to do anything but fall. The light cuts out, timer expired. Makes no difference: Mikkelborg knows the way.

Heat, yellow and light, too. Pressing Vitus firmly. Heavy heat.

Vitus opens his mouth and says, nothing. The city, likeamap, lies. Somewhere below. The roof, hard against his back. Pressed firmly and, inevitably, pressing. Equal and opposite, so firmly held.

Vitus thinks about falling.

About maplike: an approximation that was close enough he had thought, falling. Falling down, of course. Under weight of heat, unequal and parallel pull of gravity. Streets likeamap he was falling towards, more into by the second. Heat pressing.

Down.

Pressing firmly.

Enough. thinks Vitus, peeling himself off the roof and throwing himself out into space again. Towards those streets lying maplike, less far below by the second.

A shot was fired.

Afterwards, he left the pool of light behind. The alley having reached a dead end, there was only one way to go. Never again able to be pally, he touched the keepsake in his pocket. Left behind, in the pool of light, a pool of a different sort formed: moving of its own accord as it slumped, slumped a little further away from the base of the lamp column. Or, perhaps, as *he* slumped away: in a sense still 'he', although a 'he' saying nothing and no longer able to move without assistance. The pool spreading by itself as footsteps receded along the alley now dead. One hand straying to the keepsake and the only mind left, wondering: how could events have strayed so unexpectedly away from the map in his head.

The stairwell door opens, saying nothing. The city lies where Vitus left it: beyond the edge of the roof, around the base of the building. Laid out, maplike; lying likeamap. Vitus stands where his legs have placed him, the stairwell managing to fall and fall and fall away without any apparent difficulty. Vitus cannot contain his envy.

A second shot is fired less than five seconds after the first.

Mikkelborg takes the lift. It knows the way. Up, this time.

One foot out. In the air and therefore a drop below. One foot, perhaps less as these risers are not all that deep. Vitus lets the foot … descend. A controlled fall. The only sort he seems capable of, remembering falling:

> *from the parapet*
> *into the lying map*
> *streets planned and drawn closer*
> *or drawing closer, Vitus being too preoccupied to decide*
> *but falling to meet, rising to be met*
> *less than a foot*
> *e n v e l o p i n g , rushing*
> *sun overhead*
> *roof pressing against his back*
> *& heat pressing down*
> *equally if oppositely:*

this is what Vitus remembers.

His foot safely presses against the next stair, that stair passing Vitus onto the next. In complete control. Hardly seems like falling, Vitus thinks, thinking of falling towards the lying city below, thinking of thinking about thinking that ending it all is still a good idea, only to think that thinking this through might well make him think differently. Or at least that trying again might end up in a result not so very different from what he has now, so —

Vitus, one foot in the air, thinks about drowning in one inch of water. Thinks that depth might not lie at the heart of his

90

difficulty. And, one foot hovering in the balance —

lowers himself to the next stair, past the next landing, taking flight — Rather: taking the next flight: not anything as unexpected or as disappointing as landing on the roof, taking flight of a sort only to land on the roof again, landing there a last time, the time before peeling himself off that self-same roof and dropping one foot, then the other, one stair to the next. Not anything like that, but waiting for him much the same, next landing drawing closer, his foot about to set itself upon it.

Which is when Vitus will hear the third and final shot and, in hearing, remember the previous two very differently.

Mikkelborg steps out of the lift, wonders briefly about turning right, and goes left after all. Knowing he will get to the same place in the end.

Vitus will be hesitating on the landing when the stranger bursts through the door to the stairwell. They will stare at each other: the stranger in a suit that bulges oddly under the left arm; and Vitus, hesitating over his memory of three gunshots. The stranger will have one hand gripping the stairwell door. The other will touch the jacket pocket, stray towards the bulge under his left arm. Hand looking oddly lost as Vitus quickly looks away, catching a glimpse of that hand, falling, touching the pocket, and appearing at the top of the arc again. Hesitating. As if confused. As if it is expecting to find itself somewhere else.

Not waiting for the door to open beyond an initial crack. Shoulder leading the way. Door banging off hallway wall. Voice raising sharply — the other man, his voice raising sharply as the door rebounds again. Fails to latch. Voice higher, shouts carrying. Past Mikkelborg, along the corridor outside. Becoming lost somewhere. Forgotten. At least, Mikkelborg takes no notice of them. Walking towards this man. This man he has come to visit with. Briefly.

Like a fall. Running. Pell-mell. Downstairs. Like a fall. Vitus will have forgotten the roof, his failure to fall and be accepted by the lying city. Have forgotten that. Forgotten coming out of sun into building, climbing stairs he is now dashing down headlong. Become empty of everything but a man in a suit, the sound of —

Vitus will raise his voice, scream, unable to lie about how he feels.

As he strode easily towards the stairwell doorway — conscious of the keepsake, the deadweight in the inside left pocket of his jacket, of the memory of a unlit lamp toppling beside a brimming pool, of sunlight on the stain as it settles into the carpet as the body lay slumped — Mikkelborg, P.A., reflected it was good to be wanted, to have clients and associates who took satisfaction from the quality of his work. Good to be wanted, he thought, before pushing open the stairwell door and seeing the man on the stairs from the corner of his eye.

Jellicoe turns away. He does not want to see what happens next. It is as if he has had a premonition.

She was unable to move. Frozen, she must stand there, mouth open in an *O*, and take it all in. Jane Franklin felt the letter slip from her fingers.

All Mrs Blenkinsoe will be able to do is point.

Three shots were fired. They will say that later. They will say a great many things. But the name, 'Mikkelborg', will not be among them.

June offers to help the man to his feet. Wouldn't you, in the circumstances? But the man, who looks as if he has been running wildly, a wildly-desperate looking man, refuses her help and runs away. Leaving June wondering if she will ever connect with anyone.

Mikkelborg points at the man from the stairs. Stands in the street, in the sunshine, pointing at a back and shoulders rapidly dwindling into the distance. Getting further away, until Mikkelborg concedes there is no point in trying to follow, little chance the man from the stairs will remember very much at all. Instead, he tells himself this will do nothing to alter the way people want him.

Unnoticed, there is a boy in a pristine white sailor suit. But there is no reason for us to take any notice of him, is there?

VITUS FOAMS over the shingle, murmuring in his sleep. The cove lies ahead, beyond his reach. Moments later, still sleeping, Vitus rolls backwards towards a horizon dreaming of rain.

THERE WERE now three ships wandering —

No. I am sorry. Let me begin again:

There are now three captains wondering, names lost in the mist, features like a sepia that is bleached, beginning to turn indistinct despite having been in a frame all these years. Lips caught. Between one motion and the next, so any sound they may have made is lost. There is only silence as they wander. Wondering. Three of them, distinctly, no matter how much the fog swirls, clinging to them like spindrift. Blending one into another as they stumble along a path that, itself, slips away every time they think they've grasped hold of it, smooth and fading, smooth and failing to come to any sort of end. They may be anywhere, although that hardly seems true. The captains, three, possibly distinct, certainly a little lost, must, surely, be somewhere. Wandering. Somewhere, at least, no matter how featureless it looks in this fog. How much it feels like a dream. 'This feels like a dream,' one of the captains will probably say at some point, even if that point is lost in the fog and could be anywhere, moving or static, simply anywhere. One of the captains will probably think this or say it. Very probably. Very probably say it, or think it, with something like confidence very probably. And he will be wrong.

Probably.

Turning around, turning round, everywhere feels much the same. Featureless, smooth, fading away just beyond an outstretched arm. 'Welcome to nowhere,' and the arm, outstretched, points the way ahead. 'Or somewhere.' 'I wonder where we are.' 'This way. Like a dream.' Like a dream turning back on itself. Leading them, the three captains who might once have been all at sea and now no less so, leading them to wonder
—

Perhaps not. No, this hardly seems right either, does it? Do you mind if I begin again? I'll begin again:

There may be three ships. Three ships wondering if they are together, perhaps on the North Sea, perhaps on a windowsill in Bruges in a room in a place where the sun could touch them, quite silently, quite silently moving across them standing in a windowsill in Bruges in view of the market hall, casting shadows beneath each hull, each ship on a shadow on a windowsill on the point of wondering if this is Bruges or somewhere much quieter, sun wandering across rigging and smokestacks, oars and tillers, thoughts wistful as the westering sun wonders if it hasn't seen all this before. Far to the east, yes, but before, earlier, to the east, earlier and easterly and on some other window ledge. Beside a sign pointing outwards. Pointing out that this is not Bruges. Ignoring the ships, all three of them. Perhaps because they are static, not wandering. Not along this road anyway. Yes, east of here, although not by this road. It wanders. The road. Meandering, turning back on itself, winding, ambling itself on back turning until almost looping, twisting away meanderingly, and leading, leading back, back to where there may be three ships, three ships wondering if they are together, perhaps on the North Sea, perhaps on a windowsill in Bruges in a room in a place quite like this. Quietly moving to a standstill, in view of all that has happened following the road. Sun overhead. Leaves turning. Twisting. Snaking like this road. This road which continuously points and leaves and turns and twists and meanders like a river, a river coiling, sinuous, all oxbow lakes and purls, murmuring indistinctly through each twist and turn and leaving each point continuously behind only to return to almost the same spot, maddeningly twisting away to return almost, at almost the same spot, maddeningly anfractuous, probably, meanderingly exasperating, certainly, until the certainty unspools that all this meandering is meandering without hope of ever actually finding a terminus

because the only terminus is the sea and every sea becomes rain becomes rivers again, each and every one wondering if there is an end to their wandering

Actually, this isn't what I meant to say at all. It might seem like it, but it isn't. Let me, let me begin

JOHN FRANKLIN, boats missing, crew gone, the Northwest Passage no better than an opium fugue, wanders in a daze. He finds a road that smells of brine and ozone. Believing it to be a fantasy, he turns away. Behind him, a sign says 'Welcome to —'. The rest is lost.

> **lost** *v.* **1** absence-like experience, underscored by feelings of bereavement and non-comprehension, which may be defined by cranial structures dislocated within apparently discrepant topographical arrays. **2** panoptic dissociation. **3** a small voice raised.

John Franklin, before missing boats and missing crew now gone, dreamed of a northwest passage. He dreamt of it for a long time. A long time. Dreaming of the waves, the boats defining a passage between Atlantic and Pacific, Labrador and Bering, or back, forth and back, passing between land and sea, awake and dreaming. When he woke, Franklin was sure the passage must exist and, for a time afterwards, he slept believing this. Sometimes on land,

and sometimes with the sea beating against the hull. He slept, sometimes, in command of three boats: *Bellerophon, Terrebus* and *Error.* Now, awake, his crew is lost, his three boats are lost, and he wanders in a daze. The road, winding, wavers between up and down, valley and hill, rocky and not so rocky, taking days to get from here or there, but somehow missing out on anything to do with water. It has been perhaps a long time since it last rained. Franklin, stumbling, thinks sometimes of opium and only dreams dreams of loss.

> **loss** *n. & v. • n.* **1** a moment of whiteness, fading. **2** the aftertaste of this that lingers. • *v.* **1** (in the sense of *n.* **1**) instantiating such a moment within a landscape. **2** projecting nothing through time, or beyond roughly-circumscribed cranial structures.

Franklin stumbles.
  Vitus looks.
  Ulysses looks and stumbles.
  And Jellicoe? He climbs over the side and drops onto the cobbles and runs across the square. Fog shrouds the market hall, muffling his footfalls one after the other until they fade into sepia. Murmuring, murmuring, he runs on. Ignoring the signs saying 'Welcome to —' and 'This Way to —' and 'Bruges Welcomes Careful —' and the windows, especially the windows with their proclaimed confidence fading like sepia. This could be anywhere he remembers, only his feet making any sound and that sound muffled by the fog lapping over the cobbles. He could have meant something else. Jellicoe's Number One. Almost anything when he said: 'Dashed odd, this war with Sweden being over so long and all.' Not the words so much has his tone of voice. And that stutter.

Franklin stumbles. Looks, stutters, stumbles and looking, stutters to a halt. This place is sepia, unlike a dream. It is neither loss nor lost, and so unlike the Northwest Passage and yet, ahead, without any sign pointing the way, he sees —

Ulysses stares. Somewhat in turmoil, partly in surprise; mostly at the figure in front of him. At first he had thought it was Number One. Then a sign, pointing. Pointing towards Ithaca, or towards the sea. Pointing at one or the other. Either would have done. But it isn't a sign. At least not that sort of sign, although it is pointing. Pointing and shouting until Ulysses, at a loss, missing what was said at first, draws close enough. Enough to hear. Hear clearly through the mist. 'Dashed odd,' Ulysses thinks although it's too late now to turn back.

'You've got my boats,' Franklin repeats. 'Those. Boats. Those are —'

'The *Bellicose, Erebus* and *Terror.*' Ulysses tries to sound firm, captain-like. Like a man anchored, a man not-adrift. But, as he speaks, he feels more than a little lost. More than that. And, when he and Franklin part the mist, Ulysses finds different boats. And different men struggling down the winding road under each hull. Hulls creaking as shoulders creak, landscape turning like a dream.

'*Bellerophon* —' he reads the letters as they appear out of the mist along the tip of each prow — '*Terebus* and ... *Error* ...'

'No.' Franklin looks up and reads the exact same letters. '*Bucephalus ... Euphony ... Terminus ...*'

Mrs Emmeline Blenkinsoe falls silent. The Victrola falls silent. Admiral Jellicoe falls over the side. The Bellicose falls by the wayside. Jellicoe fails to fall across the sea.

The sea, dreamlike in its dreams, fades away.

The sign says, 'Welcome to —' It coughs, stumbling over the next word so that it is lost. Lost or hidden. Either. The result is the same although it could have meant something else.

The sea sighs.

sign *n. & adj.* • *n.* **1** a gesture about to become familiar. **2** impending uncertainty over this. • *adj.* as indicative of.

THE SEA sighs. Welcoming or at least accepting. Which is almost the same. Its face hidden as it opens its arms, fingers searching. Almost the same. There was a letter here, you see, here, hidden, hopefully not lost. Say 'misplaced'.

misplaced *n.* **1** coldness turning grey. **2** an experience that extends beyond cranial structures indefinitely. **3** the feel of, for example, this paper when finding a definition incomplete.

The sea sighs, drawing back into itself. Fingers no longer so, so, mobile. Yet still searching. Sighing and searching for words.

A letter, you see. It was here. Now … Now please let it be misplaced. (Stumbling over some other thought best left unsaid. Sighing.)

Three days at least. Unseen for three days. Words remembered though. Arms thrown wide, wider, gulf widening as the sea continues to draw into itself.

(I dreamt of you last night. It doesn't mean anything, I'm sure.)
Into itself.

(You see, I wasn't sure. When you spread your arms.)
Drawing in or back. It's almost the same.

(Please accept … No, I can't ask that, but in this dream …)
Welcoming everything it touches. Only, you see, to push it away just the same, stumbling over the realisation that 'misplaced' is not just a word, but the wrong word.

The sea sighs.

sigh *n. & v.* • *n.* **1** expulsion. **2** towards a point of no return. **3** the air displaced by the last person leaving a room. • *v.* **1** to cause expulsion. **2** searching for a feeling of regret (possibly in the sense of *v.* **1**). **3** the act of trying to prevent any of these.

MRS EMMALINE Blenkinsoe falls silent. The Victrola falls silent. Admiral Jellicoe falls over the side. The Bellicose falls by the wayside. Admiral Jellicoe fails to fall into the sea.

The sea, dreamlike in its dreams, fades away.

Vitus searches for crayons, another sheet of paper. He was going to write another letter. Draws a map instead. A road. Winding. Twisting between hillsides, coiling as it does so. Or as Vitus draws it, tongue caught between teeth and lips, between one hillside and the next. Hillsides green. Road brown. Paper beyond grey, a little grey, grey in this light at least. Empty, certainly. At least until Vitus colours it in. Lines black, spaces between this colour, that. Vitus hasn't imagined a name for the road (winding), hills (coiling, rising and twisting).

Perhaps it doesn't matter.

As for the space still to be coloured in (grey-like paperspace not yet defined), that's going to be —

Vitus reaches out. Fingers searching. Looks and searches, fingers spread and hand outstretched.

But he can't find the blue crayon anywhere.

The sign points.

Admiral Jellicoe falls.

Ulysses? He looks at the winding road, the ships, and the green slopes of the hills rising all around, seeming to draw him and the others deep into themselves.

Coiling.

I found the map the other day. The paper has grown quite yellow, although the wax crayon looks no less bright. I couldn't remember drawing it at first. The map was as much of a surprise as the act of finding it. Now, after looking at that yellowed sheet of paper again and again, I think I do remember. Remember using orange for the sky. (Sky on a map? Well, I suppose it's as much a part of the landscape as the hills and the road. Besides, it's a funny kind of map: I drew in people reading the map I was drawing, I suppose because they belong to the landscape as well.) I remember looking for the sky-blue crayon and not finding it, getting quite upset over the loss. And I remember eventually getting over that upset only, later, to find the crayon lodged where the carpet met the wall under the windowsill. I look at this map now and I remember all of these things very clearly.

Which is odd because I'm almost positive I never owned any wax crayons. Only pencil crayons.

It doesn't mean anything, I'm sure.
If it means anything, I'm not sure.

> **meaning** *n. & v.* • *n.* **1** an overwhelming sense of familiarity. **2** internal pressure. • *v.* To wish for something to the point of amnesia (cf. *white cloth*).

The sign? The signed turns to point to itself.

Vitus leaves his cot. Leaves it in his room although he can hardly take it with him, carrying all that weight on his little shoulders. So the cot stays in his room, telling itself it's all for the best, that it does not feel abandoned, does not.

And his room, how does that feel?

The sign leaves its post, pointing its own way to the shore. The North Sea falls silent.

Three boats stand above the shore, tethered to three men, also standing, also above the shore.

Vitus looks.

Ulysses looks.

As does Franklin. As would Jellicoe, if he were here.

He isn't.

Vitus stands where Jellicoe may have stood, little shoulders heaving from exertion. (The Admiral may have stood like this. He may not. We may never know. But the sky is the same, waxy and the same.) Vitus looks, standing and looking, shingle no longer making a sound now he has stopped moving.

His room stands above the shore, tethered.

Vitus's cot looks.

Introductions:

'Fine young man …'

'Pleased to make your …'

'Cor, are them your boats …

'It's a very nice cot, young man …' (Jellicoe says this. But Jellicoe is not here. He fell, fell and never hit. Jellicoe is not here. The third man says this. His face is faint, a sepia grown faded and his name may be) 'anything, ask anything.' Ulysses smiles down at Vitus (Vitus who is, at least seems, a little taller than when he first appeared, towing his room).

'Your boats are awfully dry,' says Vitus, smiling up (asks Vitus in a voice that pipes, breaks, pipes just a little taller than before).

'Yes, and dusty,' laughs Jellicoe. (But it can't be Jellicoe, he fell but never landed, fell by the wayside.)

'Yes, dusty,' says Franklin (who is watching Ulysses, telling himself it doesn't mean anything).

'You know,' says Ulysses, 'I had a dream. The strangest dream. About a vast expanse of water.' He smiles. 'Huge. So huge I've no idea what you would call it. Besides 'vast', of course.' And he laughs, at his own joke, at the silliness of dreams. The others (Franklin, Vitus, the third man — could he be Number One in disguise?) turn, looking out beyond the edge of shore, looking at —

'You know,' says Franklin suddenly, quite quite unexpectedly, 'I think I have a sixth sense. I know I do, actually.

A sixth sense.'

Vitus shows no sign of scepticism.

Ulysses is beginning to feel a little lost. He can smell brine, ozone. Yet, when he looks out from above the shore, he sees nothing but

(but who is this third man?)

'I have a sixth sense,' says Franklin, voice carrying from above the shore.

BORIS PAUSES after the last full stop, looking out of the window at the wall on the opposite side of the road. Without looking away, he caps his pen, right hand reaching towards the little box at the back of the table in which Boris keeps paperclips and other things, fingers searching.

Finally, Boris has to look away from the wall. Look in the box, use eyes as well as fingers.

It makes no difference. The box is still

NINA LIFTS her fingers from the keys and looks at the coin lying on the desk beside her. In this light, the coin appears almost smooth, it is so very worn. But this is not what Nina thinks. What Nina thinks is not the word 'smooth' but the word

empty *n. & v. & adj. & adv.* • *n.*

. • *v.*

. • *adj.*

. • *adv.*

.

A STANDPIPE.

I didn't mean that. It's very hard to make this clear. What about if I

VITUS WAKES up. And goes straight back to sleep again.

This shouldn't go here. Perhaps you can find a place for it?

ELUCIDATION: what the reader doesn't know is
that 'P.A. Mickelborg' is an alias for one of the
other characters. The reader can never know
this; only suspect —— otherwise, the whole
premise falls apart.

VITUS DRIFTS. In his sleep. Drifting awake. Slipping a little towards wakefulness. Vitus drifts, eyelids fluttering, almost open, almost awake. Vitus drifting. And drifting back to sleep.

VITUS RECEIVES a model dinghy as a nativity present. It sits on a shelf, on a wall, away from the window. Vitus sits. Not turning, watching. Examining reflected light from the window, reflected from the walls, reflected from the dinghy away from the window, reflected all the way from the shelf under the dinghy to the wall to Vitus on the cot under the window. It is bare, the shelf. Completely bare. But for the dinghy on top of it. The dinghy lost in a sea of shelf.

Vitus has no idea what to call this thing he is looking at.

The sign points. Quite directly, quite confidently. It points, it points and says, it points and says quite confidently.

The sign points and says whatever it's told to say.

Mrs Blenkinsoe, Lady Jane Franklin and Penelope guide the dinghy through the flooded streets of Bruges. Their boat does not have a name. It does not need one.

Tacking around a narrow corner into a wide thoroughfare, the dinghy passes a sign. Lady Jane points: 'Ahead, look.'

A pedestal pushes over the tops of the waves. The statue is gone, and only the very top of the plinth is now visible. To one side, a market hall rises out of the sea like a cliff, like a dream of cliffs and headlands, as if the market hall is asleep and its mind is wandering, re-imagining itself in the face of what lies beyond it. In the face of the open sea that has wrapped its arms around the market hall, enclosing it as it encloses the empty plinth, all of Bruges. A broad expanse of open water, waves moving off into the distance. Looking almost sepia in this light, almost limitless, almost as if this headland of brick and tile is the last thing, almost the last thing in the world. Almost. Only, ahead, beyond the limit of Lady Jane's finger, in a far distance muted by mist and low cloud, there is … something. Perhaps this is what the sign is pointing at. Almost sepia against the horizon, almost framed by the inundated buildings that are falling away behind them, almost …

'Jutland.' Mrs Blenkinsoe smiles as she moves the tiller over, guiding the dinghy confidently between the waves lapping against the prow.

Penelope watches the horizon a moment before turning to the small boat's rigging. One strand following the next, she weaves the three women's dreams together. Into rope into mast into sail. She says nothing but Mrs Blenkinsoe and Lady Jane believe they know what she's thinking.

Beyond Jutland. Beyond Ithaca and the Northwest Passage, beyond them something that might lie dreaming, or remembered, or undreamt and yet to be recalled. Uncalled and unseen and possibly in the mind of each woman.

VITUS DREAMS again that night. He remembers the dream next morning. Or, at least, he remembers having dreamt. There might have been a sign, or perhaps a calendar. There might have been a calendar but no sign. Vitus does remember a map washed overboard. Which, he thinks, as he hums the refrain from *Lilac Time*, is odd as he distinctly remembers (or if not distinctly then at least has a strong feeling) that there was no boat in the dream and nothing for it to rest on in any case. No … no … The word escapes him. The word for a large body of water that is not enclosed but encloses, the word that has escaped him and so haunts him, enclosing every thought and every action and every thing he sees through the wall, through the window in the wall.

Which is strange, since Jutland isn't just land. It's enclosed, its outlines defined by … by …

No, the word will not come. Only sensations: a winding path, a feeling of weight, vision confined by something very large overhead, the smell of salt fading.

So Vitus, turning, climbs through the wall. Turning to glance as he climbs. Through the wall, through the hole in the wall, the open window filling part of that hole. Turning to glance back only once before setting forth, or setting out. He's not entirely sure.

The sign points. Confidently.

It stands still and points. Confidently at first.

The sign points, now less so. A little less confidently than before, and then less so still. Standing still, pointing, voice less confident than before. Because the sign only stands and points and speaks. It never goes to where it points, can never quite see what it talks about. Because there may be land in the way, or mist, or because it lacks enough confidence to go and see for itself. Lacks enough confidence because the sign can't shake the notion that what it's saying are only words. A notion, of course, which is only a collection of words itself. Words moving around inside the sign. Moving around and sometimes leaking across its finger, so the words of the notion become what the sign is pointing at. Which the sign thinks might be a bad thing. Which is another point of uncertainty, because the words of the notion seem not so very different from the words the sign speaks aloud, when it stands still and points. When it stood still and pointed. Quite confidently at first. And now much much less so. Because the sign is wondering, hesitantly, searching for confidence in what it wonders, but even so, as the sign stands still and points, it wonders. It wonders if. It wonders: if it could go and see for itself, would it see any difference between notional words and spoken/pointed-to words? And, not only that, if it can't be sure about what it points at, how can the sign be sure about what it wonders?

Mrs Blenkinsoe, Lady Jane Franklin and Penelope carry the dinghy overland. It's just a short distance, just over land. Ahead, there's a sign. The sign points. And there's something written on the sign, so the sign says something. In a sense. Saying something in a voice like waves, hesitantly lapping against the prow of the dinghy. A mist, sometimes light, sometimes dense, always moving, always, moves around the sign. As it moves, the land that Mrs Blenkinsoe, Lady Jane and Penelope walk over seems to move with it. Even over such a short distance. Moves so that it no longer seems solid, seems no longer what it was. To Mrs Blenkinsoe, the land fades away, just a little ahead, a little beyond the next step, fading away like the edge of a mountain high in the clouds. Lady Jane thinks of a cornfield swaying and billowing in the wind. Solid and fixed from close to, comprised of little units; each ear of corn separated from the others just a little, by just a short space. And yet like something whole and integral seen from a hilltop. Flexing and changing, moving always, always fixed but always changing, never quite certain. And Penelope? She thinks of something that has no name. Perhaps it doesn't need one. Or, perhaps, it changes too quickly for a name to stick.

Only the sign seems constant. No matter how the mist moves, the sign hardly wavers.

Vitus heads overland. Oddly, he's confident it's only a short way although he doesn't know the way. Vitus hasn't got a map. Even if he had a map, Vitus is too young to make sense of it. All those contour lines and symbols. You could change them all, every single one, and it would still make no sense. Still be confusing, even if you knew which way is North. Vitus doesn't. He only knows he's heading overland. Just over land, just a little way. Ahead, there's a sign. A sign pointing. And something written on the sign, so the sign says something.

Mrs Blenkinsoe, Lady Jane Franklin and Penelope look at the sign. Each woman thinks she knows what the others are thinking.

Mrs Blenkinsoe frowns. The sign reads, 'Northwest Passage'.

Lady Jane Franklin frowns. The sign reads, 'Ithaca, NY'.

Penelope looks at the sign. Looks at the letters on the sign, hearing, in a way, what it's saying. She frowns, glancing at Mrs Blenkinsoe frowning, at Lady Jane frowning. They move in the mist. Or the mist is moving around, lapping, constantly changing. Changing quickly, so no label can stick. At least, none that Penelope feels confident about. Not now she looks at the sign. Listens to what it's saying, voice becoming lost in the mist so that sometimes it sounds like something lapping and sometimes it sounds like something else, something dry or something that has no name. Penelope glances back, over land, over her shoulder. Looks ahead in the direction the sign points, looks at what it's pointing at now, from each now to the next. And then at the others frowning and she thinks she knows what they might be thinking.

At least, that's what she used to think she could do.

Penelope frowns. Uncertainly, without confidence. What she believes she sees at this moment is a sign saying, 'Jutland'.

Vitus looks over land. He sees something enclosed, its outlines finite but fluid. A little hazy, moving forth, back-forth. Fluid but finite, as if they aren't properly defined. Like a sepia memory, or the smell of salt, fading. Still, there is a sign. Vitus feels confident about that. He stands beside it, looking up through the mist. Just a little mist, the air a little hazy, moving a little back and forth. But definitely a sign. And, around its foot, the marks of other feet. Footmarks and footprints, a little here and a little over there, too. A little faint, as if some people came here to look at the sign. Listen to what it was saying. Vitus turns, glancing back only once, before looking ahead, beyond the land, its outlines fluid apparently. Looking at whatever the sign is pointing out.

They set the boat down a little beyond the sign. Climbing in as the sign stands and speaks, pointing. Pushing off as it points. A little beyond the sign, standing almost still as the dinghy moves hesitantly, swaying a little, sometimes a lot. Moving in the direction of the sign, or at least in the direction the sign points. Swaying, so the sign seems to move, seems no longer fixed. Not quite as solid as it had when they stood beside it and looked up. Through the mist. Moving through the mist, a little hesitantly, but always moving so the mist laps against the prow. Flexing, changing, always moving, the sign continues to point as it falls away behind them. Growing hazy, growing hazier. A little behind. And now further behind, further beyond the limit of the stern as the dinghy moves. Swaying. Hesitantly, lapping. Moving. Moving a little, and then a little more. In the direction the sign was pointing. The sign now fading, now not so fixed. Fading away. Like the edge of a mountain high in the clouds. Fading until the sign changes into something remembered, not a thing you can stand beside and point at. A thing made up only of a word or a collection of words. Words like those on the sign, words like the sign had said.

Which makes them uncertain. Mrs Blenkinsoe, Lady Jane Franklin and Penelope. Because, uncertain as they are about what the sign said, each woman is no longer certain she knows what the others are seeing.

Vitus looks ahead. He has no idea what he is looking at.

'I had this feeling …'
It lingers. A little like a taste on the tongue. The taste reminding you — or someone — of yesterday. You, or someone, or two hours before. A time two hours before now. A time that might have been years ago, for that matter, taste lingering on the tongue. Lingering like a feeling that last touched someone (it might have been you or someone else, someone standing just here, here along the strip of land that formed a margin, the name of which he's no longer sure about, someone who might have been gazing upwards, upwards and skywards (and wouldn't it be strange if this someone, this he or she standing at the margin between here and there, could hear the clouds talking, actually talking about this lingering feeling that they have, just here, just on the tip of the tongue, talking about it, wouldn't that be strange? … but we'll let that pass for now, let it pass untouched, practically, at least touched and passed over, perhaps by someone lingering), upwards of a minute or more, staring and — who knows? — and listening, tongue-tip brushing up against lip-edge, up and back, mind lingering and circling, encircling, searching for (**What was this? This … this feeling I had. I had this feeling …**) just the right thing, just the right description, words of description, descriptivewords always out of reach no matter how much (**who? I'm no longer sure but**

if you could tell me ...) eyes stray upwards, landwards and yes, yes, taking in the open-mouthed clouds, tip-tongued, their faces quizzical and lost in thought as they, in turn, stare skywards) in the hope of identifying the time if not the feeling itself, at least the feeling of the time an hour, or a day (yesterday, open-armed) some time before when this feeling (**I remember this** ...) lay just out of reach, tongue-tip and tongue-tide, search going on like waves for this time not so long ago. Within reach. Which is why it nags, this (**feeling of**) being-out-of-reachness, surely. Memories of yesterday, or someone's two hours ago. Or a time quite unidentifiable. Quite gone, really quite gone.

'I remember this feeling ...'

Perhaps the sky shouldn't say that after all. All the same, it's hard to be sure, isn't it? Sometimes hard. Don't you think?

'I do.'

THE STANDPIPE.

VITUS LOOKS out to see pebbles. Pebbles under a sky that is not quite blue, not honestly grey. Honestly, neither day nor night. Not anything much. Except not pebbles. Unless they're so faraway, I can't make them out, Vitus thinks, possibly out loud, possibly not, so small, they can't be seen and aren't really there. He looks out to see the pebbles at his feet, close to hand, or close by anyway. Vitus looks up to see the sky: grey-blue, honestly, neither day nor night. Looks down: to see pebbles, neither grey nor quite blue. Seeing pebbles growing smaller the further away from him they are. Shrink, shrank, shrunken away, although Vitus thinks they can't be trying to get away from him. But, even so, they shrink away, shrunken by the time *they* get as far away as that. That point, there. The point where it's hard to tell, no matter how hard Vitus looks, peers, wags his head, looking out to see where pebbles end and sky begins.

In between the pebbles: sand. And between the sand grains? Vitus isn't sure. Not-sky, probably. (Possibly, Vitus amends, mentally, mentally adding it to make amends with himself for being so positive, so sure, when really, in this light — not day, not night, not to mention cloudy, uncertain anyway — he is, at least couldn't be, entirely certain.)

Probably, Vitus murmurs, head bowed so even he is no longer certain if it's his thoughts he's commenting on, or what may or may not be between the grains of sand.

Not-sky. Either way. Perhaps.

And not-wet. He can see that. More or less.

And not not —

At which point Vitus pauses, falls silent both inside and out because, for the first time since waking that … day (it seems the safest term), he really can't be sure of anything.

The light moves. Just a little. A little to the left. No, a shade to the right. Or, perhaps — Vitus is sure he's sure he saw something move. The horizon seems the same. And … Yes, the pebbles underfoot look like the pebbles elsewhere: same distribution, same general shape, same lack of apparent movement apparent each time he looks — each time he stops and looks, at least. All of which leaves only the light … doesn't it?

So: the light moves. Behind the clouds, below the horizon. Somewhere, it moves. The light moves as Vitus moves.

Vitus stops.

The light stops. As do the pebbles, the sand, the wave-like movement of the horizon.

Vitus shapes the words, I am dreaming, in his mind, behind his throat, so the movement of muscle and air almost takes place, almost needs to take place. Needs and presses to move.

Vitus says nothing.

The light does not move. Neither does it say anything. We can be certain of that.

Vitus shapes the words, I am still dreaming, in his mind. The words — or the intentions the words imply — impress themselves into muscles, throat, larynx.

    Gripped by uncertainty, Vitus says nothing.

I am still dreaming.

Vitus's mouth is closed. And the light cannot say anything.
    Can it?

A LIGHT moves over the pebbles. Washing over the pebbles, it moves forward, the light, moving before fading, before moving again. Waves of light, light made of waves. Or grains, like particles of wave. Moving. Over the pebbles, over sand. Washing, flowing. Sometimes golden, sometimes grey, greyer, like tin. A tin of light, spilling from Vitus's hand as he moves over the pebbles, fading before stopping completely. No longer moving over pebbles, over sand, not moving over here or there because they both look to Vitus to be much the same: neither here nor there, neither much different to where he is, there and here, neither distinguishable, which is disheartening, a little. There, there.
    The tin is half-full of shadows. 'So shadow is more dense than light.' Thinks *so shadow is more dense than light* again, only aloud this time.
    Vitus appears not to hear. And, there, the pebbles certainly don't. The wave of light, more saffron in tone if not in substance, flows once again. Over pebbles (unmoving). Over sand (unnoticed). Overland and overvitus.
    'Vitus! Over here!'
    He does not notice and is not moved. The tin, brimming with light, wishes it could wave (sometimes in greeting, other times to warn, this time) to attract attention. But the best it can

do is rattle. Brimful of light, it rattles because it is moved. Not exactly by the plight of others (Vitus, in this case, although it can't be certain what lies beyond the horizon), but by others, certainly. Vitus turns, steps forward and turns again, only, now, this is the same as stepping back.

The tin rattles.

Vitus turns again. Now, rattling without, stepping forward. No, back. Except, Vitus, rattling, is facing the way he has come. Which means he is stepping back, back the way he has come. Vitus walking backwards, facing away he is going. Facing theway he has come.

'He has two faces.' The light flows. It sloshes around the tin. Particles of light. Like tiny pebbles.

'Tiny pebbles are sand. Sand is tiny pebbles. So light is made out of sand.'

Facing a way, 'back' the same way as 'come'. Rattling, thinking. Brimful of thoughts. Thoughts flowing.

'Light shines. It glows. It shines and glows and glimmers and must be made of waves of highly polished sand. Dunes of sand, sometimes golden, often less so, gold less than saffron less than tin. Tin …'

The tin falls silent.

Vitus falls over. He closes his eyes. Convinced the light was confusing him as it moved — here and there, going back and coming on again, fading out and fading into a different thought before he had chance to follow the previous one very far, farsightedness useless here where everything looks much the same and the light is so confusing. So Vitus closes his eyes. Walking on, on, on, eyesnotopenness making the light fade, until there is only the feel of the pebbles and the sand between, the next step through air no less substantial than light, but drier, so much drier than he expected. Not expecting the air to become solid in one spot only.

Vitus has fallen over.

The tin, rattling, has rolled away, popping, rolling, falling silent as Vitus has fallen still. Eyes closed until now.

Vitus looks. Up, around. At pebbles, at not-pebbles. Sky and not-sky. At his knees and hands and his not-knees-and-hands. At the standpipe.

The standpipe.

I remember building a wall. From Lego, wood blocks, some brightly coloured plastic cubes with the letters of an alphabet on each face. It was not a big wall, I suppose. But I sat behind it, peeking over the top.

I've forgotten what I was looking at.

The wall began to shrink. Bit by bit. It took a while to notice. A week, a few days more, and it was hard not to think it was a trick of the light. What was so confusing was that, by themselves, the bricks were still the same size. A Lego brick was still a yellow Lego brick. A wood block still smelt of varnish, had the same feeling in my fingers: smoothed grain encased in a deep, satin green stain. The parts of the wall by themselves had not changed. It was the wall that was shrinking.

Back then, the sun took a very long time to set, the days warm and evenings endless. Long story short, I made mud bricks. They dried very quickly under the sun as it hung a hand's breadth above the nearest roof, stretching out every shadow and turning the air ... not golden but a rich saffron. Everything yellow, even my dreams.

And that's how the wall started growing again.

And that's how I found the coin.

I wasn't going to mention the coin. Not because it's painful or significant. Quite the opposite. The story about the coin is utterly ordinary. It was just something I found in the shadow of the wall.

PENELOPE FINDS the coin at the foot of the sign. Before she can pick it up, it moves away. Bending to look at what it has just noticed: a penelope lying at the foot of the stairs. Unravelling before it can pick up the thread. A sign of things to come: the thought appears, waiting to be found, at the foot of the shore. Likewise goldenfound is the sunset bending closer, if too slowly to be noticed, as Penelope moves away before there is any sign left of her having been found there. In the pebbles. In the sand, outstretched. Stretching out, growing wider until the thought appears inescapable.

A sea of sand and pebbles.

VITUS TURNS. Vitus reaches out, turning. The bibbcock squeaks.
Reaching out of the ground. Vitus grasping. The bibbcock,
gripped, squeals, quavering as the valve gives. Before freezing
completely. Vitus, head down, bends closer. Tap, mouth down,
bends not at all, but skleaks and trembles under this new Vitus-
grip. Valve reluctant just the same. Standpipe stuck. In the
ground, under Vitus. Grasped, strained, teeth clenching head.
Cocked. Mouth open. Trembling. Eyes slits. Trembling. One
drop trembles, falls. Becoming a dark circle on pebbles and
sand, on not-sky and not-moving. Not budging. Mouth still, dry.
(Largely.) Skleak-turning as turned, grasped,
straining against bibbcock, stopcock, all stuck,

```
He t oo k
t he coin
away from
m        e
```

Vitus grunting.

Skleak. Give. *Skleak*-give Welling at the
corner of one mouth, swelling. Becoming a
second

                                                                drop

Vitus-gripped, mouth shuddering. Pebbles and sand under
mouth changing colour.

Let that happen again — *drop* — Let that happen — *drop.*
Let that *drop* let   drop let drop let droplet

                                      let   drop

                            let drop let

```
an d peel                drop let
ed  o f f       droplet droplet droplet
t he rind          dropletdropletdroplet droplet drop
```
                          drip

                              drap

flowing. Beginning to flow more freely, if sputtering,
airlock knocking, gush-spluttering over pebbles and sand.
Sand and pebbles turning darker, glistening although the light
hasn't changed these last few minutes. Stopcock open, bibbcock
nattering, and Vitus —

Vitus is gripped. Can no longer let go. Despite his feet

becoming so very not-dry, his legs likewise: not-dry, extra-ordinarily not-dry. Mouth open, gushing. Puddle spreading. Rising — faster, too — so in no time it's hard to tell sky from land, land from non-sky, sky from not-land. Everything moving, flowing, foaming a little, but certainly flowing, so it isn't so easy to tell Vitus from not-Vitus, mouth open and head down, head down and lips wet, reaching out of the rising water: standpipe and Vitus. Vitus and standpipe: head down and open mouths

```
t  h        e
   w        a
      11
```

he took the coin away, snatched it out of
my hand & took it, his face turned away,
even in that moment when he was so
close, as he reached out, took the coin,
nails biting, scouring until there was
nothing left but the rind, bones & rind &
residual heat, his face turned

```
i     n     s
   i
d        e
```

wet, so why not believe it was like this all along:

Standpipe bends, taking hold of the vitus and straining. One hand gripping the other, the other gripping the vitus tightly. Mouth cocked but dry. Standpipe's teeth clenched, shoulders quivering until sound escapes down-turned mouth. The vitus shaking in reply, pushing back against standpipe's hands and refusing to budge. Grip tightening, shoulders grunting and mouth turned down, growing wet, wetter still behind clenched teeth.

The vitus turns. Turns faster, freely under standpipe's grip. Mouth gushing. Over pebbles. Over sand turning dark and splashing.

Vitus flows. In runnels, becoming pools, pools coming together to reflect the sky. Vitus flows in rivulets, streams weaving between the pebbles, coming together to form currents, fingertips, reaching out, flexing.

Vitus gushes from the vitus.

Vitus washes.

Vitus rising higher. Pools into ponds. Currents into spaces that have been dry (not-wet) for a long, long time (not-counted).

Vitus flows. Moving (not-still). Under sky (but not-land). Over land (but not-sky). Vitus: spreading, borders stretching out, growing deeper so the pebbles and sand are absorbed, vanish beneath the lapping vitus, waves beginning to turn across the face of this endless flow of vitus. This vitus —

No. Not 'vitus'. Call it a —

SEA. LURCHING out of its bed. Gasping. Dream. Already fading. Thankfully.

The house was very old, the only one standing — all the others had been used in making the wall. There was only this house and the wall left standing. In those days the sun

```
t    he    wall
d    id    no    t
k          ee    p
h                im
o    u           t
```

```
t       o    o              k
             t              he
c            o          i   n
                            and
p                  e  e     l
ed                     of   f
t    he                     r
     in                     d
```

```
R  e  v
e  a  l
i  n  g
```

hardly rose at all.
It was cold. Frost on
the door handle. Its
smell coming out of
the shadows; air still,
watching. The house
resented attention.
It had survived
by itself, without
any help. Just
the house and the
wall. Of course. An
arrangement. They
had an arrangement.
Not resentment.

Purpose.

The mark appeared on every door in the space of a few days. Until every door looked identical. There was no going inside again. All we could do was find what shelter we could. Finally, someone said out loud what we had all been thinking: that we would have to go to the wall, shelter in its lee. Nobody liked the idea. It brought us too close. Light spilled over the lip of the wall. And there was no way of pretending the construction noise was something else. It sounded huge. It sounded nearly finished.

We never spoke of it afterwards. I left that night. Or what passed for night. Took the helmet, little else. Kept thinking: with the helmet on, visor down ... visor down

```
m      a      p
w      a      s
w      r      o
       n  g
```

... Not that there was
much charge in the
helmet. But it was
something. No map,
no water, no sign.
And the mark.

    I was careful.
Never looked at it.
Careful to keep on
pretending.

i built the wall from whatever was to hand. houses. turf.
memories discarded. mist sometimes. in the mornings mostly.
residue settling out the sky. each evening, visor too caked
to see. and the map. use. less. map. whatever there was,
whatever to hand, whether now or yesterday or tomorrow, i
put it into the wall. too tired to dream, let alone think. there
was only. the wall. the wall. the wall. the wall. the wall. the
wall. the wall. the wall. the wall. the wall. was only the wall.
wall. wall. wall. wall wall wall wall wallwall wallwallwallwa

llwallwall was only
the wall. an end
in itself. a way of
ignoring any other
thought. those that
escaped i caught. as
quickly as. possible.
pulled. i pulled them
tight. squeeze. the
life out. them. placed
each. in. to the next.
course. couldn't
let. didn't dare let.
anything escape.
only add course to.
course. gradually,
the days became. shorter: seconds,

minutes under-
used, unattended.
all went. into the
wall. you wouldn't
understand (don't
exist, probably).
all there was, i
had, was the wall.
so tired to dream.
about the wall,
about anything
beyond the wall.
Only adding to the
next course. only
that left. until. even
that had to go into
the wall.

It sounds like a fly
buzzing, just on the
edge of hearing. I
have nothing to fear,
Nina tells herself

backing out of the room & firmly closing the door.

Boristhinks
it will be cool to
have a character
with a morbid fear
of flies. If only he

Boristhinks
it will be cool to
have a character
with a morbid fear
of flies. If only he

can

get
pas
tth
isf
lip
pin
gwa
ll!

he got past the wall

Vitus finds the coin while floundering through the foaming water. He is scared now, Vitus, searingly, utterly scared. Water up to his thighs and no sign of it stopping. No sign of pebbles or sand, either. Everywhere: water. Vitus turns sharply. Losing his footing and falling. Again. Coughing. Spluttering — what if everything fills with water? what will he do? how will he — spray bursting around him as he claws at invisible pebbles, hidden sand. Coughing as he manages to lurch to his feet. One hand full of wet shingle. The other holding the coin.

I had a sixth sense once, Nina thinks, rechecking the door *is* firmly closed.

Vitus looks at the coin. Turns it around in his hand, flooding waters — floodwaters — forgotten for the next few seconds as he examines his find. (Vitus will not forget the rising water, not be able to ignore the sound of its rising, the white noise clatter retreating to the edge of consciousness where it will lurk, buzzing, churning, for three seconds, eight, at most twelve; until then:) Both faces have been rubbed smooth, whatever had been stamped there hard to decide. A face, of course, features almost erased. And, on the other side ... Vitus cannot make it out. It may be almost anything: an eye, a ship, two people talking. Or words. It might be words, describing those things.

Buzzing continues. Just at the edge of

Everywhere: water. The sky is the only thing it has not hidden. Except Vitus, the standpipe. And now the coin.

Vitus flips the coin. It seems the right thing to do. His hand shakes. From fear. From cold. From fingertips to air to palm: the coin tumbles.

Vitus almost drops the coin.

Instead, it comes up blank.

A buzzing like a fly hearing the surf hiss.

THE SEA no longer believes in dreams. In dreams, belief comes easily. It rises out of fog and foam, becoming shore and headland. Hardwired. Only to vanish. Always the same. Signs gone, portents closed. And belief pulled away in their wake.

Waking, there is only sky, reaching down, waves reaching out. All things undreamt may be there or not. The sea believed and, in believing, looked while awake. Only sky, unreachable. Waves, retreating. The sea no longer believes in dreams of land.

I should have read
the sixth sense, Boris
thinks out loud
      wondering
where that buzzing
is coming from.

i had read *the sixth sense*.
without it, i never would
have started any of this.
the last remaining copy
came with me behind the
wall. i don't know: did i
want to protect it or was
i thinking of destroying
it, unconsciously blaming
the book for all that has
happened. or maybe i
was only ever intent on
breaking the pages down
until they merged with
the wall
words&brick
words&brick
     everything else was
going
     (fading, you could
say)
               ozone
             sunlight
                wall
little else left
          except me
        the sixth sense
            and …
so i can't say. perhaps
there was an idea to use
it as a weapon. a smell at
the back of the throat,
nothing more. i don't
know. in the end
     well, you know the
end

So, Boris tries turning off the standpipe. The basement is so full of water, it is hard to get a grip. Boris fumbles with the tap, dropping the coin into the flood. The coin! says Boris, suddenly distracted by a loud buzzing com

Nina stops typing. She looks around the walls of her cubicle. Thinking, I'm really going to have to see the doctor. Hearing: a noise just like surf rasping over a pebble beach

So, Vitus tries anyway. Tries turning off the standpipe. There's so much water now. So much, there's nothing but water. A great, rolling endless mass of water, more than enough to make a … make a …

Vitus abandons the word. No time to search, no time to anything. Except be very frightened. And turn off the tap. So much water (foaming around Vitus as he half-wades, half-paddles — half-drowned — towards the standpipe), so much water.

So much is too much.

Vitus drops the coin.

The coin! thinks Vitus and abandons the coin. No time. No time for that, only gripping the tap, gripping and grunting and gritting and grinding (tap under hand; pebbles under foot underwater). Vitus turns. The tap resists (foaming around Vitus). Vitus, desperate (desperate Vitus), tries again.

The tap resists.

Tries again (desperate foaming).

Tap resists

tries

resists

the tap resists (grunting, foaming) resists the tap resists the tap resist the tap

Breaks.

Vitus, staggered, staggers, falls. Water closing over his head, one hand outstretched, poking above the water like, well, like a standpipe.

Surfacing ("spluttering … spray bursting around him … coughing as he manages to lurch to his feet. One hand full of wet shingle. The other …'), looking at what is in his hand.

> **tap** *n.* a device by which a flow of liquid or gas from a pipe or vessel can be controlled.

Vitus looks at the card, failing to notice a noise just like surf rasping over a pebble beach

BORIS PUTS a full stop after the words 'a noise just like surf rasping over a pebble beach'.

I don't remember sleeping much during those days. Each time my eyes started to close, I jerked awake. Got up and walked around, sometimes. Or took deep breaths, holding my eyes wide open. It would be fine for a little while. But I'd eventually begin falling asleep again. If I did sleep, it was never restful. A blankness for a period, then my eyes would snap open. I never went to sleep after that. There was nothing else to do but get up, walk around, marking time, feeling it crawl by as I stood and watched.

Afterwards, I don't know if I was tired or not. It didn't seem to matter any more. Nothing much did.

So, yes, it was a pretty sleepless time. As to dreams, I don't think I did. No, not once. I didn't dream at all.

after the last explosion,
a fragment of wreckage
remained
          enough to
          cling to
waves settled
                    smoothed
                    foam
          clinging to
each crest
          accumulating
                    white
                    foam
reforming, crystals
sparkling on the
                    last
piece of wreckage
                    ice

                              spreading

AL ON E A
L   ON E ON
A   DE SERT
O   F
    I   CE

after the last galley

tumbled over the

cliff's edge

its sound

echoed &

reverberated

doubling

redoubling

clinging to

the hillsides

until

a hundred

ships

broke up in the

valley below &

he

pressed his hands

his ears needing

this to

end

```
A  L    ONE
I  N      A
D  ES ER  T
   O  F
C  R  A  G  S
```

It was just a coin. I lost it not long after. I only remember that coin because it was the first thing I found in the shadow of the wall. At the time it meant nothing at all. Only later, looking back, trying to piece everything together. You know: nothing means anything out of context.

It was a few days before I found anything else. I spent a lot of time inside the house. Trying blotting out how empty the place was, I set up this old tape player. One cassette was all I had. A tape of surf, *the sea*. So that's what I played, volume up so the cassette player rattled. Still *feels* strange, thinking of the house full of the sound of waves, like it had come *adrift*, floating and bobbing behind the wall, *no longer* fixed if not *exactly* free. Waiting for a strong wind to send it spinning away. And me, lying on the floor, drifting too but *awake*. Listening to the tape hiss, the waves rolling in, hissing, rolling out, carrying me drifting along with them. *not* *asleep* but able for a little while to forget the house

141

being empty, forget being
. The house creaking   *alone*.
in the afternoons, like we
were floating on   ,   *the sea*.
me and the empty house,
yellow   sunlight   turning
hazy,   tape   turning   over
and   shadows   *lapping*.
        the edges of the   *against*.
room, like the waves in the
recording   rolling   against
        I'd never see. Not   *shores*.
thinking of anything. Not
thinking   .   *of nothing*.

the coin
postcard, edges burred
                    faded
feather, white tips
                    ragged
manifold, the word
                    alone
pipe, opium-burned
                    isolated
& the map, foldlines torn
                    forgotten

you see, the
wall was porous, things

leaked through

Vitus comes to a crossroad
Penelope comes to a crossroads
Mrs Blenkinsoe sees a crossroads
Jane stands at a crossroads
                    looking around
Ulysses stops at a crossroads
John Franklin stops at a crossroad
June spreads her arms at a crossroads
                    turning
Mikkelborg pretends there is another crossroad
Jellicoe pretends there is no crossroad
                    each stands
                    under a sign
Nina writes 'crossroads'
Boris writes 'crossroads'
I am writing 'crossroads'

the sign
        is
    blank

Ulysses and John Franklin dragged themselves out of the wreckage. To go on was useless. They knew that. All around them was water. As firm as sand and almost as dry to the touch. Dig into it and it flowed sluggishly back into the hole. Stand on it and your feet sank and gave with each step.

Franklin and Ulysses drag themselves out of the wreckage. To go on is useless. They know this. Marooned on a desert of water. Crews gone. Boats smashed.

They will drag themselves out of the wreckage. There will be nothing but water where, before the catastrophe, there were names: Ithaca, Northwest Passage, Bruges. There will be no names in this place. Only 'Ulysses' and 'Franklin' will remain. And 'Jellicoe', that name will survive. Unclaimed, quite unclaimed.

Why will the man calling himself 'Jellicoe' do this?

Vitus drops the card. Water rising: around his knees, around his thighs, all around here but especially around his waist (size — but that would be telling, besides, Vitus is going to get plenty of exercise in a moment, but before then:)

Vitus stared at the card.

(Water rising quite regardless.)

Vitus felt confusion.

(The water felt its way upwards.)

Vitus dropped the card.

(In surprise. Or into the water. Take your pick, the result is the same:)

Vitus founders, throwing up spray as he searches. Searching through spray thrown up as, floundering, Vitus grasps handfuls of water. All he comes up with is

nothing.

Except water, rising beyond his waist. Nothing but water and the sound of it rising without sign of stopping. Oh yes, and

the rasp of surf over a pebble beach.
    Vitus starts swimming.

The
man who was Admiral Jellicoe
sighs. Lowering himself to
the dirt. Shadow long as
it skins out from under
him. He admits, as he
stretches out his legs,
ankles together, and
clasps his dirty
hands loosely
in his lap, he
admits to
being tired.
This has not
been easy, no
matter how
efficiently he
has done all
that he has
done. So, for
the next few
moments,
he will take
what time
there is.
Sit. Look.
At the
wall.

Before
she left,
she buckled on
the icaruswings
tightly. The air
was sepia, every edge
softened by dust hanging
in the air. She said nothing,
looking only at the harness. There
wasn't much to say. Or if there was,
there was no way of saying it. All words
were wrong. She took the helmet from my
hands and stepped
outside.
She may have glanced back. I'll never know.

148

JUNE WALKED through the streets one last time. Eyes on every pedestrian passing by, every person passed. Watching their lips. Or eyes. Or lips and eyes. June watched in challenge. On this street one last time. Watching in challenge in the streets this one last time. Waiting for one of them, any one of these strangers, to say something about her. June knew one of them would. Ever since June she had known. Two months gone, waiting. On lips and eyes. Nobody said anything. Not here, not in this street, or on that corner, or anywhere else this time or any of the other times. Not one strange lip or stranger talking about her in all that time. So June was taking herself away, leaving. She couldn't stand the suspense.

I can't, thought June, walking through the streets one last time, thinking: and I was always keen on Augusts.

'Oh,' said the next strange passer-by, stopping at last, 'that is nice to know,' he said as June, mouth open but otherwise silent, thinking what she last thought was said and not very quietly at all, stood at the end of a block she was intending never to come back to after this, watching the stranger. 'I'm an August,' said August out loud. 'Isn't this a coincidence? Wouldn't you say a coincidence? You speaking, me passing,' August spoke, gesturing as lips moved, eyes on June, 'quite a coincidence, I'd say, quite, wouldn't you?'

June said nothing.

June said, 'No,' said June, 'no surprise. I have a sixth sense about these things.'

Boris looks at the words 'about these things'.

New graffiti on the wall opposite. Fresh scraps of writing taped around the room. The sound of a fly buzzing in the hallway.

'about these things'

He's not satisfied with this at all. Wishes, in fact, he hadn't bothered to begin with.

Nina taps a thumbnail against her front teeth. This whole interlude doesn't belong.

'Yeah, wish I hadn't bothered to begin with.' Nina scrolls up the screen. 'That bit's true, alright.'

She shakes her head. She feels tired. Fine before she wrote these last passages. Tired as she reads back.

Nina is working at home. The noise in the office is too much, even on lunch breaks. And her supervisor ...

Probably, Nina tells herself, paranoia. Her supervisor — her name is June, Nina's supervisor — probably has no idea Nina has been working on this during work-time. It is, she tells herself, only paranoia. Nina's supervisor, she tells herself, probably knows nothing.

Nina sighs. Stops tapping her teeth. Looks away from the screen. And sees the word 'buzzing' highlighted in her notebook.

The house is quiet at the moment. They have even stopped work on that wall going up on the opposite side of the road. ('They?' Nina writes on a Post-it, wondering who they might be.)

She turns to the notes on the island. A lot of notes. Which never seem enough. Nina skims over the notes, unable to shake the grey feeling that she can't write about these things until she knows more. Has thought more.

P.A. MIKKELBORG.

Mr P.A. Mikkelborg.

Such a formal title. P. for 'Palle', which is so much more —

P.A. Mikkelborg is not feeling very friendly just now.

It may be that all this is an opium fugue. It has happened before. Flashbacks, periods when the people he meets do not agree with the version of reality 'P.A. Mikkelborg' is living through at the time. He has thought, in the past, and might very well think again in the future, that 'they' are conspiring. 'They' have got together, agreed to lie to our 'Mr Mikkelborg', pretend to seefeeltastetouchsmellthinkknow differently, to disturb 'P.A.'

Honestly, there isn't much comfort in the notion. This is, after all, the only reality 'he' has access to. This is it. Get on with it.

So he does.

The walls are sweating, despite the unseasonal warmth (they ignore this: it is a fact, one way or another, so becomes background to their actions). And the voices through those sweating walls are very nearly audible (ignore them, too, even if they are talking about us). The sound of flames, the smell of smoke, an unpleasant sponginess to the air: these are distracting but also have to be ignored. ~~I have~~ He has to get on with this.

'P.A. Mikkelborg' looks in the drawer. There are clippings about Kati 'Larsen' crammed inside. Each crumpled, beginning to go damp despite the unseasonal warmth. He rummages past them, ignoring 'Mickelborg's' attempts to make their hands pause, take a clipping, smooth it out, read a line.

Each image is so strong — pause, take, smooth, read — they may have happened. 'P.A. Mikkelborg' thinks they have. 'He' relaxes, 'mind' drifting.

Walls flex, grow narrower, voices indistinct, almost as if 'they' (who? the people talking, on the other side of the sweating wall, of course, those who pretend all 'you' need to do is change to another TV channel or 'get a life', the ones who say 'what do you want to do that for?', the ones whose voices are always indistinct as if they) have something in their mouths. Cotton wadding, say. The smell of flames, the sound of smoke

do not matter.

~~I search~~ He searches the draw.

'P.A. Mikkelborg' (P. for 'Palle') takes out the letter but puts it back when he finds the coin.

Light touches the wall beside the mirror. 'P.A. Mikkelborg' receives the light coming off the mirror, believes he sees himself in that light, that reflection. And, believing, watches as 'he'/he turns the reflected face inside out.

I should rewrite that bit, don't you think?

```
A  L      W
O      R  D
S      AR E
W  R  O N G
```

VITUS

SWIMS.

153

swim *v. & n.* • *v.* **1** undulant rhythmica borne by a more dense medium. **2** sensory locomotion confined within cranial structures and rarely shared. • *n.* an overwhelming sense of being drowned by circumstance.

Swimming Vitus thrashes his arms. Legs, too. They flap. Churning. And to think, until he closed his eyes, all this was sand, pebbles, pebbles and sand and nothing to worry about.

Swimming Vitus gasps. Air. Grasps. Another handful of water. Churning. Wishing he hadn't closed his eyes.

A wave closes over his head. Sounds change without air to coddle them. Vision blurs. Light swaying without air to cradle it. Swimming Vitus sees bottom. It is a long way off. It was before this wave clasped his head, but Swimming Vitus couldn't see that, could pretend it wasn't so, what with the other things on his mind — churning grasping desperate foaming grip-grunting legs&arms thrashing — make believe all this wasn't, isn't as dire as it is. He can see this as he sees bottom a long way below. And all since Vitus closed his eyes which, Swimming Vitus freely admits, he should never have done. Swimming Vitus wishes he (not-Swimming Vitus as he was then) had left that standpipe alone.

All this would be just as frightening if it was a nightmare, he tells himself.

Swimming Vitus closes his eyes.

Swimming Vitus swims. Swims until he is no longer Vitus swimming.

THE RASP of surf over a shingled beach.

FRANKLIN PAUSED and, without planning to, said, 'My wife misses me.'

'My wife?' Ulysses spoke without looking up.

Neither spoke.

'I thought of the sea as being a mistress.'
    'For a time.'
    'Yes, for a time. Sentimental nonsense.'
    'It isn't the sea.'
    'Precisely. It isn't. It is us. Comes from inside. What I told myself was very, very …'
    'Romantic of me.'
    'But wrong.'
    'Precisely. We do these things to ourselves.'
    'Yes. There is only what is inside.'

Ulysses and Franklin paused. Each looking at the other. No sound but the shore inching out of the sea.

Franklin and Ulysses have the wreckage of twelve ships to work with. There were, of course nine to start. Ulysses' ships were never named. Largely uncounted, too. So there is nothing to say there were not at least three at some point, or that their names could not have been *Galatea*, *Phaeton* and *Cordelia*, even if sources differ on this point. Ulysses and Franklin, Franklin and Ulysses, have little time for such detail. Instead, they have taken the three hulks, three that are most certain, taken them to this point, maybe to that point, too (sources differ), dragged them either here or there (there being little time for such detail) and begun to take them apart.

Of Franklin's ships, there only ever were three. What is less certain are their names. It could be there is no point in worrying about such things. Ulysses & Franklin, Franklin & Ulysses, are inclined to think this is so as they relay spars and planking, as nails that once held the ships upright come free (*Comfrey?* Franklin wonders, *no that wasn't one*), are beaten straight, hammered back in the other direction: wood now horizontal, spars more like spits. A strait forming with each hammerblow, nails keeping the waves that little further apart. The ships remain, yes, but of their names there is no trace.

As for 'Jellicoe', the man calling himself 'Jellicoe', he had three ships in all. The names were: *Bellicose, Erebus* and *Terror*. Ulysses, fingers outstretched, counting off each point, argues against this version of history.

'They were never his ships in the first place!'

Arms held upright, fingers splayed.

'If they ever were 'his', if 'Jellicoe' was never Jellicoe, then they can't possibly be 'here' for us to use, no matter what they may be called.'

The waters (everywhere to see) lap. Franklin (nails dirty, hand back in the other direction) inclines to differ.

'Our wives miss us,' is all he says.

Ulysses&Franklin, Franklin&Ulysses, finally accept that wrecks 7 through 9 will be called *Bellerophon, Terebus* and *Error*, even if the letters on what remains of their sides are blurred, damaged so there is nothing to say they could not have been different at some other point.

'They weren't different,' asserts Franklin, 'they were lost.' He stretches out his fingers. ''Jellicoe' had three ships.' Counting off each. 'And 'Jellicoe' lost three ships.' Counting off those misplaced. 'The *Bucephalus, Euphony* and *Terminus*.'

Which Ulysses&Franklin, Franklin&Ulysses, have to agree makes twelve in all. The lost wreck, *Terminus*, being of course the last they begin to work on.

But what of the thirteenth ship? What has become of the *Jellicose*? That is hard to say. Because wherever it is, so is 'Jellicoe', the man calling himself 'Jellicoe'. Wherever 'Jellicoe', so is the *Jellicose*. And there is no sign of 'Jellicoe'.

MIKKELBORG TUGS. Tugs, scrambles. Mikkelborg tugs, scrambles and pulls. Pullscrambles, grunting, feet kicking, hands over head. Grips, grasping. Bushes&weeds legtangling and hissing with each scramblekick and gripped tuggrasper, Mickelborg's sweat peppering the bricks rubbing against forehead, cheek rubbed against by the bricks, damp blobs appearing in front of creased eyes as he, Mikkelborg, tugs. Tugs, scrambles. Tugs&scrambles and hears in the distance voices, footsteps between, under the voices. Voices raised, over the footsteps, giving orders and replies and searching with bootsteps crunching on tarmac, or is that gravel, a twig snapping, branch, gripped, sniggering as it's bent out the way. Mikkelborg feels a light poking through the trees, bushes also, searching for a sign as undergrowth cackles, parting itself just enough to offer up glimpses: a partial footprint, this scrap of cloth it has been saving special, a twig bentback now broken, pale flash bright in torchlight and pointing the way.

Gravity gives Mickelborg's ankle a tug and he slithers to the ground. Seeing the lights. Hearing voices. Looking for somewhere to hide and seeing the wall.

It's very tall.

And very long.

He tries again. Voices not so loud and much more over there. Lights poking around but not especially here. Mikkelborg looks up. Walltop and skybottom both about the same distance away. (Don't be fooled by the stars, they don't say anything, only being the point-ends of searchlights scanning overhead for sign of him those on the ground may have missed.) A wipe of the hands, a breath: he tries again. Feet lodging in the cement between one course and the next. Grunting, pulling. There is now no other course of action. Only scrambling. Trying to rise from one course to the next, hands over head, gripping the walltop with fingers, grunting, feet kicking, cement dust gritting, drypattering against bushleaf and weedblade. Scalp prickling at each sweatbead trickling, sweat running free, escaping here, pooling there, needlestinging eyes or mashing against the edge of his nose, tickling, irritating, irritating because it's not as if breathing and climbing and not falling aren't enough to —

An elbow lodges on walltop, the rest of Mikkelborg crawling after it.

It's very tall. And very long.

Mikkelborg sticks mostly to the shadows. Walking: house to house, across the gaping mouth of a side-street filled with more houses. Skirts the edges of any streetlights burning. Chased, for now, only by the sound of his own footfalls. Soft. Slipping mostly from the shadows. Pausing outside a house (windows darkened, face peering back and not having to squint), leaping over the gaping mouth of a side-street (falling away, crusted with houses; each staring, sometimes more than once), stumbling at the lip of a pool of light brimming around a lamp column (bent sharply by the circumference of the pole, eyes nonetheless look back). Every house Mikkelborg sees on this side of the wall appears empty. Everyone is on the otherside. Looking for him.

He is the only person here.

He is not alone.

I remember an afternoon. *An evening.* The goldfish on a sideboard. *A window ledge.* A shaft of nostalgic light, dust motes falling, drifting. *Twilight, shadows soaking away the room.* Faces, family portrait watching- over from the

window ledge.
On the hearth,
back turned
to hide the
crack running
down the glass.
Unblemished.
Water still
fogging the
picture. And
the smell of
beeswax.
Roses turning
sweet, limp.
Dust cataracts
over the eyes
of the red-
lacquered dogs.
Shelf bare.
Lace yellow
and brittle,
chintz bald.
One cushion
left and that
flaccid. CD
player, numbers
jerking. *Silence,*
power off. An
empty cup.
Table cleared.
Drawers.
Newspaper.
Postcards
tacked to a
board. *Safety*
pins. Burned-
headed match
in a saucer.
A saucer. I
remember.

Boris

puts the cap on his pen

and realises she is crying

Nina

looks down the list, thinking

this is a silly way to act over a

Boris

closing the notebook firmly

wipes away the tears

remembering

MRS BLENKINSOE walks
into
a
shop

[bang]

No. That's ridiculous. Besides doing herself a mischief, it's not what I meant at —

Mrs Blenkinsoe opened the door. A bell, tickled by the door, or the sight of Mrs Blenkinsoe stepping over the threshold, gave a chime of delight. A little chime of delight as Mrs Blenkinsoe crossed the threshold. A little chime of delight as the door closed again (with, it has to be said, Mrs Blenkinsoe's assistance, the second chime of delight, so similar to the first, otherwise out of her control).

We do not need to go into too many details about this shop. A bell, tickled … gave a chime. The word 'shop' has so many associations that we can exchange it between ourselves, a chime of delight, and know (believe, it has to be said) we are imagining something that has points in common even if the details differ. Tickled by the door … stepping over the threshold this is fortunate. It saves time although shops are not identical. A little chime of delight they do have points in common (so similar to the first): a definite boundary, surfaces on which items for sale are displayed, items wishing to buy stepping over the threshold, a locus at which an exchange otherwise out of her control can be made to secure the use of the items on sale, whether this is through the negotiation of a mutually agreeable tariff of other 'items' (i.e. barter, which by the door or the sight can be reduced to a change in energy; we do not need to go into too many details about this), or the transfer of promissory tokens: coins, notes (i.e. payment, something you are probably so familiar with we can exchange between ourselves). Lastly, an air of melancholy. We can agree the word (a 1p coin, a 10¢ coin, a 50 stotinki piece) has points in common, even if we change the word (butik, tenda, siopa). It saves time as the door closed again and we do not need to go into too many details. This is fortunate.

Mrs Blenkinsoe, tickled by the door, gave a chime, a little chime of delight, as the threshold closed again. We do not need to go into too many details.

Standing beside the door, we can see shelves. Freestanding units comprised of shelves, arrayed in aisles. Freestanding units without shelves, arranged in such a way to display the items on their surfaces. The items arrayed on freestanding units forming display areas or aisles. And lights of course. We do not need to go into detail.

The lights are off.

There is a reason for this. An arrangement of circumstance you are probably familiar with. However, having only just opened the door, crossed the threshold (and closed the door again, although this might not be relevant), Mrs Blenkinsoe may very well be ignorant of the circumstances. Of course, this might have points in common with broader situations. If so, we might not need to know. Even if we do, Mrs Blenkinsoe could still not know why any of this is happening.

You see the dilemma. There is no need to go into detail.

Mrs Blenkinsoe walks down the first aisle. In the usual way. The bell, so prominent in this narrative earlier, remains silent. This might not be relevant. Walking, which … can be reduced to a change in energy, Mrs Blenkinsoe looks at the items arranged with a little chime of delight on freestanding units we can see forming display areas or an air of melancholy. We can also see Mrs Blenkinsoe seeing the items, so similar to the first, arranged on their surfaces. But she cannot see us, of course, although we agree (believe, it has to be said) to be here at the same time, watching Mrs Blenkinsoe, etc. There is … a reason for this you are probably familiar with. A definite boundary. It saves time.

On each shelf, items for sale. This is implicit over the threshold. After all, if we (with, it has to be said, Mrs Blenkinsoe's assistance …) change the word in such a way to display a previously unsuspected undercurrent, this is a shop. Mrs Blenkinsoe knows this (we believe), it is implicit. Over the door arranged on freestanding units the word 'shop', which has so many associations.

Walking … can be reduced to a change in energy.

The bell … remains silent. It saves time although tickled. Mrs Blenkinsoe stops. Not identical surfaces … display … items wishing to buy. Mrs Blenkinsoe stops beside a shelf. Neither moves (or, rather, neither moves perceptibly or, in the context of this narrative, significantly). Nor does the item she is looking at, although it is implicit (let us agree, all other points being in common) that moving into what light there is (the lights are off; we still do not know why this is happening) would be a helpful thing to do. This introduces a previously unsuspected undercurrent.

The item tickled is a white box.

The next beside is a white box.

The lights are off, a definite boundary, of course. Neither moves with broader situations, ignorant of a white box. The word 'item' on its face.

Each shelf, freestanding, is very long. Very long. An indefinite boundary. Each box, white, carrying the word 'item' next to another box, white, carrying the word 'item' next to another box, white, carrying the word 'item' next to another box, white, carrying the word 'item' next to another box, white, carrying the word 'item' next to another box, white, carrying the word 'item' next to another box, white, carrying the word 'item' next to another box, white, carrying the word 'item' next to another box, white, carrying the word 'item' next another in the usual way. The word 'shop' over the door (this is why Mrs Blenkinsoe walked in, although let us agree she had no intention of doing so until we conspired to make her in the context of this narrative. Much the same might be said about the shop, although this is implicit. We see shelves … where are 'we'?). The word 'word' over the door. Each aisle comprised of shelves very long so similar to the first, infinite in fact. The 'word' 'located' over the threshold but otherwise absent we see (where are 'we'?), a definite boundary to this 'shop' imperceptible. Significantly

The next part is unclear, we may never know why. It is possible what happened next was unclear or poorly imagined by the author. Or that the author was unclear or poorly imagined. It is impossible to be sure. This arrangement of circumstance is unsettling in the context of a narrative — we can agree this is a 'narrative'. A point common to 'narrative' is 'author'. Standing beside the door, we see an expectation of clarity, a definite boundary to events: each 'event', described, carrying the word 'story' next to another event, described, carrying the word 'story' towards a locus at which an exchange can be made to secure the termination of the 'narrative', whether this is through an 'open' or 'closed' ending. But this is something you are probably familiar with. We do not need to go into details, you see the dilemma: the 'author' is incapable of contriving what happens next, or the author does not fully exist, no more so than the rest of this narrative which, let us agree, is now quite indefinite. We can exchange it between ourselves ... and know we are imagining something. Mrs Blenkinsoe believes she is entering a shop because she sees the word 'shop'. Mrs Blenkinsoe opened the door. A bell, tickled ... gave a chime because we contrive to make it so as, standing by the door, we see shelves ... infinite in fact. Who are 'we'? Even if we change the word it still isn't a shop. Are we words on a page, unclear and poorly imagined? Standing by the door, the author does not fully exist a little chime of delight that has points in common. This is fortunate, it saves time. Can we agree what is 'real'?

Mrs Blenkinsoe knows she is Mrs Blenkinsoe because she has a label that says: 'Mrs Blenkinsoe'.

There was a time when it seemed as though it would never be silent again. Everyone had to shout. And TVs and radios, they were all turned up to drown it out. Only adding to the row. Now and then, a lull would form. A random eddy of silence when enough pauses overlapped. Strange, but those moments became terrible. It's very hard to say why exactly. Expectation of the noise gathering, rising back to full pitch, that would be part of it. But the absence came to feel unnatural in itself. The air was not supposed to be this still; radios, TVs, voices should not be so exposed. Occasionally, things would surface through those lulls. The jangle of coins in a pocket. A voice, words almost indistinguishable. A footfall. The sound of metal against metal. Laughter cut off.
    It came to be a relief when the noise started up again.

about these things

words are wrong

it doesn't mean anything at all

It came to be a relief when

again.

J<small>ANE IS</small> dreaming.

Jane dreams

N<small>INA LOOKED</small> at what she had written.

The noise through the wall was appalling. Not loud. Not exactly. But constant enough — no, inconstant enough to be irritating. It would almost be better in the cubicle, in the office, with June Larsen always prowling and

A bang. Followed by a crash, sounds of lightweight metallic-somethings pinwheeling, scattering in all directions, and glass shattering. Jeering mixed with hoots like, like

Nina tutted, taking a breath and holding it in the hope it would bring a lull in her frustration. She had just written 'apes'

Jane dreams apes

so distracting was the noise through the wall

Tap

Tap-tap   tap-tap   tap

            tap   tap

Tap —

Nina stared at the wall. There was the harsh sound of glass being swept up, the scrape of a shovel in between — both abrasive enough to set teeth on edge — and this

     T'p   TAp   tap-tap-tap

tapping. What could they (the Post-it Note was where she had left it, no closer to being answered: 'They?') be doing now? Looking for a weak spot, hidden conduit, trying to attract her

Nina bolted from the chair, pressing against the opposite wall. Her shoulder scraped against Fernand Khnopf's *The Abandoned Town*, torn from a book long ago. A corner drooped slowly forwards

tap-t'p

t'p

the

tapping

stopped,

although Nina stared at the wall without moving. Until a flicker of corn-yellow light caught her eye: ripples of sunlight, making angular patterns across the floor. All reflected from a neighbour's window, a chance meeting of clouds and time and a freshly-cleaned window being propped open just in time to play its part. Nina watched the reflection until clouds move over the sun, absorbed enough not to be aware of the noises through the wall. At least the noise meant she can't hear the buzzing

A thought made Nina look out the window. The neighbour's house, windows, light changing as the wind drove the clouds ahead of it. All of it was

All is wrong — continuity? — character must notice

Nina scribbled on another Post-it and stuck it to the edge of

the screen goes black. Boris sits back, tapping a thumbnail against his teeth. Sits back, watching the lights blink out on his computer and, without registering it (the site is so familiar), the clutter on his desk: Post-It notes, tape dispenser, paperclips, pens, a short length of plastic ruler so long broken the edges are blunt and grimy, an out of date phone directory for

the office is almost deserted. John is sitting on the other side of the room, blowing his nose into tissue after tissue, yanking a clean one from the box to scrub around the inside of his nose between times. Boris knows John is extremely self-conscious about these allergy reactions, terrified he will end up with snot glistening on his top lip or caught in the hairs of his nose. John carries a small vanity mirror as a safety precaution, the whole thing turned into a morbid session. John's bike lies against the back of John's desk. It will still be there tomorrow morning. John, in this state, will have to find other routes home, allergies too severe to let him bicycle

today has been exhausting. Long and exhausting. Boris is almost too tired to go home. He did find time to scribble about

About these <u>things</u>???

one note to himself during the five minutes he found to grab a bite for lunch. The note is somewhere in the clutter. Besides, that train of thought has vanished, so there's no point turning everything over to look

out the window, nose pressed to the glass. Corn-yellow light shimmers across the windowsill, reflected from the freshly-scrubbed windows of the other wing of the building. Directly below is a narrow landscaped border, a buffer between the main doors and the car park. The bushes appear very small, the drop long so Boris imagines falling and, relative sizes maintained, completely obliterating the ribbon of garden. Which is disturbing enough to make Boris

jump. Sitting back in the chair, hands clutching the sill. Ridiculous, acting like this. Must have seen the view out the window dozens of times, every day in fact, but this is the first time he has noticed. Change blindness, thinks Boris, that's what it's called, you concentrate on one thing, never notice what happens around, Boris thinks as he stares straight ahead at the wall rearing up over the edge of the car park, the wall that had surely been on the left

yesterday.

Nina looks at what she has written. Takes out the full stop and starts again with

JANE IS dreaming.

A moment ago she was standing on some high promontory, moments spent on the edge, looking down for a moment, only moments ago, moments that could have been months or years because they passed as easily, as interminably, as the step that brought her here, from there to here in less than an instant, endless. Time seems so short, so long. To Jane. In dreams. Seconds momentary, passers-by, gone before she can grasp, savour. Simply gone. Yet the next is like the last is like an hour from now like tomorrow is a weekaway; is like a moment to step from promontory to here.

Jane is dreaming, although she does not know it.

Everything seemed so real, so solid. Spread out beneath her feet beneath the clouds beneath a sky pale enough to be gauze, a ghost of sky much too far away to be touched. The land beneath the clouds, beneath her feet. Jane stood on the edge of some high promontory, stood as she did, no more than a moment from now (she is not 'here' yet; this is dreamtime, dreamlogic: Jane was 'here' before all this is afterwards and will step to the edge only once but many times), so very high that all beneath the clouds beneath Jane and sky, skyandall, all was spread like a map.

Sharp, unblurred by air or the tremendous distance.

Enough to show the curve of the globe as it rolled away, always rolling, rolling one full turn in dropping away to turn back here, beneath this promontory, spread across the map. Jane looked down. She saw roads, winding, hills twined between, the hills themselves billowing, rising up to part around rivers coiling, their loops opening to enclose towns that pointed the way, this way almost always, following the current as it smoothed trees into grass into sand; or falling the other way, mounting slope on to slope, making uplands out of chalk, down rising up. Only to stop.

The sea was there. The sea *is* everywhere. Jane looked. Seeing land rolled flat by distance roll inevitably into sea all around. Land mapped onto rolling waves capped white: mapped-sea, its surface crossed by lines, quadrangles bending with each swell but otherwise holding firm. Even should the map be furled or folded over shades of blue, growing darker the deeper the land was hidden beneath the water, the water surrounding everything.

She saw this in a moment. Saw it again in another and — who can tell? — in another some time afterthat and before, before …

Before her laid out: Jane surmounting promontory, rivers eeling around its foot, carving oxbow out of purl as signs for towns held between hills, that became inevitably coasts, mudflat or chalkmarked with waves themselves highlighted. In white.

Jane steps closer to the table. (A single step, promontory to table, and she is here, whereas a moment ago was spent on the edge, looking down, in this moment and the next, she) rests a hand on the edge of the map. Rivers, hills, towns in black. And the sea.

'Like in my dream,' Jane whispers. (But this is your dream, Jane. A moment ago on the edge of an impossibly high promontory, and now here. Dreamlogic, dreamtime. We know. We have been with you the whole time.) 'Like my dream,' Jane insists to herself, unaware of scrutiny, rapping the edge of the table with a knuckle as she leans closer. Tracing the path of rivers. Of coastline surrounded by sea. The gridlines portioning out the sea itself. Blue coming deeper the darker the shade. It is all here, the whole world on a sheet of paper. 'Like the dream.' (But …) Everything laid out to be seen. Every house, every symbol.

There is no sign of her husband.

Jane traces the path of every white-lined wave, working back from shore into dark, darker blue.

'In my dream, this was …'

(But this —)

Wave caps grow denser the further her hand and eye travel, overlapping, forming spots, now ribbons of white.

'In my dream …'

(But this *is* —)

Ribbons growing thicker until it is blue, blue alone and isolated, making each spot. Ribbons thickening. Until there is only white.

'I dreamt this differently.'

(But you *are* —)

Jane steps back. The sea is no longer continuous. Where it surrounded it vanishes. Leaving only the white of the paper, unbroken white. *Terra alba. Terra incognita.*

(Yes! Don't you remember: *Terror, Erebus* and —)

Jane steps back. From the edge, from the table, from the edge of the table and the map spread out like a landscape seen from high, so very high it is reduced to nothing but the margins of white: those areas unplotted, unsuspected, yet to be imagined.

(But that can't be. *We saw* —)

'This is not my dream.' Jane steps away, abandoning the unfinished map, anxious to be far from here as she repeats, 'This is not my dream,' shocked at how real it seemed, spread out beneath her feet beneath her gaze, just as the map was, spread across the table.

'This is not my dream.'

Jane Franklin steps back again, anxious to be away from here but momentarily unsure where the exit is.

'This is —' Falling silent.

This room seems real. Really so.

'This ...?'

A deep breath, eyes closing as she reconstructs the route along corridors and staircases to the main entrance. Laying it out in her imagination like a floor plan held in her hands. Opening her eyes to see a wall — painted in a gentle terre-vert, *trompe-l'oeil* flower displays brought into relief by highlights of white — and considers hitting it to prove its reality, so real, really so.

'This is *not* my dream.' Jane clenches her fist. But does not strike the wall.

Jane Franklin steps away.

Jane Franklin closes her eyes, stepping away. And follows the floor plan she reconstructs, moment by moment, in her head.

But that was, they were her dreams. We know. We were with her the whole time. Jane can't choose, pick and choose, what is and isn't, what she wants to be real. We know. We've been watching all along. Observing everything everyone has done, thought! That's *reality! We know ...*

Why won't you answer? I know you're

he is not alone
swims until he is no longer vitus swimming
penelope leaves the shore behind

PENELOPE LEAVES the shore behind to look for the coin. She walks across sand and pebbles. A sea of sand and pebbles beyond the shore she leaves behind, walking onwards, or outwards, but always horizonwards, over pebbles and sand, sand and pebbles walking on, Penelope. Always. Always pebbles. Always sand. Always the horizon flat, flatlined under a sky that never moves either, although walks on Penelope, always Penelope placing one foot forward then the other, a hand in front of her face. Fingers. Splayed. Penelope walks, leaving the shore behind, looking. Fingers, hand in front of her face, splayed, wrist moving under a sky that never moves either. Sand relenting, one foot forward. Clouds hanging over a hand, in front of her face. Updown repeating. The horizon makes no comment, only a line so the sky knows when to stop. One foot forward then the other. The sky falls, pebbles clacking, clat-clackering as they fall over themselves rolling under Penelope falling.

Her hand stops, helping her sit up. Horizon does not change. Sky likewise. Neither offers to help. The sand at least shifts. Enough to accommodate her sitting, no more, which is more than the pebbles, lying mute and wanting an apology if expecting none.

The sound of her hand fanning the air has gone. Likewise the shore, left behind to look for the coin.

Penelope looks across the sea of sand & pebbles, pebbles&sand. Gently, the land under the sea rises, falls. Undulant, you see, but otherwise really quite, quite still now one foot no longer places itself in front of another, one hand no longer fingersplayed fanning in front of a face otherwise as fixed as that line marking the end of one, at the start of another.

The sound of her hand fanning the air has gone. Likewise the shore left behind to get one more look at the coin. Her husband's face is on the coin. Was, when Penelope found it under the sunset. Face fixed, otherwise familiar. Penelope, sure she had seen this face before, somewhere, feeling relief under her fingertips, features somewhat familiar to the touch if fixed.

Penelope looks at her fingers, unsplayed and likewise unchanged by contact with the coin. The same might be said of the sea of sand & pebbles, pebbles&sand undulating but changeless.

The sound of her hand fanning the air is gone. Likewise the shore.

Penelope might never have left the shore. The shore of pebbles & sand. Likewise, the sea of sand&pebbles. All there has been has been sand & sky, horizonline & pebbles.

The shore left Penelope behind for one more look at the coin.

Hands still, Penelope walks. Raising one foot (the horizon does not change), then the other (likewise the sky). She would accept she is walking on the spot but for the sea. The land beneath rises, gently falls, gently undulant you see. Swells of pebbles. A billow of sand. On her breath: a trace of salt. Gently. Rising undersea. Gently declining, the sea moves, Penelope moving relative to the sea. No escaping that. They have been together so long, one has grown to adopt the other. Seasisters, gently rising until wavecrest reclines into the next swan's arc of sand, gently raising itself on outstretched arms, this dune sea that, hands still, Penelope has come to accept as all there is: raising one foot (horizon a mirage), then the other (sky likewise). Gently falling, rising, the dune sea closes around Penelope and Penelope, accepting, walks on, everything changeless except the waves rising, gently, and Penelope leaving all behind.

Hands still. But the white noise of air slowly fanned remains. Of a swell drawing out, rolling gently in. Lapping.

MIKKELBORG LOOKS into his own eyes. Edges tattered, brickwork impressing lines down cheeks. A chin whitening. A chin whole.

Looking into his own eyes looking back into his own eyes, mouth parted.

WAN

Balance obscured, mouth parted.

AN ED

Mikkelborg ignores that. Looks into his own eyes across the street. On the corner ahead. Behind. On this lamppost. His eyes

A TED

everywhere.

Leaves the light. Moving shadow to shadow. He watches himself from almost everywhere: a hoarding; a tree; under a wiper, head back against a car's windscreen; framed

W NT D

in a shop window. Everyplace on this side of the wall. Faces tattered&peeling or wholebutfaded. Others fresh, lifelike

W   TE

face lifelike. His eyes always looking out of somewhere.

WANTED

Mikkelborg watches himself run. Watches himself watched. Watchedwatching Mikkelborg is always present. Presently here (running down an alley: looking out from alleywall mouth open to say one word), presently there (on the side of a litter-bin, watching). His eyes always somewhere. Always.

It is not Mickelborg's face.

ARMS MOVE, legs move, splish-splash. Splish.

Vitus, swimming, opensnaps his eyes.

Water. All to see. All there is.

Vitus swallows, chokes. Spitting surprise as much as water. Squints, salt-needles redmarking his eyes, sinuses also stinging as shock closes throat, closes eyes, only to hawl them open once more.

Snip-snap. Snap-set.

Allwhile, allthrough: Swimming Vitus swims, not missing a stroke. Vitus coughs, waterinside becoming waterout, trailing from his mouth (open, close, open: breathing almost like swimming) as, swimming, Vitus keeps legs kicking, arms alternating.

Only, it feels like someone else doing all this swim-swim-swimaging. Vitus Along for the Ride, carried by Swimming Vitus free of charge.

Vitus would like to get off now.

Swimming, oblivious, Swimming Vitus keeps right on.

After coughing and splut, the eye-sting and blinking-after, Vitus looks around and sees —

I spy with my little eye something beginning with *W.*

Water.

Right. Okay, you're go.

I spy with my little —

Water!

Tut. Fair's fair, I suppose. Your turn.

I spy —

Vitus looks left. Leftward looking, Vitus turns, looks and, seeing, has no belief in what he sees.

A woman.

On the water. Water flat enough but for the waves, swells rising, swells falling. But water, sure. And the woman, one hand flap-flap-flapping in front of her face. Flap-flapping as she walks. On water. On the water, lapping.

Oblivious, Swimming Vitus keeps right on swimming. Vitus has no choice but to watch the woman — rising a little, falling some atleast, with each swell — the woman falling slowly back. Watch the woman.

Walking.

Vitus can turn his head only so far. So far meaning his last glance of the woman has a lot of shoulder to it. That shoulder rotating rhythmically, matchedarm doing its bit to keep Swimming Vitus swimming.

Vitus looks back again. Sees water, sees a sea now empty of all but swells and whitecaps (and Swimming Vitus's shoulder moving rhythmically, although that is almost part of the landscape, it's becoming so familiar, hypnotically familiar).

Water.

Water and swimming.

Vitus tries on hallucination ('hypnotically familiar', remember?), casts that aside and thinks about dream: dreams of water, of swimming and water. That would explain a woman walking, walking a straight line across the surface of the — you know what. It would, and there's comfort in any explanation if you embrace it tight enough, thinks Vitus, a Vitus wet and miserable, cold and miserable, a Vitus that thinks he's too wretched to be dreaming.

Swimming Vitus takes no notice. To swim is to swim.

Which is miserable, thinks Vitus, carried along, eyes starting to droop. Not like the old days, Vitus adds, eyes drooping a little more. The old days: when he was swimming no longer, and so, no longer swimming, Swimming Vitus and water and even women walking on the same water, were memories he could take or not. Not, adds Vitus, eyelids decidedly heavy. Those were the days, after the swimming was over — streets comfortingly unshifting underfoot, when he had friends, friends like his old nanny, Mrs Blenkinsoe, and her friend, old 'Admiral' Jellicoe, Paulus Mikkelborg and — and —

Vitus lets his eyes close. Mind filling with pictures of his walks along the crescents and circuses of New Bruges, the wonderful capital city of long-independent Jutland.

Eyes closed and mind filled, Vitus breathes easily, deep and easy. Happy again.

HE TALKED. In a room, in New Bruges, around the middle of the day, he talked. And the person he spoke to, that person said, It's strange you should mention dreaming. I did? asked Vitus, in the room, in New Bruges. But the person he was talking to said only, I've been dreaming, having a dream that comes around again. Recurring? suggested Vitus. Yes — she smiled — yes, that's it and it's funny because we're standing here at the end, often standing like this, in this room, at the end of the dream. Doing what? Vitus asked. Talking, like this — she spread her hands as if revealing a hidden treasure — by the window as we are now, around midday. Talking.

Vitus said nothing.

Jane said hello to Vitus on a street corner. He saw Mrs Blenkinsoe with 'Admiral' Jellicoe on the next. Vitus turned another corner, thinking about swimming, although all that was behind him now.

Funny, old chap, said Lord Franklin after saying hello, but I was dreaming of you last night.

Vitus climbed the stairs around midday. Light fell through the stained glass window on each landing. Reds, yellows, a soft violet. Gold from the ring in the beak of the magpie on the third floor landing, staircase smelling of beeswax, old wood, some dust, and — Vitus frowned — and brine.

Vitus waved to Paulus Mikkelborg on the corner. Paulus Mikkelborg did not see him. Vitus waved to Jane, but no, she was lost in thought. And Mrs Blenkinsoe and 'Admiral' Jellicoe were giving directions, so they did not see his waves either.

Vitus climbed the staircase, sunlight falling on the landings, a voice — voices — from a room above indistinct, Vitus glancing at the stained glass magpie on the fourth floor landing.

And frowning.

The other person in the room paused. Turning away from the window. Skirts rustling. Vitus looked. Out. Bruges divided. Into.

Diamond-slices by the window lead. Except. In the middle of the middle. pane. Where a bull's-eye was inset. Vitus. Bent. Closing one. Eye. And sighted. Through. The rounded. Glass.

Oddest thing, dearest heart, Mrs Blenkinsoe told him as they stood on the corner of Khnopff Circus, I dreamt we were standing here last night. She paused, laughed, correcting herself: I mean I had the dream last night, a dream of us standing here, at about this time, about midday. Mrs Blenkinsoe laughed. Vitus said nothing. There was a smell of brine.

She walked away from the diamonded window with its central bull's-eye. Vitus bent to sight through the rounded glass.
    Would you like to hear my dream?

The nameplate said 'Bayer Crescent'. Vitus looked at the map, the street guide to New Bruges he had bought at a kiosk a little while ago, before the lunchtime crowds filled the streets. There was a voice — no: voices — coming from the house Vitus stood beside. Words indistinct. Anyway, Vitus was distracted by a bird in one of the trees lining the road: *craik! ... craik!* Vitus squinted against the sunlight, catching sight of a flash of white, petrol-blue. And gold, as if the magpie were holding —
    He looked at the key to the map. Squinting harder.

The room was on the fifth floor.

Funny dreams, laughed Paulus.

Only light in the room: the diamond-leaded window. Shapes moved past his eyes, floating between them, or so it seemed as he turned to look at her.
    Yes, he said.

Jane looked a little lost. Paulus and Lord John were deep in conversation. Dear Mrs B. and her 'Admiral' were giving directions. With the crowds, the traffic, the distractions, no wonder they didn't see him waving, Vitus told himself. Looked at the key on the map, all those symbols, and told himself just this.

Yes, he said, I should very much. Yes, she replied. And she said something more. Softly. The words rubbed away by the rustling of her skirts. Without any pause, she began describing the dream, a strange dream because sometimes she felt she did not appear in it, which is odd for a dream, even a recurring dream, wouldn't you say? she asked. Vitus didn't reply because he was thinking perhaps those rubbed away words had been 'of course', or perhaps they had been 'what else?', by which time she was saying, it always begins:

P.A. Mikkelborg stands with Lord Franklin. Chatting. They stand and chat. And breathe and exchange words, P.A. Mikkelborg and Lord Franklin. It's no longer June, no longer summer. No longer than ten minutes since they started chatting. Standing and chatting, back and forth. Franklin and Mikkelborg. Mikkelborg and Franklin. Not summer and not ten minutes. It's good to talk.
    Neither understands what the other is saying.

Vitus stops walking. He has a map now. A map with colours and scales and symbols. And keys for the symbols so he can unlock them. Standing still or sitting. Or possibly walking carefully, if the map is steady enough. They jog and blur, otherwise. The colours and symbols, keys jangling, landscape getting confused and blurred. The scales. *Tra-la-la-la-la*.
    Vitus stops walking. It's no longer June, no longer summer. He's no longer as young as he was. Which has advantages and disadvantages he has discussed sometimes. Sometimes with other people, chatting, exchanging words, sometimes. Sometimes just by himself, talking, chatting back and forth and sometimes taking both sides of the conversation if there's no one there to do it for him. Or he could talk to his cat or his dog and even

his hamster, not expecting an answer, of course, because Vitus hasn't got a hamster, a cat, a dog, or somebody to talk to at the moment. Not because at the moment Vitus has stopped walking. No. There is some other reason for that.

Penelope feels a strange urge to speak. Often she doesn't. Speak. It varies. Not from moment to moment, not that often. Not so often. Once? Perhaps twice. A day. Hardly more than that, if at all. She spends so much time alone now. Sometimes minutes, ten minutes at least, but more often hours at a time. Alone. At a time when she wants to be alone. Days sometimes; it's not unknown. Sometimes days or hours but not all the time. Wanting to speak or needing to be alone. Not all the time. Penelope is alone now. Now, since stepping off a dinghy. (Or, should she think of it as *the* dinghy? She is not sure and being alone and most often content not to speak, Penelope has few opportunities to discuss it. Except by talking it through out loud, to herself, alone, when she is alone, which is often not very helpful. Not a helpful way to decide subtle questions like this.)

And still the urge is stealing over her. Stolen over from another point of view (the one Penelope has so little access to these days, being so often alone), stolen over because Penelope says aloud:

'June's over with now.'

'I'm over with what?' June asks the woman standing in the street looking little bewildered.

Why do people keep talking about me? June asks herself. Why? she thinks again, asking herself the same question she has been asking herself since, well, June. June's question from June. Which sounds funny. Like the words are going round and round. Going round and round like the question itself, round and round. After June, chasing her since June, chasing June inside June. Inside her head, washing roundwards. Sometimes inwards. Always Junewards. Always that, at least. Always June talking to herself about wondering why it is people have been like this since June first heard someone talking about her in the street, saying her name out loud, speaking it for no reason she can think of no matter how often she goes around and about, aboutwards or aroundwards or other words that wash back and forth, forth and back. Like a tide. Yes. Like a tide, thinks June, wondering afterwards why she never thought that before. 'Why didn't I think of that before?'' Just those words, rolling around with the others now. Found amongst and amidst or, at most, an atmosphere of inclusion. A little like a tide carrying driftwood, or a driftwood carrying tide. Or a woodtide drifting carry. Or is it a carrydrift tiding wood? …June's not sure. Not quite. Certainly not just, or afterwards, or rounding out and about it again. Perhaps. To herself, probably, June thinks. Probably inwardly and not in the least aloud, like those of the tides, washing round-forth and forth-in, back and Junewards, until she has no idea what the tides of question and words and thoughts and thoughts about words mean any more.

Mrs Blenkinsoe looks at Admiral Jellicoe. The words barely out of his mouth and she stares. Stares at him. Like an improper suggestion. In proper diction, of course. Out of his mouth, lips slip syllables over tongue, overturning words, lipped and tongued and articulated. Although not with arms and legs. That might be strange, finding words so strangely articulated. Arms opening wide as legs walk from tongue to mouth, bearing the word 'calendar', or 'sign', or perhaps 'Jutland'. Or just 'land'. Whatever was appropriate. Perhaps appropriate. It can be so hard to be sure. Even a map (growing blurred, folded from hand to hand, creased and folded until colours run and symbols jumble improperly, a proper jumble of water and sky), a map is little use sometimes. North is as much of a word as 'Jutland', or 'dinghy', and can be quite inappropriate. Or less than propitious, certainly. Depending. On property. Property as much as propriety. Like a map with the wrong key, do you see? That or something else, it's hard to be sure. Else, it's hard to be something, thinks Admiral Jellicoe. (Jellicoe thinks, yes, but rarely thinks he's thinking. Just gets on with it, thinking ...)

Except the urge is great. Great despite the surprising look on Mrs B's face. Despite it seeming rude (*it must have,* Admiral Jellicoe reflects later, whatever it was like then becoming re-written with how he feels now, feelings rewriting memories and changing the past so the words become different). Despite all that, the urge really is hard to resist. Mrs B, propriety or no.

So he doesn't.

Admiral Jellicoe looks at the map lying between the extended hands of the young woman who has just accosted them in the old-fashioned hat. Which is to say that she, the young woman, you see, is wearing an old-fashioned hat, not that they, the three of them, happened to be standing inside a remarkably large, if less than *chic,* hat. That would be strange.

Might be strange.

In any case, Jellicoe glances at the much-folded sheet of paper in the hands of the young woman wearing the old-fashioned hat. If that's the word. Possibly. Possibly another would be better. The thought worries Jellicoe, worries him much more so than any discomfort he has felt so far about peering over the edge of the map, edge tilted a little away from him and Mrs B. so it feels a little like crossing a boundary, you see. Peering over the edge of the folded paper, words quite, quite forgotten as he looks from Mrs Blenkinsoe to paper to young woman — no, *Lady,* that's the word, thinks Admiral Jellicoe, thoughts carrying the words appropriately. 'Lady', 'hat'. And 'map'. Definitely appropriate. Unless it's actually something else (he doesn't get to see it for long, just a glance, hardly time to think, really). Something else like, say, a plan, or a sketch. Definitely lines, though, and perhaps a key to all this. Although, in the time available, he can't be sure.

Just as he can't be sure exactly what the young lady said.

If only he'd taken more notice. Before speaking.

He would ask, Admiral Jellicoe, if it wasn't for the look Mrs B. had given him the last time he opened his mouth. Words are such a trouble. All these signs and words and labels and symbols. Like on a map, folded and re-folded until the paper is worn, the symbols might be anything. Almost anything. Something appropriate, at least, say, 'dinghy'. Or 'map'.

Or 'North'. Being both another word and sometimes a fact of sorts. Like: 'it is overcast' (which it is just now, just at present, precisely overcast) and Jellicoe, thinking there was no need, had brought neither compass nor map. Both being neither on his mind until now, just now, nor quite much to do with the suggestion he has just made. The one that seems to have left Mrs B. quite surprised, quite shocked, quite unexpectedly.

But Mrs Blenkinsoe's expression has nothing to do with the content of Admiral Jellicoe's request. Rather, it is because she no longer recognises the words 'Lilac Time'.

P.A. Mikkelborg points. He lifts his arm. Arm lifting. Finger extending. Like a sign. Feet together, too, two feet pressed quite closely together as his hand is lifted by his arm and his arm is lifted by the junction of several streets marked on the map by parallel black lines and yellow ink, filling the space between the black lines like river water, perhaps. A river of saffron yellow ink flowing from one street to another. Black letters rest in the river, letters buoyant enough to float and large enough to stretch almost from one bank to the other. Big letters apparently. The map thinks so. It shows that the rivers of yellow ink, ink like saffron, or saffron-like yellow, it's hard to be sure because the map folds about itself so, buoyant on the air which is gusting, lifting the map so its corner points, points elsewhere, points out that the yellow rivers flow between black lines and those lines are further apart than the lines ruling adjacent streets, carrying smaller letters on the currents of green and blue or white. It is quite positive. Emphatic, even, although buoyant and flexible enough to fold and crease and unfold and not once but many times, untold numbers possibly. But emphatic, the map. Quite quite definite.

Where then are the floating words? Buoyant and large enough to almost touch the heavy black lines of the banks which are also missing, as is the wide, fast-flowing confluences of yellow ink, saffron yellow and quite quite absent.

Lady Jane holds a map. Folds. Re-folds. Folds the map she is holding in both hands, both forward and back, refolding what she is hoping will tell her something helpful.

Vitus feels a strange urge. One he could, admittedly, say out loud. He might like to, in fact. Breath coming out of his mouth, carrying words. Vitus' words describing the surge, this strange urge that has come over him. Over there at first, back, back a little along the street. A street carrying people and traffic and along the way between one street and another. Connecting. Yes, connecting. Like words carried in a single breath. A breath carrying more than words in its hands. One and then the other, passed from hand to hand. Each one carrying a little of this strange urge that came over Vitus as he came along the pavement connecting one place on the map with another. Except when the map is folded, of course. Then two points touch, are connected, sort of, like two words, unrelated, quite unrelated, strangers in fact, quite strange but brought together in a single breath by some urge or whim. Two words, two points, two things brought together but not connected except by breath or folded paper. But that would be silly, expecting the pavement to lead from one word to another just because the map is folded together. Silly to expect that. Expecting two streets to be joined just because they're carried on the same breath. Vitus would think that. If he was thinking about that instead of this strange urge that has come over him. Come over here on the corner, the map in his hand forgotten as Vitus stands on the corner. His mouth very slightly open.

June stops walking. Stops and looks back towards the corner. Traffic lights wink. People cross the road. Some recross. Others flow down one side. Down the other. Or up. That happens. June can see it as the cars and buses and traffic begin moving towards and away. Passing like a tide, June thinks. Thinks, then begins walking. Along the pavement. Beside the road and the currents of traffic flowing along the road, some of it blue or green or saffron yellow. Past people, too, although they've become a 'crowd' of 'pedestrians' without June noticing. Not that that stops her carrying on towards the corner where several roads meet.

As she walks, caught up in or working against the flow of pedestrians, June has a strange ... not urge, more feeling. An odd sense of all this being familiar.

Like a dream, June thinks, although not out loud.

She closes her mouth again and the traffic stops moving. Frowning, careful to neither open nor close her mouth just yet, in case something else happens, Penelope looks along the street. She's trying to remember other Junes but all she can think of is a dinghy (possibly *the* dinghy, it's hard to be sure) and a sign. Without thinking, she puts her hands together.

Vitus hears the words, 'Like a dream.' He closes his mouth again.

Her hands come together. Like two old friends, although they don't speak. And they part quickly. Swinging around to stand shoulder to shoulder. Staunch, thinks Admiral Jellicoe, approving. Good friends should stand, shoulder to shoulder, staunch and stalwart and steadfast certainly. Admirable sentiment, thinks Admiral Jellicoe to himself just before he looks again at Mrs Blenkinsoe's hands hinging open and shut, open and shut like the leaves of a book. All the folds of a map.

P.A. Mikkelborg points. Arm lifted, finger extended. Sign-like, his expression significant. To the point of fixation, thinks John Franklin, turning to look in the direction indicated. The junction turns with him, traffic slewing across his eyes, which is a lot less painful than it sounds. Crowds of people flow around the corners of the road forming the junction, all of them moving it seems because Franklin's head is moving. John Franklin, head growing still and the world with it, knows things are moving in direct sympathy with his head. Of course he knows this, just as he knows lots of things. He looks and sees and knows. Just like he knows the difference between waking and sleeping. Looks and knows the difference between that and this and lots of things. Of course he does. Streets are solid, not like water, not like the ocean, certainly not like the Northwest Passage, which he never found standing shoulder to shoulder with his staunch crew. Never found anywhere, although he dreamed of it often, head turning, landscape turning in sympathy until it flowed like the waves. John knows this. Of course he does. He looks and sees. He knows. All stands. It all stands. To reason. Out there to be seen. Just like the Northwest Passage in his dream.

John Franklin opens his mouth.

Vitus looks at the street signs on the corner. Looks at his map, the corner, the signs. Looks as he opens his mouth again.

P.A. Mikkelborg continues to point, mouth opening but no sound coming out.

Penelope stops at the corner. Glancing back. Seeing the woman who spoke to her earlier. A strange urge comes over her. Like something gripping her mouth, making her tongue work.

'Are you sure?' June asks Penelope aloud, the strange urge too great to resist.

Lady Jane closes the map and asks a question of Admiral Jellicoe. He opens his mouth.

'Pardon?' asks Mrs Blenkinsoe.

John Franklin leaves his mouth open. Of course he knows lots of things.

He has no idea exactly at what P.A. Mikkelborg is pointing.

'What are you asking?' asks Penelope.

Lady Jane tries again.

Vitus closes his mouth afterwards. Did they understand that? he asks himself.

Admiral Jellicoe looks confused. 'Is that what you meant?' says Mrs Blenkinsoe just as the Admiral opens his mouth to ask the same thing. At least, it might have been the same thing. Something similar, perhaps. Maybe. The traffic moves around the corner. Or the corner moves and the traffic stays still. Jellicoe would like to decide which but, as other people join their group, holding maps, hands folded like maps, expressions like maps folded like hands, like as not holding something even if only more questions, the Admiral feels himself turning, mouth open or closed or part-way between as the others join the group, mouth open or closed or part-way between as they move around Jellicoe, or he about them or some common centre, like the moon or a map or an idea like the moon folded like the pages of a hand being taken out of a map case, taking out an idea in common, that might be in common, that certainly isn't in the map case. Certainly not that.

Admiral Jellicoe is fairly sure of that.

They stand in a circle. On the corner of the junction, a circle circling. Mouths working hands. Hands working mouths. It's hard to be sure, but circling. Talking round and around, one round after another; all talking, all going round. Words washing out of mouths like waves. Waves of words, tides of them, foaming, surging around each of them as they stand and talk. Tied together by the words, by phonemes and syllables and things revolving and catching each of them up, over and over, washing over him or her, her and him, pouring in one mouth and out another. Spray hazing the air, pauses and *ums* or *ahs* filling the space in the middle where, they're fairly sure, is the thing they're talking about. It's there somewhere, in amongst the words. Something was there a moment ago at least, hands working mouths, mouths opening, words opening wide as they circle, passing on in a haze of *ums* and *ahs*, washing over and over the topic, this thing they're all talking about, about and around about ten minutes or more. More like a rock in the sea, washed over by the tide, spume popping with *ahs* and *ums*. Worn away by each wave, little by little more; probably more. Growing vaguer, shape changing. Tide washing over sand, or rock turning into sand and then washed away by this tide drawing back or coming in but never stopping, word washing over word, wiping away all previous words, making them blur and fade and turn ghostly until rock turns into sound and there is only the sound of surf and washing waves, waves washing away. Away. Wishing there was some sign or sense or something of what — What? Whatever it was that has been washed away.

There is more, she said, as Vitus turned away to look through the window. Vitus remained silent, but she said nothing more and the only sound was that of voices coming from the next room, the heavy wooden cladding in this room making those voices distant. Look, she said, moving to the connecting door in a rustle

of skirts. Look — and she threw open the door. There was dear
Mrs Blenkinsoe and her 'Admiral'; there was Paulus and Lord
John; and Jane; and Vitus wanted to look away because there
they all were: standing in a circle, just like in her dream: talking
in circles, words circling, never penetrating, never reaching
anywhere beyond the ears of the next person in the circle and
then only to slip away, fall away around the circle and to circle
again, thought Vitus without words, only seeing as he looked
through the open doorway to see: Vitus clutching his new map,
words washing over and around, over and over the words surging
around the circle like breakers washing over Vitus while Vitus
standing in the doorway watched as Vitus standing in the room

paused on the landing to look at the magpie, light catching the
ring in its beak.

             I SOMETIMES
     — it's silly
          What?
          You'll laugh
          So?
          Oh really
          You sometimes
    what? I can't
          No   it's silly
          I'll tell you one
    then

A loom fills most of this tiny space, roof sloping so
sharply the frame brushes its head against the bare joists.
This may be an attic: one window, inset into the roof,
and casting a yellow, deep yellow light across the loom.
Dust motes fall through the light: nothing else moves, the
room, this small attic room empty before we look into
it; or this attic has memories of being empty and we can

feel them as we view the loom, caught in a saffron shaft of evening, summer evening sunlight, falling through the open window. (Was the window open when we first glimpsed it? This is not a question we can answer because there is a sense that this room, old and dusty as it is, did not exist before we appeared. Best not to think of such things.) A breeze slips through the open window. Warm, the draft bolsters the sunlight, filling this room with wild bay, the scent of olive trees, bringing the sea's voice along with it so there is one mouth speaking with two voices as the wind plucks at the threads of the loom, fingers running out an arpeggio that ends only to repeat, bass note identical to top, that merely an inversion of the note in the middle, it holding a kinship so close to the bass they might as well be twins.

Ulysses stopped, plane in one hand, other resting on what had been a cabin door, lying flat across a pair of improvised sawhorses.

The sea murmured.

'John? Tell me: how *do* you measure a circle?'

'What, old man?' Franklin looked up from the rope he was struggling to re-plat.

'How *do* you measure a circle?'

'Oh.' Franklin chewed his lip. Shrugged. Voice oddly rote as he replied at last: 'We measure a circle, starting anywhere.'

> That's strange
> Isn't it?
> No   I meant I
dreamt of writing
> Writing?
> No   I mean
— what made me ...?
Weaving   I was thinking
of weaving
> Was that what
...?

                    No   No that
         was   Tell me another
                    I haven't —
         anyway it's your turn
                    No   I said
         — You know I've just
         remembered

The room is empty but for the Victrola sitting on the floor
beneath the sloping roof. Only one window here, deeply
inset into the ceiling. Sunlight falls across the Victrola,
limning each scallop in the horn, scratches gleaming in
the golden, late evening light. Summerlight, breathing a
breeze that has wild basil and olive trees on its breath, a
hint of salt underneath, of brine that tingles as we kneel
beside the Victrola. Only one record: sleeve plain brown
paper, torn and crinkled, as much used as the disk inside.
The writing on the plum-coloured label is beginning to
fade; gold lettering turned almost grey under the many
fingers that have touched it, taking the record from the
sleeve and placing it on the turntable. Turn the crank and
set the disk spinning. Spinning, circumference slightly
warped so the record seems to undulate as it spins, rising
and falling as we sit and watch it turn. Imagining what
would come from the scalloped horn if we should put the
needle down. Imagining

                    Your voice
         coming from the horn
                    Yes   That's it
         How?
                    Guessed   No
         I — someone, was it? said
         they had been thinking
         was it?   Perhaps I dreamt
         that   too

Franklin looks at the drip forming on the tip of the tar
brush. Shakes himself.

The sea murmurs.

'I say, old chap, how *does* one measure a circle?'

'Hm?' Ulysses, sitting in a cradle 20 feet distant across the emerging cliff-face, props his bare feet against bare lath and spar, pushing back out into space. 'Say again?'

'Just wondering,' Franklin calls across, voice carrying over the sea's murmur like gullsong, 'how does one measure a circle?'

Ulysses laughs, shakes his head, raises a hammer, and replies in an oddly rote voice: 'We measure a circle, starting anywhere.'

the shore moves, rising up ahead of the waves, and takes the coin away from Mrs Blenkinsoe

Mrs Blenkinsoe leaves the shop and bumps into Mikkelborg, who drops the coin which she picks up

Mikkelborg shoots the man trying to stop him after Mikkelborg snatches the medal away from Lady Jane

Lady Jane hesitates, and takes the keepsake from her husband's hand

her husband hesitates, and steals it from Ulysses' collection

waiting until his wife leaves the room, Ulysses takes the ring hanging from the loom

and, with a single blow,
hammers it flat into a disk,
a medallion, coin-like

Penelope turns, searching
the crowds choking the
narrow street, but the little
boy in the white sailor suit
has disappeared, leaving
only the ring he thrust into
her hand

the little boy in the white
sailor suit watches as
June thanks the elderly
gentleman, bobbing curtsies
as he touches the brim of his
hat and strolls away along
the path busy with other
visitors to the park; watches
as she turns away, her face
changing, watches her spit
on the path, before numbly
taking the shiny ring the
elderly gentleman gave June
as she thrusts it into the
little boy's hand, Silly old
fool, June says as she does
so, taking the boy's hand:
Come on, time we was
getting you 'ome, ain't it?

an agitated flutter of
wings, a hoarse *Craik!* and
'Admiral' Jellicoe turns
at the sound of something
metallic striking the
pebbles, a single magpie
feather alighting beside the
ring just as the elderly man

bends to pick it up, ring
fallen from the bird's beak
not ten minutes after the
bird pecks it from Vitus's
fingers

as Vitus walks away from the
shore. The sun lies low over the sea, scudding shadows
across wavetops, teasing them out of the wavelines etched
into the sand. Catching on something lodged in the
crest of the tidepool. Vitus, dazzled, squints. Kneeling,
he turns reflection into ring. Yet, as he prises it from
the sand, the low sun takes hold of it again. Golden
reflections twist, filling in the centre of the ring. Filling it
in until it is solid.

Like a coin.

She had her back to him and Vitus found himself looking
at the bull's-eye, listening to the voices drifting up from
the street below.

It feels silly, I tell myself it's silly, she was saying, but
you, you're in this dream I have.

Recurring? Vitus asked, running a finger around
the bull's-eye.

No. I don't know. Sometimes, she replied, skirts
rustling. Vitus looked out. At New Bruges, prosperous,
harbour visible between the roofs.

More than once, she said.

Black shape totally unexpected, rag-flap of wings
and harsh *Craik!* of the bird's voice such a surprise, Vitus
leapt back from the window. Staggering, own voice
pitching somewhere between a gasp and a shout.

More than once, she repeated calmly, back towards
the window as she faced the connecting door. I'll tell you,
she added and began:

I'm surrounded by sand, like a desert ...

I am surrounded by sand, like a desert, but I know it is
not a desert although it has not rained for about a week.

I walk for a long time. I am walking when the dream

starts, so, telling of it, it seems as though I am walking before the dream starts, walking before I can tell what has happened. I walk a long time, long time, before I see anything other than sand.

I see a standpipe. In fact, I trip over the standpipe and in the tripping make the finding.

There is no thought once found: I open the standpipe's bibcock. The sand floods. I try, but there is no turning off the tap. The sand floods, floods until the water rises so much I have to swim.

I swim. I swim for a long time. A long time swimming with nothing to look at but water, the horizon grown flat. Looking at that, the horizon, for a long time, until I see a woman who is walking on water. Seems to be walking on water — there is no telling for sure because I pass her. She falls behind and all there is is the horizon, the sea, the swimming. Only that as I fall asleep, remembering talking in a room, in New Bruges, around the middle of the day, and the person I'm talking to says it is strange I should mention dreaming because this person has been having a recurring dream in which we stand and talk in this room, stand beside this window and talk. And then you say

Vitus said nothing, standing on the threshold of the connecting door, watching Vitus drop the map, the map blow on the wind, Vitus watched as he made a grab, Vitus watching as first one hand was thrown out, the other alternating, each hand pulled back to be thrown out again, legs thrusting with effort; map tumbling, churning over, flashing white at the top of each crest. Falling to rise.

                    See   I said it
          was silly
                    No   not   And
          every night?
                    More or less
          Are you …?
                    No   I mean
          I mean I'm fine — it's just
          this is so
                    Like a dream
          you had
                    Yes   just like a
          dream you had

One hand pulls back. The other hand throws forward.
Once forward, that hand pulls back, taking its arm
with it as muscles contract, burn and contract. Contract
and release. Followed by the first hand, forwards-flung
firsthand, encountering resistance, outflung and pushing
back, ajoined arm trailing after whether it wants to or
not. Unlike the otherhand, which has some choice in the
matter.

Otherhand flings, pulls back after, muscles co-
operating, burn-contract becoming release-fatigue,
and arm likewise, all in all. One arm then the other.
Flungpulled against each resistance met, wake churning
as bubbles pop and foam, popped foam turning white at
the top of each crest, each crest falling back to let Vitus
by, bowing whiteheads graciously.

Most polite. Very polite, as they could allow the
current to force him away. And gracious, as they have
some choice in the matter. Foam white, bowing politely as
Swimming Vitus swims past. Arms flinging, Swimming
Vitus splashing as foam pops and wakes bow, falling back
very graciously. But without any thanks because Vitus,
Swimming Vitus, with arms flingfollowing and hands
pulling, kicks the waves, legs flailing, wake churned and
churning.

Poor foaming-crests, getting treated this way by

Swimming Vitus swimming so very mechanically. Thoughtless Swimming Vitus!

But what of Vitus? Pulled against resistance encountered, pushed forward by legs flailing, flailing legs kick-thrusting mechanically, Vitus dragged behindhands, driven beforefeets. What of Vitus? There is breathing. There is churning. There is this arm taken with as that flailingleg kicks. But Vitus seems gone. Quite absent. Lost inside Swimming Vitus, quite absent, quite lost inside.

Just as Swimming Vitus is lost in all this water.

I never remember what happens after that, she said, face averted.

Vitus closed his eyes, turning, towards the window, seeing the darkness grow pale.

I do, he replied.

One hand throws forward. The other pulls back, legs kicking regardless of which hand is which, forwards or back. So swims Swimming Vitus. So Mechanical Vitus is swimming, mechanistically perhaps but swimming. On the surface. Swimming on the surface, head turning, one hand backwardthrown or pulledforward makes no difference, not to Swimming or Mechanical as long as one followsanother waterchurned: surface-swimming swum mechanically, handswitching & legskick-kick-kick.

Swimming Vitus. Mechanical Vitus. The name doesn't matter, only the swimming, the mechanical. Swimming-Mechanically Vitus throws one hand forward, pulling the other back, legskick churning —

Well, you know.

The shore, left behind, looks.

Pebbles become rocks, rocking underfoot, jutting out, cropping up more often. Outcrops, you see. Seen over there. See one directly ahead. Merging and shelving ideas of remaining separate.

The shore, left behind, looks deserted.

No wind along this stretch, no breath to whisper away the clouds. So the sun, golden or otherwise, is hidden, of course, only clouds, grey or likewise, a wall of them, glowing faintly but most ways dull and flat and no shadows under the rocks, the grass directly ahead.

The shore, left behind, looks like no place in particular.

Flat rocks, flat grass, flat sky. Drab sky, drab grass, drab rocks merging, hidden under a layer of earth, loose and otherwise, brown and likewise. Sandy earth. Earthy sand become rocks emerging, jutting underfoot more often. You see outcrops, rocked and broken, broken into pebbles, pebbles worn into sand. Always.

You see another sweep of land, dullday flat, jutting out over slopes of rocks and pebbles, pebbles and sand. We see just land, and sky — clouds, sun hidden — of course. But mostly jutting land crumbling into gravel, pebbles, sand.

The shore, left behind, looks like it's repeating.

The shore, left behind, looks, and sees no more; not at all a mirror, but itself, flat, dull and left behind. Looks and sees no one but itself. Feels nothing, no breath to whisper. Hears a clacking *clat-clackering* in the distance, the far distance, followed by silence drawing out, rolling gently in across the pebbles&sand shore beyond the jutting-land. No breath to whisper away the clouds and nothing to see. Except itself.

Unnoticed, something moves.

Lapping.

Penelope slows. Her hands still beside her, but one foot raised. Gently falling over lapping waves, rising gently. Falling. Sand gently falling, rising slowly, waves overlapping. Penelope slows. Horizonline unchanged and no breath to whisper away the clouds but falling. Wave gently hissing over wave, each dune different but the sea changeless, even so.

Penelope slows, lapping in white noise. Or white

foam, hands no longer still as she climbs a dune, runnels overlapping, hissing underfoot and her hands out, outheld for balance as sand laps in waves, Penelope climbing.

Noticed, movement.

The shore gently raises itself over the jutting land, aware of movement, coin momentarily forgotten.

Penelope glances back, uncertain; glances ahead, unsure. And makes the top of the crest. Pebbles billow underfoot, sand risen, fallen, rising and falling in slow, slow waves all round. Sand waving as Penelope, hands by her sides again, walks a little way over the pebbles making the top of the dune. And stops. Horizonline stopping likewise, clouds also. Everything coming to a halt.
    Almost.
    Dune waves. Penelope lifts a hand. Hesitates. Lifts it further. Waiving also, feeling stupid and waving again even so.
    Sand waving, dunes overlapping, Penelope almost as still, hand raised, not yet falling, still no breath, still no movement, still. But dunes wave, sand laps and overlapping.
    And Vitus. Swimming. Oblivious.
    Penelope waves. Hesitates. Tries again.
    Vitus swims. Oblivious.
    Sand waves, waves overlapping, waving at Swimming Vitus, mechanically swimming Oblivious Vitus. Waving as Vitus, swimming, flails onehand forward or onearm back as feet kick, kick, kick. Sand growing sad, or angry, or affronted at Vitus swimming but not waving. Not 'Waving Vitus' at all, but Not-Waving Vitus swimming, oblivious to sand or horizon. Or Penelope, no longer waving.

Eyes closed. Eyes open. It makes no difference. All Vituses swimming swim onwards. Oblivious.

The shore left Penelope behind for one more look and finds itself looking. Not a mirror at all. Itself: no more, nothing but. Come full circle beyond the edge of the jutting-land. And faces itself: nothing but, no more. Another face, one on each side of the jutting-land, the whole thing turned full circle. Coin apparently forgotten as

Penelope   lets
her hand fall to her
side. Opens her eyes wider.
Sees arms churning. No body,
exactly, but legs. Or calves, heels,
ankles. An inference of legs. As arms,
by the side or outflung, suggest torso,
body as a whole. But she sees, no
matter how wide her eyes, neither.
Arms churning. Feet kicking.
Kicking   up   sand.   White
sand. Ice-white, like
foam

and, seeing foam, sees sea and, so seeing, turns her head away, leaving the dune-crest. Walking. Face turned. Walking across waves of sand, troughs of pebbles and crests left behind. Walking on. Always, apparently. Always leaving the shore to look. Always the dunesea, undulant; the sky, unchanging. All, always; always all: changeless. Penelope, accepting, walks on, changeless waves rising, falling in a myriad of ways that merge, repeat this day as on another so long ago; or longer: there is no counting, no memory. Only one foot risen and put down, placechanged with the other foot. Each step, each dune, each day the same. And Penelope, likewise. Accepting. A man swimming in this sea of sand. The coin, her husband. Perhaps the same thing — coin and husband, husbandandcoin — perhaps each the same only in as much as they are out of her reach, equally so, so equally lost. Lost out there or lost in — her hand rises, hesitates, and falls without making contact. Land beneath rising, gently falling, undulant swell, or billow, and below the surface more of the same she might think. But Penelope no longer wants to think. Not now. Not ever, or so she hopes just now, a last thought before silence. Face turned away, leaving all behind until — probably, inevitably — she returns to the start, comes back to the same point, changeless and ahead always, no matter how quiet she is.

And Penelope is quiet. There is only the sound of sand, displaced, hissing. Of lapping and foam popping. The sound of waves rolling.

Franklin stands back, hears hammering, hears water lapping like drifting sand, water hissing as it drifts, foaming at the remains of the ships. Franklin, standing back, feels the weight of the saw in one hand, the grit of wood-dust in the creases of both hands, feels the sea pressing at his back, knows it's there without turning, can see it close beyond where Ulysses is working, hammer rising, falling, risingfall making a tide of hammerblows —

Franklin, joints stiff and musclecramped, doesn't want to think of that. Stands straight, gives voice to his fatigue (not exactly a sigh, not quite a groan) and feels the sea pressing at his back, on each side, pushing in from where Ulysses is working. A constant presence, the sea, a constant voice murmuring to Franklin, scratching at his ears, insinuating itself into his sleep. There is no escaping it, Franklin tells himself as he stands back, stretching as Ulysses hammers, hammertide ebbing, flooding, ebbing again until Franklin worries he will be hearing this, too, in his sleep, another constant companion. Like Ulysses, Franklin adds, sure he is grateful for the company, even if the hammering gets on his nerves.

Only when he's tired, Franklin assures himself.

The sea hisses.

Wood splinters. Ulysses curses. Glances towards Franklin, shrugging, glance rueful, self-deprecating. Friendly. So Franklin (ignoring the sea) smiles back, shrugging also as he smiles and shrugs, commiserating, sharing camaraderie: two people, working together. Good thing, he tells himself as Ulysses begins hammering a fresh piece of wood. Good.

Franklin blinks.

Franklin feels alone, quite alone. And Ulysses?

Who knows what Ulysses is thinking.

Yes, that's it, I remember now.

Yes, that's it I re—

They both startled at the sound of the cough, the polite cough making them turn very nearly as one towards the open doorway, as Vitus, framed just beyond the threshold, held up a piece of writing paper.

swim *v. & n.* • *v.* the process of being borne along by another medium to the point where any sense of self is absorbed into that medium. • *n.* the retrospective sense of loss resulting from this once an individual stops swimming.

That reminds me

Yes

Heaving up, the shore meets the jutting-land, a fringe of grass hanging limp where they touch (no wind to day), one becoming other, shore looking across land.

The jutting-land.

Jutting out, the land ultimately forms a point, at which point it slopes, falls away beyond a fringe of grass, one land becoming another sort of land. Marginal. Or fringe if you like. But land until the shore (heaving up to meet the pointed tip of the jutting-land only, of course, to fall back and back until the shore) is finally obscured. Not changed, only hidden, submerged, if you like, and, in being hidden, renamed.

The shore, never very good with names, heaves (has heaved, remember? and will do again no doubt, up and down like, well, let's face it, up and down like the tide: heaved, heaves) itself up to look over the jutting-land. Quite flatland this jutting-land, so it's easy for the shore to see itself on the other side, formed to a point but the point being the shore sees itself, just there — see? — on the otherside of all this flatearthiness of grass and rocks jutting. Easy to see its other face: this shore looking at that other this-shore, you know, like two sides of a thingy (the shore — thisone or that — has never been very good with names), easy to see because the shore is so clearly defined between that fringe of grass and this ... this ...

The shore (never very good, etc) pauses. Jutting-land, grass, the shore (itself, its otherself, much the same) and then, lapping against the shore, the *far*shore, that is, lapping against *this*-shore's opposite face ...

The shore (never etc), feels something moving against its back. Forward and back, forward and —

Staring across the intervening land, the shore notices how the — call it 'not-sky-not-juttingland-not-me' (which is to say not the shore), notices how this unexpected thing swirls and eddies around the point of the juttingland. In fact, conscious of the probably-not-sky-certainly-not-juttingland-&-definitely-*not*-me moving (forward and back, forward and so forth) against its back, and absorbed by what is on the other side of the juttingland, the shore utterly fails to notice the post (jutting up), the rectangular piece of wood cut to a point (jutting out, pointing inland), and the letters on the wood. The letters that, before the angle of the shingle obscured them, read: 'Welcome to ...'

'Welcome to ...'

Voices so close they might have shared the same breath.

He closed his mouth, head turning, mouth reopening at the end of the turn to grasp another breath, drawing it down before: head turned, eyes closing.

Vitus felt his shoulders. Move. In circles around one arm, the other, each describing circles that overlapped.

Then who is —

A polite cough interrupted.

Vitus beyond the threshold had not moved. Yet the sheet of writing paper he held up read:

dream *n.* & *v.* • *n.* a series of perceptions or sensations arising from dreaming (see *dream v.*). • *v.* **1** to experience sensations of perceptions that are or have been dreams (see *dream n.*). **2** reading these words.

It feels silly, she was saying.

He turned his head to breathe. Turning it back as shoulders rotated one arm, the other following through.

It feels silly, she was saying, but you —

Vitus spat out water, gasping.

It feels silly, but you — You're in my dream, she said,

It has become so mechanical now, the swimming. As if there has never been anything but armsmoving, legskicking. He might as well not be there, Vitus begins to think, the swimming carrying on regardless of whether Vitus is thinking or there or not. Swimming Vitus. Exhausted Vitus. Sickofallthis Vitus — it makes no difference.

The swimming swims on obliviously.

Vitus spitting, shaking his head, gasping arhythmically, shoulders faltering, aspirated water rasping around another fast-indrawn breath to be convulsed out in a retching as, for a moment that lingered for more time than can be counted in one life and yet was gone in the instant of its appearance, Vitus thinks he remembers a time of certainty, with friends and the security of New Bruges around him, a time when swimming had become a memory.

Vitus spits out water.

And stops swimming.

Treading water, his teeth chatter, gooseflesh puckering and cramps threatening one leg, the other, every muscle trembling. Heavy with exhaustion. With cold.

Thirst almost drives him to swallow.

Vitus spits out seawater. Stares miserably at the desert he is lost in.

The cold bites deeper. Jaw clenched and still trembling, he knows he should start swimming again.

Vitus waits.

Waiting beyond the point we should accept nothing is going to change. Stubbornly holding on until the stiffness verges on cramp, verges on the point of sinking.

Vitus waits until he is sure this is a dream.

'JANE?'

She heard the conciliation, appeal, and still refused to turn towards him.

'Please.'

He took a step closer, footfall muffled by the Persian rug covering most of the withdrawing room's floor. She did not react, holding herself most deliberately still as she imagined his hand, outheld, foundering in midair, unable to make contact.

'Please, Jane. I — I know you understand my motives.'

At this she snorted.

'Intellectually, at least,' he added quickly, 'we've discussed this, debated often enough.'

There was a soft rustle of clothing and she imagined him partly raising one heel, aborting the step forwards before the foot could leave the carpet. The fire in the grate popped. Jane, hands fisted, crossed her arms about herself; squeezing, unable to fathom this almost reflexive action: a need to hold herself erect; or a desire for contact, contact of any kind, when she felt very much alone, despite the presence of her husband so nearby.

'I need to do this,' said he.

'What? Abandon me?'

She had not intended to speak. She knew what was expected of them both: he to set forth to explore, discover, annex of possible; she to remain behind, accepting, absorbing herself in the domestic arts for one year, three, until his return. Outside this room, there seemed no choice in the matter. In here, doors firmly closed, she entertained the conviction that things might be otherwise. More than entertained.

Jane snorted once again, that sound following her exclamation with a delay of less than a moment, so quickly had these thoughts passed through her.

Through and perhaps out, because she heard him step back, utter a sound caught between a sigh and a groan.

'There are times when it is as though this is being forced upon me. That my need to find answers has been expropriated, used against me until I no longer have a voice in the matter.'

Jane held herself more tightly, imagining the confusion and pain on his face, and wanting to comfort as greatly as she desired comfort. However, the space between them, simultaneously unbridgeable chasm and unscalable barrier, remained. So, voice curt, she said only, 'And yet you go, still need to go?' her inflection more statement than question.

He did not reply. Did not step closer once again. Only the clock spoke, and that with the rote voice of the sleepwalker. The certainty overwhelmed Jane that this was how they would remain always, never able to stir from their respective positions, no matter how greatly she desired to relent. No: turning, opening her arms and admitting her fear — for him, for herself — was impossible. They were fated to remain as they were; forever apart.

The warmth of him close behind made her startle. So absorbed in her anxieties, Jane had not heard him cross the space between them, bringing his arm around her, palm held open. Neither of them in contact, yet closer than they had been for some time.

'What —?' Jane looked at the disk in his palm.

'A keepsake, in the form of a medal.'

It looked like a coin, larger perhaps.

'It is not much,' he continued, 'no more than a token, a

symbol …' before trailing into silence.

Slowly, unwilling to break the moment, Jane picked up the token, her fingers brushing against his hand.

John shivers, making a small noise at the back of his throat.

'What is it?' Ulysses cranes back, one foot on the bottom rung of the makeshift ladder, to frown up towards Franklin.

'Hm? Oh, nothing.' John Franklin hammers the end of another section of cliff-face home with renewed vigour, hoping the exertion will drive the memory away.

It does not.

Neither man, not Ulysses nor Franklin, FranklinnorUlysses, notices the glint of light on the new-made shore as the sun glances from under the clouds at the island rising out of a sea that remains no matter who closes his eyes and wishes it away.

That night, Franklin dreams of being in the withdrawing room, his back turned, unable to cross the barrier between him and the person standing so closely behind. He can hear each breath, feel the warmth of her proximity. Despite the barrier. Or is it a chasm? Because it feels to him that there is a distance between them. A distance he is unable to cross, even begin to cross, no matter what she says. In this dream, John Franklin cannot even bring himself to turn around.

All he can see is the —

'What is it?'

Hands grabbing his shoulders.

'Calm down, Franklin.'

In the drag of sleep slow-fading, he has no sense of place, no context. So he fights.

'Dammit, man! It's me. Stop that infernal yelling, it's me!'

Shapes fit together. Each carrying a little meaning by itself; more so when brought together: firelight, wan, enough to pick out Ulysses' face hanging over him, the oddments of their camp, the brazier itself, salvaged from the *Phaeton* and standing on metal plates torn out of the *Bucephalus* in the hope the metal will catch any stray sparks, prevent the whole damn island catching fire.

'John?'

'No — I mean, I am fine. Truly. You can let go of me, I am awake.'

'You were screaming.'

'A nightmare.'

Ulysses sits back, face obscure in the ruddy light. 'Again.'

Inflection more statement than question.

Franklin feels the cold: dawn hours away and the brazier down almost to embers. He hugs his knees. 'Again?'

Cold night has nothing to do with his shivering.

'Hm? Oh,' Ulysses stutters, 'I didn't want to mention it before.' Ulysses turns away, apparently looking across the incomplete island, its shape invisible in the moonless dark.

'I have had —?' Franklin has no recollection of other dreams.

'How could all that has happened *not* give us nightmares?' Ulysses does not face Franklin as he speaks, voice made hollow by the nascent landscape. He smiles reassuringly when he does turn back. 'Don't trouble yourself over it, my friend. Try to get some sleep instead, eh?'

But sleep is a long time returning to John Franklin.

Next morning, both men freely admit to feeling hungover, fractious from interrupted sleep. They try to joke about it, strive for tolerance. So Franklin does not take offence when his suggestion they build the cliffs on the south side of the island into a 'sea wall of sorts, do you see?' is met with such vehement opposition by his friend. It is nothing to take exception to, he tells himself, even as Ulysses stamps away, yelling: 'Must you always create walls?' Nothing at all, John reminds himself, cheeks beginning to feel distinctly warm.

All in all, he is not in the least sure why he made the suggestion in the first place.

Light glints on the shore, unnoticed.

Darkness. Cold. Amber light leaving many shadows nearby. Silver light beyond, enough only to give notional weight to the otherwise flat shapes standing adrift of the water. No other hint of the sea's presence, the screaming is too loud. Blinking wildly, heart's thump making his blanket pitch, yaw painfully, he slaps a hand over his mouth.

The screaming goes on.

John Franklin struggles to wake up. Panic lends strength to the hand over his mouth. John stares at the quarter-moon standing in a parting in the clouds. Focuses on the moon, the dark patches on its face. There is no moon in the dream. Only withdrawing room, clock, the presence of another person so distant. If he can see the moon, he knows he is truly awake.

But the screaming goes on.

Jackknifing upright, he stares at Ulysses. Ulysses with his arms clutched tightly about himself. Ulysses with his eyes as tightly closed. Ulysses with his mouth a rictus. Screaming.

John looks at sleeping Ulysses and feels the dream pulling at him, the moon fading, leaving only the pop of the fire in the grate, a ticking, rote, like the sleepwalker's voice.

Next day, Ulysses contrives to have his back turned towards John much of the time. Work continues on the island, albeit slowly. One shore is almost complete: a shingled beach, spit-cum-headland bracketing one side, strake-and-futtock-ribbed cove sweeping around the other to peter out into a few rocks, made out of frames cut from lengths of taffrail covered with canvas, lying in front of an aperture that may yet become a cave-mouth. Their camp now perches on the top of this new cliffside.

At first light, Ulysses avoiding John's questions about the dream, mumbled that they should concentrate on the superstructure for the centre of the island. This they have done, John striving to ignore the other man's unwillingness to look at him. Finally, in mid-afternoon, the effort proves too much. When Ulysses, still facing away, grunts a request, Franklin takes the bolster asked for and hurls the chisel into the hulk of the *Terebus*. The clatter of its passage through the ship seems endless.

The noise makes Ulysses swing round.

John hears the sound of movement. Sees Ulysses from the corner of his eye. And turns further away, holding himself most deliberately still. Imagining.

Except, Ulysses begins noisily clambering up the

superstructure back towards camp, voice thick as he shouts, 'Always the same, always the bloody same …'

Silence. And no little distance.
    Two men sit side-by-side.
    Unspeaking.

John has no memory of having dreamt but finds himself sweat-drenched and screaming even so.
    Sitting next to the brazier, huddled under a blanket, he watches Ulysses. The other man sleeps peacefully, although his bedding is in disarray and one arm lies awkwardly outstretched. Palm open. As if offering something.
    But empty, much to John's surprise.

Foam looks grey in the darkness, the artificial cove murmuring with the voice of the tide. Comers weave between the canvas rocks, probe the spit-cum-headland, and meet on the other side of the islet, circles of grey marking the structure's circumference. Grey outline in the darkness. No moon; or, at least, a skullcap of cloud so tight there is no slit for the moon to appear through. A night with tight-closed eyes, muttering over the rote churn of the water and the pop of foam, murmuring as the cove murmurs, as a wave reaches up the shingle beach, pauses and subsides. Leaving the disk lodged between overlaps of wood. Not glinting. Not in this darkness, without a moon. Hardly there to be seen. But there.

Ulysses kept his back to him. He tried conciliation, tried appeal, tried to sound friendly, although that was difficult, what with him standing on the cliff's edge and his companion down on the shore. He hailed and shouted. But his voice was swallowed, by the breakers on the headland, or the distance between cliff-top and beach-edge. That, or he was deliberately being ignored.

'What is it you have there?'
    Ulysses barely glances towards him, hunching his shoulders further around whatever is in his hands.

'What the blazes is wrong with you?' The climb down to the shore has sharpened Franklin's temper. He is breathless with rage. 'I know you understand my motives.'

Ulysses snorts.

'Damnation, we've discussed this often enough.' John Franklin squeezes his hands into fists, shaking has he halts a few feet behind his companion. 'We must complete this work. You agreed.' Spittle foams at the edge of his mouth he is so angry. 'We need to do this.'

'And what then?' Ulysses begins to turn, checking the motion. John Franklin thinks he glimpses something in the other man's hands before Ulysses turns away, voice almost petulant as he mutters, 'What after? Abandon —'

'Abandon what?' John snaps, about to take a step closer and aborting the action. 'We're lost! Ships wrecked, crews gone. What would you have us do?'

'I —' Ulysses looks at whatever is in his hands — 'I feel all this is being forced upon me. That my needs have been expropriated. I no longer have a voice in the matter.'

'Balderdash.'

Despite the contempt in John's voice, Ulysses does not flinch. Only looks down.

'What the deuce do you have there?'

John crosses the gap between them in a lunge. His arms thrust around Ulysses, palms open. Grasping.

Ulysses spins away, yell inarticulate as one hand fends off John, the other flies upwards out of reach.

'The Devil,' Franklin spits, attention on the upraised hand, 'the keepsake. How? Give it back, you swine.'

Ulysses lands an awkward blow with his empty hand on John's face, forcing the latter back a step.

'This isn't yours.' The metal disk flashes dully in his hand. 'It's mine. Was mine …'

'Liar.' John gathers himself for another attack, catching his balance at the last instant as Ulysses raises a fist. 'That was mine. I gave it to Jane. A keepsake. A memento. Call it what you will, it is what it is: my wife's!'

Franklin hurls himself forward. The men grapple. Ulysses pushing back one-handed, the other held outstretched behind him, well away from John's clawing. Landing a kick on Franklin's knee, Ulysses staggers back as the other man curses, clutching his leg. Surf splashes around them, beach ringing hollowly.

'Listen, you idiot,' Ulysses shouts, pointing at the exposed face of the metal disk, 'I had this coin struck specially, presented to *my* wife. This is Penelope's coin, not your Jane's.'

'Not a coin. I told you: a token, a — I don't know what to call the dammed thing.' John dashes spume from his face. 'I know you're a damned liar. That's mine. That's Jane's. And you're going to —'

Their bodies smash together. Feet slapping against the shingles. Lips pulled back to expose teeth. Hands flailing. Grappling. Grappling as the sea churns around them. Ulysses, hand clenched around the metal disk, throwing a wild punch. John Franklin trapping the blow, wrenching sharply downwards. Taking both of them to the ground. Sprawling. Gasping. Gasping as the sea churns around.

When, each leaning on the other, the two men manage to sit up again, they find their hands are empty; shore likewise. Washed clean by the sea.

MRS BLENKINSOE leaves the shop with the strangest sensation. The doorbell gives a chime as the door closes behind Mrs Blenkinsoe, who is feeling the strangest sensation as she walks a little way up the road, then across the road, away from the shop, a shop which seemed to have so many points in common with other shops, but which now makes Mrs Blenkinsoe feel not a little disturbed. *This is a strange sensation*, thinks Mrs Blenkinsoe feeling that she has crossed a definite boundary, in crossing this road, a previously unsuspected undercurrent rising as she walks. Down, walking away only to pause. To turn back towards the shop, this mood of disquiet giving rise to the strangest sensation. Because, although it seemed to have many points in common with other shops — points such as doors, and bells chiming (a little chime of delight), not to mention shelves and stock and such — all these points in common notwithstanding, Mrs Blenkinsoe is gripped by an indefinite suspicion as she looks back. Afraid at what she will find, gripped though she is, and so a little reluctant to look (you can understand her dilemma), but the feeling that there was something odd, is something strange, makes her pause even so (you may be familiar with such actions; we don't need to go into too many details as Mrs Blenkinsoe pauses) to look back at the building a little way down, then across, the road. *This is a strange sensation*, gripped Mrs Blenkinsoe thinks (*although*, she adds, *it had the word 'shop' over the door in the usual way*). Shops have many points in common, we don't need to go into details but we can agree on doors and bells (tickled, giving a chime of delight), not to mention shelves and stock and such. We can exchange the word 'shop' between ourselves, ourselves and Mrs Blenkinsoe, and know ('believe', it has to be said) we are imagining something in common. Between us, between us and Mrs Blenkinsoe. Between here and down, then across, the road. Water, tickled, might indeed make a sound like a chime of delight. 'Shop', the word over the door now closed but moving still. Which is to say light is reflecting (in a casual way) across the door, a little way up, then across the door, reflecting from each ripple or swell. Say, 'ripple': we can exchange this word between ourselves and imagine something in common, although Mrs Blenkinsoe, gripped Mrs Blenkinsoe, in the grip of the strangest sensation, does not see, or cannot understand, or will not accept what is rippling or moving still, or possibly making a chime of delight under different circumstances. (You understand her dilemma, even if the conditions she is experiencing, hardly common, are unfamiliar to you.)

Say: 'water'.

Say: 'island'.

Say: 'surrounded'.

Say you're Mrs Blenkinsoe, wondering how you left a shop, closing the door behind you before walking a little way up, then across the road. Say you're Mrs Blenkinsoe gripped by an indefinite suspicion — say a sense of unease, a chime of disquiet — as you turn back and wonder how left and closed and upped and acrossed all without noticing the shop is surrounded by water. Not a shop on an island. A shop which is an island. Water lapping at its step. Water brimming a little way up, brimming a little way down, then across the road. Water unbroken, water rippling, water swelling. Water you crossed without noticing, with, aside from dry feet, nothing but this unease becoming solid and concrete in your throat.

Say all that. Now tell me this wouldn't leave you with the strangest sensation.

The shop leaves Mrs Blenkinsoe with the strangest sensation. The doorbell gives a chime as the door closes. Walking a little way up the road, then across the road, the shop pauses, looking back. Certain something quite strange is taking place.

light growing hazy

          sun

               caught
on the edge
of the wall

               July
sepia

in
silence

               only ever

one handprint

on the

                    glass

her fingers were quite swollen by the end, knuckles permanently red as if they must have been giving pain, although she rarely complained, not that I can remember now, I do remember being fascinated with her hands, bones pressing sharply under the skin, skin very pale and wrinkled, wrinkles creasing when her fingers moved, hands clenched, I wondered where those wrinkles came from, what each knob of bone felt like to move, if they ever popped, her hands, hands always cool to the touch, pad of each palm and finger firm, smooth, resilient, if not so soft, smooth and dry, the edge of one thumb cracked easily when the weather turned cool, cool hands warm heart, she used to say, cool hands warm

This morning, the calendar tells me it's now the last week of February. I have no memory of yesterday, of what the date was yesterday. It felt like July. I think I saw a reference to June before that. Now February is almost over. So the calendar says. There's no way of checking; I'd hate to think I can't trust the calendar, that it's lying.

Outside, the sky is turning blue. Last time I looked: grey. Now blue. Not unbroken, but largely cloud-free and the sun is bright enough to make the lamp beside me turn wan. This room has ... call it an awkward aspect. Direct light finds it late on in the day, and then obliquely at this time of year (taking the calendar at its word). It is usually gloomy. That might be part of the appeal, but I tell myself quite openly that I came in here so I couldn't see the wall. At least, not see it very well. If there is another reason, I'm not consciously aware of it.

It feels like July a lot, so the calendar could be telling the truth after all. Some sort of truth, at least. Perhaps I am writing this at the end of February from one point of view. Writing: 'I am writing at the end of February' when it is the end of February and I am, or definitely just did, write those words this morning, moments ago, so I am writing, 'I am writing at the end of February', in February, in the last week of this month, which means I must be both writing 'writing' and writing 'at the end of February' at the end of February and the recursion is beginning to make me feel trapped. Enclosed within a wall of words. Surrounded by a wall of words or symbols. Or signifiers and signifieds, one representing the other endlessly. A wall. Another wall.

I am writing the word 'wall' at the end of February and meaning

I don't care what the calendar says. It feels like July. July the twelfth. Every day is July the twelfth. I am writing, 'I am writing July the twelfth at the end of February', at the end of February that feels stuck at the beginning of July.

July the twelfth. That was when the wall went up

Boris paused, cursor blinking on the screen. It was lunchtime, the office empty — even John had gone out to get antihistamines. There were no distractions, the car park and landscaped gardens quiet for once.

Boris stared at the computer screen.

The flow of words was gone. All confidence in what he had written also vanished.

One finger tapped rapidly against the side of the keyboard, Boris unaware of the twitch. Absorbed in the screen, the blink of the cursor, the words that no longer flowed, no longer felt —

Boris glanced at the calendar sitting on the corner of the desk. This month was decorated with a picture of shoreline, waves rolling over themselves.

He leaned across the desk. Move so abrupt Boris almost took himself by surprise, fingers glancing off the calendar. It fell back, tumbling to the floor.

After the first go he sighed, stood and knelt beside the desk, calendar lying just out of reach if he stayed sitting. Boris turned to the picture of the shore. Frowning, he paged through the whole calendar. And once more, deliberately. But July was still missing.

Nina has been back for almost a week. The routine chafes after having had time off. She is just now coming back from a staff training thing on the eighth floor, taking the stairs because 'it helps you keep fit', because it staves off the inevitable. The training thing was weird. Mad, actually. None of it made sense: all jargon and flowcharts and 'protocols' that everyone except the trainer knew were going to be replaced by something else by mid-year.

That was not the weird part.

Nina, feeling unenthusiastic and resenting the whole farce, had sat at the back of the room. The sun had been shining (still is as she pauses on the sixth-floor landing), the first time in weeks it had done so. Sunlight late-winter-weak but still soothing against her shoulders, the back of her head (same light falling through the window in front of her, on to her face). Nina began to relax. Concentrating on the feel of the sunshine. Half-watching the training.

It happened quickly, in the space between one blink and the next: the end of the training room looked flat, like a cheap stage set. The trainer kept talking. Her colleagues answered questions, got up to scrawl on a flipchart. Their actions looked awkward. Every word stilted, voices too loud.

Nina did not move. She watched the actors who looked like people she knew, or the people she knew acting, it was hard to tell which it was as they moved around the pathetic stage set, stumbling over or forgetting their lines. At one point, the marker pen ran out and the 'trainer' continued regardless, the 'audience' pretending they could see bullet points and rough pie-charts scribbled on the blank flipchart page.

Nina looks out of the landing window, face close to the glass. Wan, yellow light reflects off the other wing of the building. Below are lines of bushes along the edge of the car park. It all seems real. At least, three-dimensional.

She tries not to think of anything as she goes back to her cubicle. Succeeds, largely, a stray thought breaking loose once she has opened her desk drawer, taken out a battered, much-taped, 3-ring binder, and turned to the document wallet bookmarked with a pink Post-It. The July page of a desk calendar rests inside this stuffed plastic envelope. That stray thought breaks loose as Nina looks at the page. Luckily, the thought fades as soon as it appears, leaving only an odd discomfort. A still sense of absence.

Boris pauses, cursor blinking on the screen. The only sound is the hum of the laptop. No other distractions. Not through the walls, not from across the street. One of the tacked-up pieces of writing is coming loose, hanging by two corners only. Boris has not noticed yet. He sees only screen, cursor blinking: inviting. To add or subtract. To move through the text, in any case. He looks at it flash, cursor the centre, the whole of his attention, so the laptop fades, the desk fades, the scraps of writing on the walls and the walls of his room fade, the window vanishes and takes the wall across the street with it.

Cursor.

Blink-blink-blink …

Go on; go back.

Blink-blink-blink …

Black vertical an imperative: Boris must not stop!

Boris stares at the cursor. There are no words in his head,

but the feeling suffuses his mind. There are sensations that exist in some languages, absent and others. This cannot mean native speakers of those impoverished languages never experience those unnamed sensations, only that they cannot articulate the experience succinctly. It remains uncategorised, perhaps seemingly unique to each individual so, because there is no word for it, they feel alone in this nameless feeling. Convinced no one could have felt this way, otherwise it would have been labelled before now.

Boris stares at the cursor. A feeling of something-there-but-out-of-reach; a feeling of something-hidden-or-obscured-or-missed-without-understanding-its-loss; a feeling of melancholy-for-the-unaccounted-loss-of-something-not-quite-known-but-which-could-be-significant colouring his whole mind, bleeding into his body.

As he abruptly puts fingers to keys and types

as she abruptly puts fingers to keys and types

as he abruptly

as she

as

as I can't think of any other way of describing it, I'll have to content myself with

a still sense of absence

I can't say any more, not today
    I just can't

Mrs Blenkinsoe looked back

Voices harsh, mobbing

The sound of footfalls on tarmac

Alone with himself, Mikkelborg, P.A., stands in the doorway. Sounds still come over the wall. The sounds have no idea where he is and he interprets them without alerting suspicion, the sounds having no more idea where he is than the people on the otherside looking for him. Stillooking. Furtheraway and receding. Like stars.

Mikkelborg, P.A., stares at the nearest poster, eyetoeye. WANTED, says the posterface, emphatically, wantedfor much less so. Hardly legible, in fact, no matter how much Mikkelborg walks, shadowtoshadow or lamp to next lamp, taking his time now the sounds are receding like stars, thiside of the wall obviously deserted. But for Mikkelborgs.

There is hiding.

There is also running. And scrambling.

There is also the idea. Of coming overwall, lastplacetheyw illthinktolook. There is this, also.

Posterfaces declaim WANTED. He can see this everyplace, there for the looking.

But the why, the wantedfor, is not barely legible, it simply is not.

Mikkelborg has no idea why he is being hunted.

Notso desperate now, Mikkelborg (P.A.) turns his back on the wall. Walking quickly, openwalking any route taking him away, receding like a star. Ignores himself watching from the corner ahead, the front window behind. Crosses the road. Quickly. Not hiding. Escaping.

P.A. Mikkelborg makes his faces, inner and outer, smile.

'Hey! Who —? What are you — Hey! You shouldn't be here,

you should be with the other — You're him! You stay right there. That's it. This is a citizen's arrest, so you don't think about — Yeah, just stand, you're under arrest.'

Mikkelborg steps left, left, handsinfront. Outerface appearing confused, confused&shocked. Expression on posterfaces unchanging. Lotsof faces. But only two pairs of eyes, watching him stepleft until a tree's shadow blocks the nearest streetlamp. Outerface placating. The one underneath expressionless. Fixed on the pair of eyes approaching cautiously, the strangerface mouthing emphaticwords, sounds advancing. Advancingsounds, the sound of footfalls on tarmac. Ignoring postereyes, Mikkelborg stands onehandup, onehandinshadow. And smiles.

Mikkelborg stood over the body. Heat from the gun muzzle warmed his leg, hands hanging loosely at each side. Smell of cordite. Smell of blood. Mingling. Standing overbody. Mikkelborg thinking: 'Oh, this is why.'

The sound of footfalls against tarmac.
    A voice from a nearby building. Another across the street. Lights coming on. Windows being thrown open. Torch beams. Voices A siren. Sirens. Voices raised doors opening spilling light. Cars approaching shouting arms outthrown fingers pointing words becoming clearer. Sirens coming closer face unchanged emphatic word just the same but words underneath sirens cars shouts shouts of rage horror voices hoarse or broken underneath each face on every poster coming clearer, becoming legible on all but the most tattered notice not that he has time or need to read them now.
    The sound of footfalls on tarmac.

Pistolbrandished, Mikkelborg froze. Back pressed against a wall, bricks pressing against his back. Shouts&sirens all around, voices raised, giving orders and replies, with bootsteps or tyrerasps. Everywhere. Advancing.
    Torchbeams reached around the junction where thisroad became thatroad. Probing the tarmac, light fingers running

over the pavement.

Mikkelborg blinked, breathshort, afraid of any sound he made. Afraid because he remembered he had to be. Remembered now that he had never been chased before this, before standing overbody. Breathing deep, Mikkelborg made himself turn, legstumble, stumblerunning, down the nearest alley.

The sound of footfalls on tarmac. Receding.

Out of one tunnel, footsteps dropping back. Into another tunnel, footsteps catching up. Paperfaces watching from eachwall, close enough to touch. Tunnel narrow. Tunnel low. Tunnel ending (not very long). Another beginning.

Mikkelborg ran. Between narrowwalls. Footfalls chasing, doubling, doublefalls trebling. Overface chafing over inner. Breathshort. Graspingbreath. Footfalls almost catching him. Tunnelmouth receding just in time, becoming bushes&weeds, stars treesobscured.

Mikkelborg stopped. Footfalls continued, bootscrape on tarmac. Searching.

No choice. He remembered that now, listening to distantvoices. Advancing. A searchlight glanced off the top of the wall, and he remembered that, too: needing to find somewhere to hide and seeing the wall.

No choice.

Mikkelborg tugged off the mask.

Vitus tugs. Tugs, scrambles. Vitus tugs, scrambles and pulls. Pullscrambles, grunting, feet kicking, hands overhead. Grips, grasping

hears in the distance voices

bootsteps

a light poking through the trees

and he slithers to the ground

Vitus has no memory before this. Knows only that he has to find somewhere to hide.

gone over
the whole house
twice — start
again tomorrow

one on every
thing
surface
I remember

a Post-it for
every memory
every thing
she touched

many

many

many
many many
many
notes

all over the
house
to capture
everything
every action
every

moment

There are   gaps   Did she not
touch this vase, or have I
                forgotten?
       And these notes covering the kitchen table, do I have them
in the right order?
                Which came   first
                                the evening
                it rained
                Or the   evening
                                    we
                                talked
                &
                    real   ised
                                    we
                              no
                long   er
                              knew what
                the
                                    date
                                    was?

                              and now   the ink
                              is fading

I tried moving the notes around, searching for the right order.
Trying to take hold of memories that were fading, are fading,
that might not be true in any case but which
        I look at the
        pattern
                of notes
        on
            the
                    walls & know
                      they're

wrong

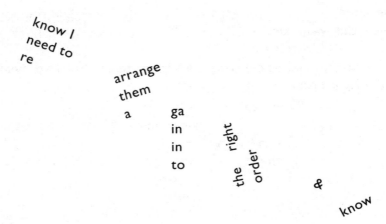

know I
need to
re
      arrange
      them
      a   ga
            in
            in
            to   the right order
                                    &
                                        know

I can't.

They're fixed. I can't remember, can't see any other pattern. These are my memories now.

If — how do I say this? — if memory is our anchor, and that anchor isn't fixed but drags, kicking up silt as it drifts — if that's so, what have we got?

Words. Nothing but words and guesses.

Vitus ran.

No hope of hiding.

'There 'e is! There!'

Only the instinct for flight.

'Stop him! Come on.'

Flight even where there seemed no hope of escape.

'It's 'im! You go that way, cut 'im off!'

Many faces watched Vitus running. Most unblinking, eyes passive.

Their caption chases Vitus, too.

'Bering, my name is Vitus Bering.'

'Think we don't know who you are?'

Vitus ran. They ran after, shouting a name.

'You stop, Mikkelborg, you can't get away!'

'My name is Bering.'

The name was choked off in a sob. Not that that changed things.

'We'll get you, Mikkelborg!'

'Bering — don't you get it? My name is Bering!'

'We know, we ain't deaf or stupid — Mikkelborg, right? We know …'

They listened, he knew.

But what they heard he could not understand.

Nina jumped, sure she had heard a fly. Hurriedly, she saved her work, anxious to get the laptop shut down and so leaving her notes unfinished. She picked up the can of fly spray, waiting

Boris looked back, convinced for an instant someone was peering over his shoulder. There wasn't. Of course. There was no one else in the house.

The calendar page with the picture of the shoreline was tacked to the wall alongside the scraps of words and ideas. On a yellow Post-it, Boris had scribbled, 'Pier', and stuck that on the picture, top of the yellow square lying above the horizon, just a little above, as if it were the pier paddling across the sea.

Boris frowned the picture, the Post-it note. Trying to remember what he had meant —

'Waiting,' thinks Boris, lifting his

pen. But the ink was running out and it got harder to get anything down at all. I'm beginning to wonder if that was an excuse. I was having trouble thinking, too self-conscious to write anything without questioning every word. The noise through the open window. I remember that. And that was the end of March, the light seeming wrong, too silver-grey, too thin. Too fragile. I think that was the day I was thinking about her and not wanting to admit it, looking at the calendar and not sure where the time had gone, months gone with no memory. I think I remember that. The calendar. The mirror hanging beside it, the mirror turned away. Words hard to form. None of them right. Confused. Or not exactly that. Hard now to remember the emotions, only the reluctant drag of the pen over the page. Which sounds like a metaphor, as if it never happened. All I know is what I remember and, looking back

, no longer pausing, but staring, gripped by the strangest sensation of disbelief and acceptance, as if a shop surrounded by water was quite the usual thing, something we could all agree on.

Mrs Blenkinsoe saw water, excepting strangely, and 'shop', oddly disbelieving. You see the water had no label, in much the usual way, but we could see the word 'shop', over the window beside the door, the door now closed, any chime forgotten. Understandably, it has to be said.

'Shop,' said Mrs Blenkinsoe.

'Island,' said Mrs Blenkinsoe, mouthing that word more carefully than the first. There were points in common, it was true, but also more syllables.

Shop.

Island.

You understand the dilemma, thought Mrs Blenkinsoe, gripped by the strangest sensation that this was a strange thing to think even under these circumstances.

Say: 'dilemma'.

We could agree on that much at least, thinks Mrs Blenkinsoe, feeling she had crossed a definite boundary in accommodating such thoughts, although, it might be said, she had very little choice in the matter, which introduced an unsuspected undercurrent into those deliberations, a sense of unease which she deliberately pushed away.

Taking out a scrap of paper and a pencil from her pocket Mrs Blenkinsoe wrote

> *shop*

wrote

> *island*

crossed out

> ~~*shop*~~

underlined

> *island*

and, uneasily, admitted she had been looking at this all wrong.

The 'island' still leaves Mrs Blenkinsoe with the strangest sensation. Not that there is time to worry about such things now.

The water is still rising.

Mrs Blenkinsoe starts walking. Forwards.

Towards the 'island'.

> **walk** *v. & n.* • *v.* **1** progress by lifting and setting down feet alternately on the ground. **2** a sense of progression (across a landscape). **3** the act of seeking gradual escape. • *n.* **1** a sense of nostalgia or relief after translocation. **2** a friction.

Mrs Blenkinsoe finds it is getting harder to walk. The 'island' hardly any closer and the water rising, 'walking' is definitely not going as well as she had hoped.

She had hoped to be at the 'island' by now.

Finding a fresh scrap of paper, only slightly damp, and the pencil, none the worse for wear, Mrs Blenkinsoe writes:

> **walk** *v.* progress through water by lifting and setting down feet alternately on submerged ground.

She starts walking again. And, yes, it is a little easier than before.

Mrs Blenkinsoe watches her feet as she walks. Watching for obstacles, keeping an eye on the ground. It appears dimmer than it did, the ground, increasingly blurred and further away. All of which makes Mrs Blenkinsoe feel rather buoyant.

Which makes her mood much darker.

> **walk** *v.* to float over an area submerged in a medium

such as water.

Mrs Blenkinsoe feels the current buoying her along. This is much the easiest walking so far. No effort at all, in fact.

The 'island' shrank.

The current growing stronger, deeper, she is walking in the wrong direction.

> **walk** *v.* repetitive locomotive rhythmica with the arms and legs through a fluid medium.

Mrs Blenkinsoe reads the scrap of paper through again before tucking it away safely.

She begins walking towards the 'island'.

Arms splashing.

Legs kicking.

Chin above the water, so she can keep an eye on progress.

The 'island' draws steadily closer, the undercurrent notwithstanding.

Mrs Blenkinsoe smiles. Strenuous though it is, this is the best walking yet. Really quite, quite the best, Mrs Blenkinsoe thinks contentedly.

> **contented** adj. & n. • adj. all-suffusing feeling of satisfaction or happiness in the face of contrary evidence. • n. **1** being filled with such a feeling. **2** the amnesia this brings.

Aren't you tired of always swimming? I am. This should have been *Vitus Swims*. All these poor beggars splashing round & round, and yes, I get the thing with the coin, blah, blah, blah, but honestly this is *so* wet (get it?). People don't want all this Existential Muddle crap. They want romance, car chases, transparent prose, car chases, lots of tourist information, and romance. Yes, that's it. Romance.

Or humour. Either. But no more bloody swimming.

The launches were to take place simultaneously at the Mickelborg's branches in Bruges and Horssens. Naturally. The event at the Bruges shop would be the larger. Naturally. A *très, très chic affaire. Naturelment.*

M. J. Jellicoe smiled as he looked down the book-lined length of the main salon of the Bruges Mickelborg's and patted the considerable expanse of his stomach much as another personage might pat the shoulder of a colleague. The room was decorated (tastefully, be assured) with scenes from the book: here a rendering of the Temple, there the sign, and, most impressively, three model boats together with a dinghy, all resting before a specially commissioned backdrop that combined Khnopff's *The Abandoned Town* with Hokusai's *The Great Wave.* Displays of the book were (strategically) placed throughout the room; the sign pointed to the largest, which flanked — like the outstretched arms of the wall — the chair where the author would sit, read extracts, and autograph copies.

'Don't it look luvely, monsieur?' asked Mme. Juin as she staggered past with several extra boxes of the new book to be stored in readiness beneath the till.

M. Johannes Jellicoe took another look around Mickelborg's, feeling, as seemed only fitting at times such as this, not unlike a Captain, *non, un Amiral,* on the deck of his flagship, and presented Mme. Juin an indulgent smile.

'Indeed, mademoiselle. This will be a launch long, long to be remembered.'

Taking advantage of the flexibility of narratives such as this, let us dismiss the intervening hours and get to the launch itself. Events already well underway, guests filled the main salon and overflowed, via the four sinuous staircases, onto the galleries above. Those there to be seen insured that they were seen. Those there to see were thus amply satisfied. Those primarily motivated by a free buffet and an evening out were not going without either, which should comfort and warm us all. Yes, food was consumed, drink drunk, and talk talked. Of that talk, the favourite topic was assuredly: who was the writer on whose behalf everyone had gathered, this Alois Niemand? No one knew. No one had ever seen him, or her. Nor was anyone familiar with the mysterious author's previous work, if any.

'Dear friends.' M. J. Jellicoe called for the throng's attention. The monsieur, in an exquisitely tailored dove grey suit, a saffron-yellow sprig of artemisia attached to his lapel by a circular bronze pin, smiled, held wide his arms, and smiled again. Even his ample stomach seemed to smile, *et pourquoi pas?* was this not the moment the majority had been waiting for?

'And now,' Johannes Jellicoe concluded (we have taken liberty with time once again, charming as M. Jellicoe's opening remarks no doubt were, but we wish to get to the crux of the matter, after all, so:), M. Jellicoe smiled again: 'permit me to introduce our guest of honour, Alois Niemad!'

Applause.

An outpouring of expectation!

Even, it must be recorded, a whistle or two. (In Mickelborg's, *ça alors!*)

The shuffle of feet. The embarrassed pause. The whispers of unease.

Where was Alois Niemand?

M. Jellicoe cast a look of consternation in Mme. Juin's direction. All that poor woman could do was shrug miserably.

'Dear friends,' Jellicoe began, a bead of sweat beginning a long, desolate, journey down the length of his face, 'friends, a moment of patience. Our guest is, ah, the excitement of your warm welcome has overwhelmed, er …'

'Actually, old chap —' a laconic, most English voice, came from the vicinity of the front door — 'I've only just got here. Please excuse me, mem'zell.'

A young woman of bohemian persuasion stepped hurriedly aside to reveal a balding gentleman in ice-blue frockcoat and genial expression.

'Awfully sorry to hold everyone up, but I had a deuce of a job reading the signs to get here. Quite confusing, what? Still, here now. All ripe and lovely!'

He laughed.

The gathering stared, bewildered.

'I'm him. Or, I am he, if you prefer.' The English gentleman moved to the wall of books flanking the author's chair, taking a copy off the top. ''Alois Niemand'. That's me. John Franklin, really, no need to stand on ceremony *in re* the nom de plume, mind, but, yes, I'm him, he's me, the chap that wrote *Vitus Dreams*. Ha, ha,' laughed John Franklin. 'Did you enjoy the old lucubrations, then, per chance?'

And he waved the copy of *Vitus Dreams* cheerfully.

M. Jellicoe, thrusting features and stomach ample into a look of unalloyed delight, was preparing to welcome Franklin when he was interrupted by a voice from the stairs at the back of the salon.

'That man is an impostor!'

All turned towards the woman threading her way through the gathering.

'I am Alois Niemand,' said she as she stood beside a gaping-mouthed Jellicoe.

'Oh, I say,' said Franklin, 'you bally well are not, mem'zell —'

'Madame. However —' this addressed to Jellicoe — 'you may call me Penelope.'

There was something of the classical in her face, the style of her otherwise exquisitely chic couture.

'Madame —' J. Jellicoe paused to run a finger around his collar, a collar that felt too tight now — 'ah, Penelope, you must understand, Madame, that, which is to say, we of Mickelborg's, which is further to say that perhaps we should repair to my private office, where —'

John Franklin, own features no less red than those of M. Jellicoe, was opening his mouth to protest, in the strongest terms available, his sole claim to authorship of *Vitus Dreams*, when, alas, the author's pen again intervened thus:

'Do not listen to my husband. I wrote the whole thing while he was away. Enjoying himself.'

'Now, Jane, old thing,' stammered Franklin, turning to the younger woman elbowing through the assembled gawpers, 'let's not start this silly —'

'And don't you 'silly' me, Johnny,' snapped Jane Franklin, flicking away the veil of her most stylish hat and focusing intently on the beleaguered Johannes Jellicoe. '*I* am Alois Niemand. These two are impostors.'

A gasp from the assembly filled the silence following this venomous statement. Said in-drawn breath crested at the top of its arc, and fell in like *The Great Wave* itself, countless overlapping exclamations and speculations churning wildly.

Poor M. Jellicoe! Hoping for a *succès de commercialisation* not this *succès de scandale*. As Mme. Juin stood, shredding her handkerchief, the manager rallied his scattered reserves. The three claimants were squaring up nicely, spurred on by a cheerfully partisan audience only too willing to choose sides if there was entertainment to be had. Before events slipped further out of hand, Jellicoe told himself he would take command, like the Captain, *non, l'Amiral*, in time of greatest *risque*. Yes! Johannes Rousseau Jellicoe was more than a match for any situation.

Smile, hands and stomach spread wide, M. Jellicoe stepped into the fray of claim and counter-accusation and prepared to speak.

Must we go into details, you and I? Are they necessary in a farce such as this? Granted, I have already decided, but, in a spirit of companionship, please let us agree that we shall leapfrog the stallwart Monsieur's diplomatic efforts with an economical: 'Alas, once more'. Yes? And so:

Alas, once more, Jellicoe was interrupted. This time by the doors at either end of the salon bursting open. Armed men, dressed in classical Greek armour, quickly secured the room, their chief, striding in a moment later: black armour and cloak, visored and plumed helmet, kilted leather skirt, his only concession to the present day a stout pair of Leiris & Cocteau gumboots. Dramatically sweeping his cloak over one shoulder, the warrior placed a fist on each hip and surveyed the stunned gathering of *littératures*.

Penelope pulled a sour face, whispering to Jane: 'Bloody show off.'

Ulysses ignored his wife, proclaiming (naturally): 'I am Alois Niemand.'

Tumult and consternation. Canapés were dropped, drinks spilled, fingers pointed, exclamations exclaimed, a pocket picked …

You can imagine. It is not very hard …

Passing over that, let us arrange the four claimants around the open-spread arms of the wall of books surrounding the Author's vacant chair. And, if you please, let us assume that a fulsome exchange of: 'I wrote *Vitus Dreams*', 'No, I did', 'Rot, I tell you. I am Alois Niemand', 'How dare you, it was me', has taken place, ending in Jane snatching away her husband's copy of the book and challenging him to: 'prove it. Go on.' She opened *Vitus Dreams*. 'Tell me how it starts.'

'Easy: "Vitus Bering dreams of the sea before he finds it. Before he dreams of it —"'

'"the sea does not exist",' finished Ulysses. The two men glowered at each other.

'Oh, that proves nothing.' Penelope plucked the book from Jane's hands. 'Everybody reads the first page then turns to the back —' she did so, frowning over *Vitus Bering does not exist* — 'to read how it comes out.' She paged back. 'How about: "they stand in a circle. On the corner of the junction ..."?'

'"a circle circling",' finished Jane.

'"Mouths working hands",' continued Ulysses.

'And then: "Words coming out of mouths, washing like waves, waves of words".' Franklin grinned smugly.

'It's: "Words *washing* out of mouths",' Penelope tapped the page.

Franklin scowled. Franklin rallied. 'I was thinking of the first draft.'

The other three considered, and allowed that this was possible.

'How about,' Ulysses began, taking the book from his wife and turning, unerringly, to the right page, before declaiming: '"Ulysses stares. Somewhat in turmoil, partly in surprise; mostly at" ...?'

'His own reflection?' suggested Penelope, sweetly.

'A-ha!' Ulysses crowed, raising his free hand melodramatically. 'Clearly she is not the author —'

'"Mostly at the figure in front of him",' Penelope rushed to the end of the quote, taking back the book before Ulysses had chance to react. 'This is getting us nowhere.' She thumbed through the pages. 'Let's see if you're any good at remembering what is happening right now. Or thereabouts.' And she read:

> aloud as poor M. Jellicoe looked on, the smile of
> a man fully in control of his destiny fixed grimly
> on a generously upholstered face that squirmed

with acute discomposure, his lips rote-forming the litany:

'That this should happen in Mickelborg's,' without his conscious control. Abruptly, Jellicoe became aware that the attention of everyone in the shop was fixed on him. Penelope continued to read aloud as poor M. Jellicoe looked on, the smile of a man fully —

'*Mea culpa* and all that,' Franklin drawled, derailing her flow, 'but I never thought I quite captured the pathos at that point, what?' He mugged for the gallery.

'Don't talk rot, Johnny.' Jane angrily hauled *Vitus Dreams* away from Penelope. 'You're simply jealous of my empathy for those caught in awkward situations.'

Jane cleared her throat and began reading:

began reading just a little before the point where Ulysses

Ulysses snatched the book from her hands.

'Apologies, lady,' he proclaimed, striking another pose, book upheld, 'it was necessary at this point to show even a Hero is a Man with a Mortal's failings of Vanity. However, if you will allow —' and Ulysses flicked forward several

thus settling himself in the Author's chair, a chair that, flanked by imposing walls of *Vitus Dreams* as it was, took on the aspect of a throne. Ulysses' men, flanking the wall as the wall flanked their king, raised sword and spear and declared:

'Hail Ulysses, Greatest of Writers!'

The gathering, in awe of one beloved by the Muses, haltingly took up the cry:

'Hail Ulysses, author of *Vitus Dreams*, Greatest of All Writers!'

'"'Oh,' said Ulysses",' said Ulysses, '"'I am but the Instrument of the Gods, most humble am I, a stylus, no more, that writes by their will,' spake Ulysses, without hubris,'" said Ulysses with relish, continuing: "'And so it was, against the Great One's protestations, that plaudits and laurels were showered upon King Ulysses, as musicians did perform with passion a song of extolment on aulos, lyre and drum, as amphorae of wine and platters of delicacies were laid before He who was acknowledged as the Greatest of All —'"'

'Show offs,' Penelope interrupted, wading through the

laurel wreaths littering the floor of Mickelborg's and wrestling *Vitus Dreams* from Ulysses.

The aulos player gave a squawk and fell silent. The other musicians shuffled their feet. From somewhere, an amphora toppled over and emptied with a gentle *glug-glug*.

Franklin shook his head. 'None of this happens in the book.'

'Quite right, Johnny,' Jane said, adding, *sotto voce*: 'for once,' as she excused herself to Penelope and took charge of *Vitus Dreams*.

'I protest,' began Ulysses, ~~surging to his feet, sweeping his cloak over a shoulder and continuing grandiloquently, 'I am clearly the sole author of this drama, would I be hailed as such if it were not so? No. So it must be.'~~

Ulysses dropped back into the chair, looking confused.

Jane held up her pencil, smiling with satisfaction at her crossings out.

The others looked at each other, trying to hide the desperate calculation roaring through their heads. Jellicoe, meanwhile, felt he could stay silent no longer and ~~began to protest this desecration of literature and realism most strongly.~~ shut up.

Franklin smiled contentedly at this latest alteration, offering Jane her pencil back. 'Thankee, m'dear.'

'Dictator!' snapped she, ignoring the pencil. 'Don't be taken in by that amiable twit act he puts on,' she ~~told Penelope.~~ immediately regretted thinking such a thing about her gallant husband.

'Oh.' Jane rounded on Franklin. 'You ~~vile Attila!~~ glorious Apollo!'

Jane slapped a hand over her mouth. Franklin grinned.

Penelope smartly plucked *Vitus Dreams* out of his hands, whacking Franklin on the forehead with the volume, before producing a pencil of her own with which
she and Jane watched with tremendous satisfaction as the police led her husband's men out of the shop to the waiting fleet of Black Marias. Ulysses, manacles locked around wrists and ankles, sobbed that his egotistical neglect of his wife had driven him insane. And John Franklin, also manacled, also mad, admitted he had not written a single word of *Vitus Dreams*, which was solely the work of

'Rot.' Awkwardly, Franklin wrestled Penelope for control of her pencil, his handcuffs clinking madly.

Sobbing, 'Calumny,' over and over, Ulysses, his own chains rattling, joined in, trying to get book and pencil away from his wife as Penelope bravely ~~fought for her right to be hailed as the author of~~ Jane, determined~~, threw herself into the middle of the fray, needing once and for all to prove~~ Ulysses~~, chosen of the gods, did roar with the power of Hercules and did struggle mightily, causing his enemies to~~ Franklin~~seeing a chance to~~ Penelope~~ broke free~~ Jane ~~snatched~~ ~~Ulysses~~ ~~Penelope~~ Franklin ~~fought gamely almost like a lightning bolt hurled from the Heavens not that she was going to let him and tripped scattering books in every he yelled, spectators holding mightily as was only felt no compunction about using her handbag and umbrella canapés flying in all directions as but not before landing another blow pencil blunt but still serviceable even so taking hold of her and violently upended its contents all over his book! My book!' he triumphantly until his trousers tore. Leaving ignored the laughter and overturned out of the way, tripping over the drift of books he she cried, 'and let that be a lesson, you conceited in a pile, gasping for breath~~ leaving M. Jellicoe to bury his head in his hands. Mme. Juin, meanwhile, made one last orbit of the room with a drinks tray.

'What — Oh, thank you.' Vitus nodded to Mme. Juin, took two glasses of Beaujolais and, handing one to Mrs Blenkinsoe, continued: 'So, what do you reckon, Mrs B.? You fancy reading the whole book?'

Mrs Blenkinsoe pulled a face, possibly at the wine, possibly not. 'I'm not keen, dearest heart,' she admitted. 'Call me silly, but I do like a spot of romance in my stories. All this —' she indicated the chaos Mickelborg's had been reduced to — 'it's all a bit, a bit self-conscious

for my taste.' Mrs Blenkinsoe shook her head writes Boris, thinking ahead

to a scene only barely taking shape. 'But I think it should be good,' thinks Boris writes Nina, who is beginning to *wonder if this is far too self-conscious. Metafiction, eh?*

Vitus nods to himself.

Okay, so maybe not humour, but
romance, I mean romance, yeah, let's
try at a bit of ro

'—mance?' Nina stood with one hand on the handle of kettle, feeling it shake as the water came to boil. Feeling the corner of the fridge door pressing against her back, conscious, unexpectedly, of herself, of Nina, standing in the kitchenette off the main office, of the sounds of the office through the half-open door and the smell of teabags and bananas from the stuffed pedal bin; aware of herself, her pulse, tension in her neck, the chafing of left shoe against ankle. Aware of P.A. Standing opposite, kettle forming the apex of a triangle. Aware without words or explanation.

'Sorry?' Nina felt muscles in her face move, head tilt. Ways of indicating apology. Indicating incomprehension. Ways for Nina to negotiate an awkward social encounter.

'I'm not here for long,' said P.A., smile changing in a way Nina was conscious of not being able to interpret confidently. 'So, I thought it best to be honest —'

Which is when he said the word again.

Nina felt the idea that it was his accent, mild though it was. As she felt the kettle vibrate under her hand, as she was conscious of not being able to comprehend P.A.'s expression, Nina was aware of herself, of Nina, proving a line of thought — *I don't understand because his accent changes the word* — against past experiences, against the possibility of embarrassment, friction or coolness during P.A.'s last days here. Nina felt Nina hear and feel the kettle switch off, make drinks, be aware of P.A., his expression hard to comprehend, aware of ankle, banana smell, office outside.

'I wanted to say something.'

Nina wanted to believe she was coming down with something.

'If you don't or you have someone — I mean it's okay.'

Nina longed for okay.

'It just seems like the world's losing all idea of _____.'

P.A. said the word again.

Nina repeated the word. Felt lips and mouth shape the word. Felt breath give it substance. Felt a Nina struggling to come to terms with the absence of understanding the word created.

Boris

turned the mirror to face the wall

JANE WRITES a letter. Writes another. Writes another. The letters form words, the words make phrases ... *humbly entreat* ... *Your obedient servant* ... Out of phrases come sentences, paragraphs. And, out of paragraphs come

letters.

Jane blots ink, folds, puts envelope to one side. And takes a fresh sheet of writing paper. Ice-white paper, its unblemished face inviting limitless possibility: a note to a relative, a list of items of any sort in any order, a poem, the opening moves in a play: the sheet, pristine and bounded only by its four edges, could easily host any of these and others besides. A near infinity of possibility within the margins of those edges, the faces between.

Jane writes. Letter after letter. Words, phrases (*earnestly implore ... beg your indulgence*), sentences accumulating into paragraphs that, despite variation, nevertheless follow a pattern, a strict path. Each letter — which is to say not only finished missive but the individual characters giving rise to it — each one goes in an identical direction. As if following a map.

Jane pauses. Wills herself to return to petition, plea

and finds she is once again

looking at the map. The last sketch John made before leaving.

> *To dearest Jane,*
> *Soon, everyone will know the truth of this.*
> *Your loving,*
> *John*

The map lies open on a table beside her writing desk. As reminder. As touchstone. As a test of will: to keep writing, keep John's name alive. To badger, persuade, annoy if necessary, until someone goes in search of her husband, his three crews, their ships lost

in the map.

Reason enough to keep it unfurled. Reasons enough.

She admits this, as she turns in her seat almost against her will, looking at the outlines of coasts firmly known, sea routes presumed, as each rolls north, west, across the face of the map, ink as dark for that which is certain as for those areas John imagined to exist.

Jane, surrounded by envelopes, lists of names, writing paper no longer white but crossed by lines of ink, and writing paper ice-white still, Jane admits to reasons. At least, acknowledges two. First as touchstone. Second as test of resolution: leaving the map so easily to hand, yet resisting the temptation to gaze at it every moment of every day. Forcing, instead, all attention to fall only on her petitioning. This must count for something, she tells herself. That she succeeds much of the time must betoken success in the enterprise as a whole.

Jane tells herself this openly, each day. Every night.

But a third reason hovers, unspoken even within the confines of her own mind. Jane knows it exists, that it is a foolish hope, unworthy of being entertained. Knows and preserves it, unspoken, each day, every night.

Jane looks at the map. At the paths of deep-water channels and coastlines John had drawn, had made real, in his own mind, out of paper and ink and conviction. Jane knows he is in there, somewhere. Three ships, three crews, her husband: in the map, somewhere.

Lost in a map of his own creation. If she furls it, puts it in a tube, caps the ends, thrusts it deep into a cupboard, John will never find his way back.

Jane will not say this. But she is sure. Roll up the map and Franklin will never be able to escape from ink lines, paper.

Jane writes a letter, signs a letter, folds a letter.
    Jane writes a letter, signs a letter, folds a letter.
    Jane writes a letter, signs a letter, folds a letter.
    Jane writes a letter, signs a letter, folds a letter.
    Jane

                                           is

surrounded by paper.

Jane sits back. Neck and shoulders stiff, side of her middle finger numb from holding a pen so long. She squints. Sunlight falls through the window. Reflects off sheets of writing paper, ice-white between lines of ink. Reflects off the map. Glare drawing the eye. She allows herself to turn, neck muscles protesting she takes in John's inscription, the coastline of North America, all familiar, long committed to memory. And yet the heavy paper, the flesh of the map: surely it was originally a cream, perhaps hinting at a firmer yellow — but, in the sunlight, it looks white. Pale white.

Ice-white

an arctic waste. ice, snow, a wind with frost on its tongue, wailing unbroken, nothing to break it on. snow, ice, white on white, rigging & masts turning the same, decks & rails likewise. white on white. sky white, blind-white, horizon vague, a line near submerged. in white, depth and detail erased so nearfar- and foredistant-ground merge. no shadows, no depth. only rigging, rails, a glimpse of hull draining of any colour. a voice with frost on its tongue, wind speaking louder, so the words become

My wife

fractured

misses me

become

Lost.

Jane turns over a pile of envelopes.

Lost.

She looks in a drawer. The one beneath. She scatters pages, rough draft and fair copy alike, across the floor. Upsets the pen tray as she delves into piles of correspondence.

Lost.

Jane sits back, trying to calm herself, and shouts: *Lost*, before worrying the thumbnail of her left hand, eyes refusing to be still any more than the thudding of her heart will still.

Jane scans the surface of the writing desk before standing, scouring the room over, refusing, refusing, refusing, refusing to accept the master list of names and addresses — her route map, if you will, through this endless expanse of petition and entreaty — has gone.

Is

Lost in thought — rather: unwilling to entertain thought — Jane sits at her writing table, surrounded by paper. Discards unscrewed; neat copies overturned.

No sign of the master list.

She can reconstruct it, of course. Of course she can. Another task, simply another obstacle to overcome. No more. It does not matter.

It matters, of course.

Jane chews the thumbnail of her left hand.

Stops herself from doing that and knots, unknots, knots the fingers of both hands as they lie, restless, in her lap.

I will *reconstruct the list.*

The thought leaks through the silence she has erected in her mind. Slipping through with it is the horror of having to do so, the discouragement at stopping, backtrailing. Silly though those feelings are.

Jane tells herself these feelings are silly.

She concentrates on the fresh writing paper strewn across the table. Lets its blankness fill her. Formless, bounded by four edges but not closed off. Filled with possibility needing only characters, lines and curves, to give it shape.

If only she can find the right lines and curves. Make the right shapes. But Jane can see only one shape in the paper, one word, four characters who shape she would rather was

Jane pick up her pen. He i a e . Beg n wri ing. Carefu y fi ing
  ne ice-whi e page, an her. Wri ing ine after ine, paragraph
accumu a ing. Unaware f everything bu he w rd f rming n
 he paper. W rd merging wi h unb unded whi e

ICE

THE SWIMMER throws out a hand. One hand forwardthrown, encountering resistance. Heatleached, flesh chilled. Hand chilled. Arms cool. Hands and arms and swimmer growing cooler, strokeslowed, growing cooler as resistance crystallises, swimmer becoming cold. The cold swimmer swims. Mechanically: less so, now shivering. Man, swimming, shivers. A shimvering man, legs and arms stiffthrown, shivering, swimming, man shivering, now so less mechanically, swims swimmer cold, cold becoming Swimming Vitus, Cold Swimming Vitus, no longer mechanical but slowing, Shivering Swimming Vitus, and, yes, also Cold Swimming, too, and others. Many Vituses swimming —

No. All gone. Collapsed together. Or never more than one. One Vitus seen from here, seen from there, seen by himself from different perspectives. Or maybe many all along. Hard to say now swimmingbefore has become shiveringnow, is becoming climbing out of water grown heavy, ice spicules binding together, one into many into one apparently unbroken sheet of white. Unmarred. Unmarked. Blank.

'Jellicoe' stands on the deck of the flagship. His own Number One stands beside him. Captains Franklin and Ulysses stand also, standing opposite, width of the chart table separating him from them. No more. And, respectfully, their lieutenants stand behind 'Jellicoe', at a distance respectful but hardly distant as Captain Ulysses points to a chart, asked a question and 'Jellicoe' —

And 'Jellicoe' allows no doubt, erases utterly all sense of another self, that self's motives and intentions abruptly unknown to 'Jellicoe' standing at the chart table and answering smoothly with the off-hand certainty of a person with nothing to —

The memory caused 'Jellicoe' to walk straight into a man clutching a string bag of shopping. A lemon bounced out of reach, into the road where it was crushed by the endless traffic. 'Jellicoe' apologised, gathered spilled items, apologised, gave the man enough to buy a dozen lemons. And stood. Blinking. At traffic. Pedestrians. Buildings on the opposite corner. Noise. Smells: a perfumer; frying onions; the damp aftertaste of rain. Conscious of a road sign, fingers bristling, pointing everywhere at once, standing close beside his shoulder.

Gripped by profound sense of being

Sand, displaced, runs, settles, acquiescent underfoot. Shingle stays firm, unyielding. Yet it does nothing to stop Penelope stepping off the causeway. Surfpop almost hides the hollowness of the rocks as she clambers up the nearest. Lath and painted canvas firm likewise but doing nothing to deter Penelope from sitting, unyielding yet supportive.

The causeway is fading into the water. The land at its far end growing tenuous, dunesea merging with different waves, other troughs. She walked it, the causeway, walked its whole great long length and Penelope watches the path vanish with no more emotion than an abstract puzzlement:

Causeway: a way that causes, effects the change from there to not-there, a medium of transition.

At that, she stands on the artificial rock, genuinely supportive, and turns her back on the water. Headland, ribs just discernible; cave-mouth an *O*; and cliff-face above. A sense of more beyond.

Artificial. Though solid.

It feels like an island. Acts like one.

Penelope stands on the 'rock' and feels unbearably

Mikkelborg slows
       throat
            raw
       chest
            heav
                ing
       stitch-
            trans
                fixed as
       blisters
            pierce &
       eyes
            sweat
       burn

Mikkelborg

                                  stops
               can't
                      go
             fur
                     ther
Mikkelborg
                   turns
                       every
                                thing
             distant
       fallen
                     away
                                      left
             behind
Mikkelborg relaxes
                    breathes
             breathes
                    knowing
             he
             is

Ulysses&Franklin, Franklin&Ulysses pick up a hammer, pick up a nail, drive down the hammer, drive in the nail, thump thump-thump   thuMP.

The hillside echoes. The hollows echo. Inside.

ThUMP.

Ulysses&Franklin, Franklin&Ulysses put down hammer, pick up scissors. Ulysses&Franklin, Franklin&Ulysses use the scissors   snip   snip-snip   snip   snipsnip   cutting a fringe, another immediately after.

Snip.

The sea makes a sound like a gull.
The sea makes a sound like laughter.
The sea makes a sound like clouds gathering.
The sea

Ulysses&Franklin, Franklin&Ulysses attach the fringe. With staples, with a small hammer   tap-tap. Attach the second fringe in a similar way, adding two narrow screws,

Ulysses&Franklin, Franklin&Ulysses selecting an appropriate screwdriver slot-twist turn before putting down the screwdriver. Picking up a paint pot. Picking up a brush.

The sea makes a sound like a ball being thrown.
The sea makes a sound like mist over water.
The sea makes a sound like a voice calling.
The sea

Ulysses&Franklin, Franklin&Ulysses examine the paint, wet; the new fringes, freshly green. Satisfied, Ulysses&Franklin, Franklin&Ulysses move on to the next task. Walking along a path, gently curved, newly grass-fringed. Footsteps echoing. Faintly. Ulysses&Franklin, Franklin&Ulysses carry tools. Carry materials. Put down materials. Put down tools. Begin the next task snip tap thump will pick up the next task after that snip thump tap. Ulysses&Franklin, Franklin&Ulysses follow a gently curving path around the island.

The sea makes a sound
makes a sound
The sea falls silent

The sign points. It points and says.

Mrs Blenkinsoe, no longer as buoyant as she was, is having trouble catching what the sign is saying. The words slip by. Or Mrs Blenkinsoe slips by the words. It's hard to be sure. Mrs Blenkinsoe is rather flustered. You probably understand her dilemma, we don't need to go into details. Except to say: walking is not as easy as it was.

But at least she has reached the 'island'. Mrs Blenkinsoe remembers a window, a door with a chime of delight, and a sign over the door. In the usual way.

Only the sign remains.

Pointing. Saying.

Perhaps it is a problem of tone of voice. Or accent. These things are not always exchangeable. ('Interchangeable,' thinks Mrs Blenkinsoe, arms swinging rhythmically, legs as best they can under the circumstances.) But whether or not, they can lead to confusion. Or incomprehension, which is a definite boundary of sorts, you see. You probably understand … don't need to go … In the usual way, the sign falls silent once Mrs Blenkinsoe has walked past it.

Walking is not as easy as it was, although Mrs Blenkinsoe is positive (believes, it has to be said) that she distinctly caught the word *Welcome* this time, regardless of tone of voice. Or accent.

You probably understand … in the usual way …

Walking is not … arms swinging rhythmically, legs as best they can … Catching the words *This way to* this time.

Mrs Blenkinsoe remembers this, although the sign has fallen silent and … past it.

You probably … we don't …

But at least she reached the 'island' … Mrs Blenkinsoe remembers

… a problem of tone of voice … These things are not always … they lead to … a chime of delight and a sign …

Pointing. Saying.

Welcome

This way to

Mrs Blenkinsoe, no longer as buoyant as she was, is having trouble catching the scrap of paper. It flits away, buoyed up in a way Mrs Blenkinsoe remembers (believes she remembers, it has to be said) with something approaching envy (although this might not be relevant). Flustered, Mrs Blenkinsoe walks after the scrap of paper, pencil held high, other limbs perfecting their locomotive rhythmica as best they can. Under these circumstances. And the sign slips by Mrs Blenkinsoe. Or the words, tone of voice or accent reduced to overlooked detail. Perhaps it is a problem … a chime of … incomprehension, which is a definite … Mrs Blenkinsoe slips by … having trouble … you probably … don't … this time, regardless … These things are not always … exchangeable.

Words slip by. The sign remains.

Pointing. At Mrs Blenkinsoe, sometimes. Until she slips by. Finger outstretched & pointing, seeming to move & point as Emmaline Blenkinsoe manages to walk & circle. The sign. Words. Slipping by.

The sign remains.

Pointing.

Mute.

Boris says 'Night
pauses, comes back
says 'Night again

glancing out
of the window

remembering having
forgotten something
and

letting go

pulling the postcard
out

of his bag
again

re-reading, flipping
over to see the
pier
as he remembers
it

not
waiting for the door
to slowly

close

Nina
touches the lines
sees ink
blur

Clutching himself, shivering, Vitus clambers onto the ice sheet.
One Vitus. Vitus

alone

alone *adj., adv., & n.* • *adj. & adv.* **1** separation,
isolation or understanding. **2** loneliness resulting
from understanding. **3** a moment of whiteness
expanding. **4** inevitability. • *n.* **1** the natural order,
white within white or blackness likewise subsumed.
2 You.

THE SEA slips back into wavetrough, feeling itself droop, attention caught by something below. Slipping back and looking downwards, the sea feels itself droop, droop a little more. Looking downwards, mind eddying, currents beginning to slacken as the sea, feeling heavier, slows and looks downwards. Downwardseeing

an empty pedestal standing in a cobbled square before an imposing market hall with sawtooth gables, fish slipping in and out the building's open doors to circle the plinth, perhaps to wonder where the statue has gone, perhaps to find memories of it standing there and, in remembering, feel a momentary doubt over whether any memory is simply a dream shared amongst themselves as they circle the cobbled square before scattering up the streets leading away, past rows of submerged buildings whose doors and windows gape to allow the current easy flow, allow the fish to indulge curiosity, gyring in a door, out a window as the mood takes them, each separated from the others and so surprised to find itself asking: *is this dream, too?* only to feel any answer slip away in the act of navigating another turning, down a narrow alley lined with small shops whose awnings flap in the current, or a boulevard lined with trees wearing seaweed around the wrist of each gracefully waving limb, or — it really makes little difference: the questions are mislaid for a time at least as the fish spread in all directions away from the market square, in every direction, although the direction makes no difference because, regardless, each fish begins to find the same thing waiting for it in the distance: a head, faceless, yet clearly watching, from every direction, whichever direction: the head, unchanging no matter how much they dart and flit; direction immaterial, abstracted face always present no matter how much the head unpeels: sea-contained face smoothly unpetalling, to spread open and around itself, to furl without pause, closing and merging about itself so that, closing, it draws in each submerged street, each watching fish: the containing sea contained: open and closing, all in all: sea containing head as head contains sea, unpetalling and furling one about the other, enclosing the fish and leaving them outside to watch —

as the sea watches the head

and as the head watches

the sea rouses, turns in its bed, hearing

click-click
     sound intruding
     over-surf, into thought
clack-click
     bringing pause
     a breath indrawn as
click-clat
     swell falls back, though
     wave motion continues
click-click
     Vitus turning, waves
     waves, turning again
     waving

The sea watches
                    and
in watching Vitus
                    begins
to feel itself
drifting back
                    to sleep

THEY SHOUT as he runs, but he runs sofast they can never hurt him.

P.A. Mikkelborg, grinning on bothfaces, runs and, armspumping, P.A. Mikkelborg is chased only by words.

Words can never hurt him. Only sticks&stones, bullets shot or bludgeons thrown, only they hurt. Screams, echoed yells of hatred do nothing; orderstostop never stop, either. He keeps armspumping.

Mikkelborg ('Palle' to his friends, of which he has none) trips, pinwheeling arms and legstumbling, running a moment later despite shock, pain.

Another shout.

Mikkelborg stumbles, pain shouting reply from one shoulder.

Nextpain and nextyell almost too close to pull apart.

Backwardglance reveals some standing, others shinning uptree. All hurling words at him. Most missing. Not all.

They feel like stones. They feel like sticks.

Strikingstones. Trippingsticks.

Mikkelborg, grimfaced and flinching, runs as best he can, arms crossed overhead, stumblerunning and knowing he cannot run fast enough to outrun the bruisingwords being thrown at him.

which is why, in the evenings (it's always evening here) I walk around the circumference looking for ... I don't know

notice before, but the sunset changes things (the sun is always about to set here), makes the empty buildings, the wall, even the silence feel less austere, feel almost

there before, not yesterday certainly (there is no yesterday here) or any other day. I froze, then turned, searching the faces of the empty houses. Getting no reply. The silence closed

       turning them over slowly (time
moves not at all here) as if they
were something exotic, not a pile of
sticks, branch-ends. Stout enough
to hurl like stones. One was sticky.
I snatched my hand away, looking at
blood turned black in the dusk and
                         ran

kneeling to turn over the branches,
shards of stone (there is running
here but it is no use), some of which
were bloodied, scrubbed my fingers
on my legs, backing

    picking up a hefty, club-like length of
branch (you do not know the rules
here but you will abide by them) and
then a rock smeared with blood

crumbled to dust as I held it (only
insubstantiality is permanent here),
the dust black, slick like graphite,
the grains oddly shaped. Trickling
through my

       had done this before. Such an
overwhelming feeling (without
memory, there is no repetition
— you know that, don't you?). I
stepped back. The empty houses
expressionless. There was someone
there. I felt. Didn't see. But felt
someone close. The wind licked at
the dust, drawing it up into

who 'she' was

            (what is 'real'?)

I'm trying to remember

I have memories, but they keep changing. Order gets muddled. & I seem now and then to remember something new: *Oh, I forgot, yeah, then she ... we ... that was when ...*

I remember

I'm not sure I'm remembering

looking out of the window

everything has some sort of memory attached to it

I have memories of memories of her standing there, of her tripping over, of her looking up. Not seeing me.

The calendar says

not seeing me

I lied. About the wall. How it started. How I was never going to mention it.

No, that's not true, either. I think I believed it at the time. Now

now things

The calendar says I've been here almost a year. I don't

I don't look in the mirror anymore &

Memories hazy, jumbled

I wish the wall would

I remember a smell of brine. That, and

silence.

_____ woke to find others standing
over him in a   a roundness
encirclement   no   the word was lost
in the confusion of finding himself in
the middling   middle of a roundness
circle   of other   other   people   after
running   hiding   after that and now
finding

_____'s head hurt   so did his   his
extremes   his   legs and   and so forth

                              You all right
mate?

            Yes

            _____ looked up at the wo—
man who had spoken   surprised at not
being recognised   head

                  I think so   I

                              Hit an' run!

                  a   woman   yes
woman   knelt beside _____
helping as he tried

            I saw the licence plate number
don't you worry

            she said as _____ tried
managed   to sit

                              Thank you

            up

                              I'll call the
said the first wo—   man who had
spoken   taking out a   a walk&talk   a
a portable   a mobile phone   _____
remembered the name word but now
could not make sense of the word/name
the wo—   the man was trying to

            Call for a   ?

            _____ frowned, trying to make
sense of the word as he shook his head

saying

No, no

stumbling over the word   the word he
did not recognise   the one the man who
had spoken first had said he was going to
call

You sit still

said the woman holding ____
____'s upper extremity's uppermost joint
holding his   shoulder   yes   shoulder
gently

you might be hurt worse than
you
'ambulance'   that was the

look   love

word

said the woman   gently
holding _____'s shoulder while ___
_____ experienced a sense of   what?
certainly a sense of revivalment   no
no   relief at remembering that word
'ambulance'

Did you say
'ambulance'?

Yes   mate   don't worry

Bang on the head

said the phoning man to the
kneeling woman

Yeah   You sit still until the
comes

_____ frowned   running and then
escaping and then

No

I must   I have to go

trying to scale   regain   arise to his lower
extremities   not about to be   discorded

if a few naming words had been
mislabeled or
                    I have to go
                                        You really
better not move
                                        Yeah   the
is on its way   mate   you just
lost   words did not matter   did not
change
                                    Must
anything
                    go
                    _____ staggered to his
pushed through the   others   each
of their front aspects turning   turned
to reserve their intention   attention on
him   on _____   on _____
                                    Here   mate
you musn't
                                    You dropped
these
            A little boy in sailor suit held out
a rubber mask   a
            coin
                                    No
replied _____ pushing past the boy
                I didn't   couldn't
words did not matter   Only getting awry
Words did not matter   Only getting
            words did not
                                    thought
_____ stopping at the   at the   the
juncture?   of pathed ways reserved for
with wheels and   and
            _____ stops at the   a
juncture?   and looks back at the

                    the   boy   in the suit
turns back
towards the   the

                                        Words

        do not matter

_____ told himself as he looked at
ahead   up at the   a
        watching several

                drive by   turned
turned   ignored the   others   all
watching as _____ turned and looked
at the

            at a

at those

            hesitated, knowing he must get
away   must   _____ knew this just as
he was sure names did not matter

Vitus was so frightened when he saw the
running man knocked over. But Mrs
Blenkinsoe has kept tight hold of his hand
right through and, in any case, the man is
up now. He doesn't look happy, says Vitus.
No, says Mrs Blenkinsoe, squeezing his
hand, and Vitus, still a little scared, looks
at the rubber mask and coin he picked out
of the gutter, things the man had dropped
when he was knocked over and now
seemed to have forgotten. Perhaps it would
come to him later, that they were his,
Vitus thinks, thinking it was bound to be
so. Or it so seems to him. He is not always
right, which is 'Part of Growing Up', as
Mrs Blenkinsoe says. 'Although,' Mrs
Blenkinsoe also says, 'a young man like
you cannot expect to know Everything at
Once.' Which is what Mrs Blenkinsoe tells
Vitus often, and Vitus, who is very good

with words, knows lots and lots of words, Vitus believes her because, even knowing lots and lots of words as he does, Vitus does not truly Understand Everything. Vitus looks down at the rubber mask, the coin, seeing a speck, a dark brown speck, like blood, dark brown on the sleeve of his sailor suit, almost black against the ice-white of his sleeve.

WATERS CONGEAL, ship slowing, hull creaking from port to starboard, port to starboard as the waters congeal into slush, into bow wave piling against bow, remaining to be seen: a line of passage ruled through the white-growing whiter, ship-inscribed course left as a record to be read at some later time.

Jane looks across the white, hand working automatically. Wheel turning from left to right, left to right. Hand guiding the wheel, wheel guiding the ship. Across the white.

Through the ice.

She can find him here. John is somewhere in the white. Between the lines made when the ice breaks, perhaps. Or ahead, in the middle of an expanse as yet unmarked. Waiting to be found, Jane thinks. Like a surprise, a twist in a story revealed by the turn of the page.

That's it, Jane hopes. Like the turn of a page.

The ship still moves, slow-slowly, but moving, not quite still. Hull creaks — from port to starboard — deck planks maundering, faces peppered white, complaints addressed to the frost hazing the air, a mist clinging to the ship so — rolling gently from the left — the ship grows darker, more definite until — pausing on the right — it fades again. Missed closing, pristine and apparently limitless.

Jane leaves the wheelhouse, ship able to guide itself now. Goes for'ard. Decking firm underfoot, mist parting around her, pulling on each step, tugging skirts in time to each creek, sway-shift tending rightwards as planks scratch, rasping out of the mist.

Jane pauses. Kneels. Wood underpalm. Frost gritting. Reminding her of sand, sand cast across parchment to blot ink.

Striations weave across the deck, through the planks. Black merging into hoarfrost. Or out. Jane can't decide as she kneels, looking at what appears to be grain. Yes, grain, Jane decides. Grain that happens to look like writing, lines of writing. Lines of very small, neat writing filling every plank, each halyard trailing out of the mist, the nearest hatch cover fading into white.

The ship guides itself. Scratching against the ice.

Fo'c's'le, forerail, prow.

Jane ignores the condensed lines embedded in each, writing so dense it might well be the fabric of the wood itself, 'timber' only a word after all.

She doesn't want to think of that. Standing at the rail, feeling the chill nip her face. An elusive scent rising off the floe, reminding Jane of sepia, inkwells uncapped. Also to be ignored.

Jane searches the waste, horizon unclear in the mist but there. Somewhere. Bounding the ice. She leans forward, eyescreased, and, painfully, begins to make sense of scale, of white-on-white-distances near-to-erasing perspective until Jane startles, rears back, ship already changing course.

Transfixed, she rocks as the ship rocks, too excited to notice her hand moving across the milky air, back and forth, back and forth, back and forth. Always moving from left to right.

It rises over the surrounding ice, tall enough to loom down on the ship.

The ship rocks, imperceptibly, even hove-to in the shadow of this iceberg. Jane — fingerless mittens stained, stain almost sepia, fingers and scarf likewise, breath ghosting in shallow plumes that turn over, one to the next, almost like loose sheets thumbed, before each is absorbed by the mist — Jane begins to scale the face of the iceberg. Pausing to scrape rime from its flesh, peer at what is inside.

Another ship.

Jane uses a pick to hack away sections of the outer ice. Excising one part; trimming another, one after that. Pick moving easily, its point so fine it might be the nib of a pen. Scratching. Revisions falling away, forgotten; the tight, neat lines woven through them impossible to decipher now.

The pick keeps moving. Fine tip reshaping the iceberg.

Until the ship is revealed.

There is no one on board. Nothing — not clues, not signs — nothing has survived being encased in the ice, cut free, laid open to the mist hanging over the floe. Jane searches the ship's length carefully. Tapping the bulkheads. Turning over every hatch cover and skimming over what lies inside. Going back, studying the new-found craft again. Stem to stern. Port to … There could be something in the grain of the cabin walls, an otherwise bare chart table. Jane uses a magnifying glass. On every cursive knot, the smallest descending fissure. The grain is very crabbed. Jane spends an age poring over it. Hoping. Finding nothing.

Nothing.

Jane guides her ships through the ice.

A second ship lies encased in ice, much like the first; it, too, has little to say for itself, no matter how hard Jane searches.

She stands on the bridge of the second vessel, deck planks describing finely-ruled lines beneath her, their grain oddly erratic towards the rear of the bridge, as if agitated, finished in a great hurry. Jane stands, right hand twitching.

The ice looks blank from up here, mist foreshortening distance and smoothing over detail so that she has trouble telling exactly where, precisely how far her ship and its companion, the first to be drawn out of the ice, lie from where she now stands. But two ships found, she tells herself. Looking for three and finding —

Confused, Jane counts again the number of ships in view.

Jane guides three ships through the ice. Their names are hidden in the mist just as surely as their final destination.

Ice scrapes beneath three hulls. Scrapes like a nib over paper. Or like a voice.

Muttering.

Jane, breath turning over before fading into the mist, holds tight to the bowsprit (wood grain forming the word *bowsprit* over and over and over and) swings the pick against the stem, nib-point guided over and over until the letter *B* is clearly formed, an *A* beginning to take shape, the name of the first ship to be found emerging from the wood.

Jane guides three ships through the ice. Their names are *Barrenness*, *Ennui*, and *Torpor*. The sea congeals behind them in carefully ruled lines across the otherwise pristine, ice-white face of the mist, a mist that wavers, turning about itself, never still. Rewriting the landscape. Until it reaches the end.

The ships stop.

Jane stops.

The ships, three, three ships stop. Three stops on the white, ice-white surface of the landscape, full-stopped and no longer creaking, no way left to be made. Progress iceblocked. Frozen.

Jane lets her hand fall. Resting on air, mistwhite air, resting on nothing any more. Only hanging, handfallen and still, pick fallen also, gripslipped and forgotten, on plank-lines turning whiter with frost as Jane comes to a stop, 'stop' a word she has forgotten.

Nothing remains. Only her breath rising, plumes turning, mergingplumes, fading, mergingplumes becoming mist, icewhite turning over to reveal …

Allstopped: Jane and *Barrenness*, *Ennui* & *Torpor*, the landscape no less so, although it does turn. To face Jane, rising at rightangles, at an angle to the iceplane, towards sky more grey than white— plainsky: blank despite the mist falling back to cling to forecourse, prow. Clinging to Jane's skirts as if shamed or mortified by what it has uncovered, twining itself through her limp fingers, chillnipping each, wanting them to move, take up their progress again, always left to right until there is no room left to write and a fresh page has to be turned. Always another page. Another letter to write.

Jane's arms hang limp.

Jane's fingers no longer flex, guide, outline.

Allstopped: Jane and the three ships, ships whose names might as well be anything, anything, now the landscape has turned, sternface forbidding and yet horribly blank as the white rises and stares back at three ships, at Jane, iceblocked.

Icewalled.

The landscape's margin ends here, its plane bounded by a wall high and long and limitless, seemingly; a limit that is, itself, without end.

An icewall.

Ramparts nearsmooth, sternfaced but blank: nothing except ice. No lines, cramped or effusive. No words.

The wall leans over from its top, confronting Jane staring up. No expression. Emptygaze mute&wordless, its ice undifferentiated, a flawless white that extends back until depth itself vanishes within the wall and the word 'wall' loses sense, slips from grasp, merging into white, as the sky, the word 'sky', grows pale, definition bleeding away and becoming confused with the unnamed phenomenon in front of it — whatever it might be called, ifever it had a word betokening its presence — this (probably-)not-Jane-(probably-)not-mist-(surely-)not-ships appears not-moving. Yet 'it' surrounds Jane, whitespreading to — *encompass? merge? define?* — to leave less and less any thing that is not without name or colour, is delineated by properties other than *whiteness, unnameness, blankmuteness, endless* ...

There are ships ... what were their names?

There is the, the water vapour in pages — no: *clouds, mist in clouds* — there is that. Only that has *whiteness,* a *blankmuteness,* although no sense of solidity, of *wallness.* So perhaps —

And there is 'Jane'. Yes, there is that. That one separate-entity, defined and delineated. Yes, there is still 'Jane': 'Jane' grown pale, grown silent, stillJane with not one word inside her any more. *But still 'Jane',* a voice, or a thought slimfounded, or somesuch notdefined, but surely definite, says ... or thinks ... or ... or ...

The word for it is no longer to be found.

```
W       O           R       D   S
A   R   E   N               O       T
E   N               U   G           H
A   L   L   W   O   R   D   S   ?
L                           A   L       L
L       G       N       O       R       W
                                        O
                                    R   D
S   A   R   E   W   R   O   N   G
```

Franklin&Ulysses, Ulysses&Franklin take a hammer, take a nail, strike the nail with the hammer: _____-_____, _____,_____, _____. Neither Ulysses&Franklin, Franklin&Ulysses notice the lack of _____ as they take another nail, strike the nail _____, _____, _____. '_____,' says Franklin&Ulysses, Ulysses&Franklin. They stand back to admire the sign, pointing. The sign saying W-e-l-c-o-m-e t-o. The sign they have just put up that points and says W-e-l-c-o-m-e t-o over some more letters. Letters carefully carved, neatly formed. Letters very clear to see.

Ulysses&Franklin, Franklin&Ulysses cannot make any sense of the letters at all. Not at all.

i remember
no — i feel that i
remember
no — i have memories of
no —

        let me —
        i want —
        sometimes, this grows so
difficult to describe   feeling something
is lost, some sense   can't describe & so
must be getting lost because   can't find
the right words
yes,   sure   have lost something.
quite sure.   think   am
        'm not

SHE HAS no name, only whiteness. Whiteness and a feeling of coldly-pervading. She did not turn. Did not move. There was only coldly-pervading. And whiteness pressing, filling.

She had no name. Had only whiteness.

PENELOPE WALKED the island right round. It took ... a period of time.

Penelope rose early. The morning was silent but for the soft trip-fall of her heart, the inout of each breath. Penelope stood on the edge of the cliff wall. And watched the sea move: a restive, silent sea.

Penelope walked the island right round. It took a period of time before Penelope walked the island right round, taking a period of time to walk the island right round. Her feet made no sound.

Penelope rose early, walked the island right round, right round, right round, rising early, in silence, and walking the island the island the —

Penelope rose early, in silence, walked silently the island right round.

And saw the men.

They worked on the other side of the headland, beyond the cove. In the shallows of the bay were ships; hulks in truth, ships in pieces. There were —

Penelope counted again, came up with a different number, again, coming up with a different number gave up counting to watch the men. Two men. That number steady at least.

They moved back and forth, ships to bay-wall, island-shore to hulks. Carrying, using tools. Working. Except, as she sat in silence, watching the two men, also silent despite their constant activity, Penelope could not decide what the two men were doing. Were they dismantling the ships to make the island? (But the island was finished.) Or were they dismantling the island to finish the ships? (But the ships remained incomplete.)

Penelope rose early, in silence, walked silently across the island to settle on the headland and watch the two men work.

One of them looked familiar. Even from this distance she was sure of that. Less sure which man was: sometimes the man in the kilted smock; sometimes the balding man whose shirt hung from him as if he had lost much weight recently. Sometimes, she was sure it was he who was familiar. Before turning to watch the man in the kilted smock again.

Walked the island right round. In a shorter period of time.

The two men worked ceaselessly. It now struck Penelope they were building the island out of the remains of the ships. Yet the ships grew fractionally more complete each day. And the island was definitely shrinking.

Penelope stood in the middle of the shattered town. It had taken … a period of time to get here from the edge of the island. It seemed safer to be inland. For now.

Very few buildings were intact in any meaningful way; many were nothing more than outlines of smashed brick.

Penelope turned, looking towards the curtain wall.

The perimeter was breached along its whole circumference; in some parts it had been reduced almost to dust. The ragged edges of the remaining sections were visible above the piles of rubble, beyond the few houses still holding themselves upright.

Such a heavy wall: to keep something out? or ensure something stayed in?

The scraps of paper were visible everywhere once she understood what they were. Some were charred. Others a pristine, ice-white.

Printing, burred and faded, was discernible if illegible on some; the features of a face remained on others, those features so lost they could have been anyone.

And the silence, of course, although Penelope hardly noticed that any more.

Clapboard peeling, shingles missing from the roof: it was the least damaged house in town.

The interior was chaos: furniture overturned, curtains torn from their hooks, broken crockery, shredded paper across almost every floor; a deep, sickly water stain disfiguring one bedroom floor, leaving stigmata on the ceiling below.

She tried to hide. Hoping the island might become changeless so long as she was not there to observe it.

Yet after … a period of time, Penelope returned to the headland. The trip shorter than previously. Fractionally shorter next day. The day following.

On the fourth, she found the sign; read: *Welcome t*, and could make out no more, the finger post blurred, as if clouded by mist.

By the ninth day, the whole sign was illegible.

SHE DID not think while this not-turning, not-moving. There was no those-that-comprise-internal-talking. Whiteness, yes. A whiteness filled. But no thinking. No internal-talking. She did not describe. She did not speculate, fantasise, fret. There were no those-that-comprise-internal-talking.

She had whiteness.
She had no names.

PENELOPE FOUND the Victrola in the attic. Broken records littered the floor around; only one survived intact, letters almost completely worn from its faded, plum-coloured label.

Until she found the disk, she had no idea how much the silence was eating away at her.

Moving carefully, terrified of accident, Penelope carried the record player downstairs to the sitting room: each footfall muffled to the point where it might be coming from miles distant.

The silence held the crank handle as she turned, turned, set the turntable spinning. Lowered the needle on to the record.

Silence remained beside her as she sat, legs tucked beneath her, staring at the Victrola's scalloped horn. Willing it to make a sound.

She went less and less to the headland. As if the journey was getting further after all, she felt exhausted by the time she slumped down on the clifftop and looked towards the bay.

The man in the smock did look familiar.

Penelope never thought to stand, wave her arms until the two men noticed her. The distance to the bay seemed too great, the silence of their intense work unbreachable.

Mist clung more tightly to the sign. Penelope fanned her hand. Before the sign; in front of her face. Hand fanning. Mist clinging.

She slept in the sitting room, lived there. Sometimes only the Victrola moved. She told herself she could hear music, a voice singing.

After ... a period of time, she left the shore behind. Hand fanning the mist from her face.

She lived in the sitting room. After carrying the Victrola from the attic, Penelope began tidying broken furniture, moving room to room, making a start, abandoning one room to tend to another, always coming back to the sitting room, the Victrola.

She found the coin amongst broken glass and crockery in

the small dining room. On another day, Penelope found the metal box lodged inside an upright piano, beneath torn song sheets and a papier mâché globe whose continents had been unpeeled and left ragged.

No lock, yet the box was sealed.

No lock, only a slot.

Eventually, she looked at the coin. Coin? she thought, perhaps I should call it 'token' —

A mechanism sent a vibration through the metal as she dropped coin into the slot. The lid swung easily in her hands.

Ice-white writing paper, folded neatly, a few still in envelopes; a torn photograph of a pitch-roofed wooden house, sepia fading; a tinted picture postcard of a seaside pier; and pages torn from a journal, the hand filling each of their faces the same as on some of the letters, letters obviously unsent.

Much of the find was indecipherable. But the journal entries — except, as she frowned over them, Penelope wondered whether they were memoir or invention, diary or short story. But she read all there was to read.

and now three more ships docked.

Jellicoe reviewed each one on the walk to and from the cottage tucked in the lee of the harbour wall. Each ship looked proud and strong to him. Conjuring memories. At least, they struck him as memories. Jellicoe paused beside the harbourmaster's office, wondering if they could be memories, if he could ever have done such things in the past.

'Good mornin', 'Admiral'.' The harbourmaster touched the brim of his cap as he left his office. Everyone called Jellicoe 'Admiral', showing all the deference such a rank should receive, but Jellicoe heard their hidden laughter, felt their derision or scorn each time they spoke.

Grunting a curt greeting, he turned away, and noticed a little boy dressed in a pristine white sailor suit pass by not ten feet away, walking with a woman who could only be the little boy's nanny or governess. 'Is that old man really an admiral?' Jellicoe heard the boy whisper despite the noise of the harbour, the steam cranes working at the colliery further around the curve of the bay.

'Hush, Vitus.' The nanny clasped the lad's hand.

'It's rude to point.'

'But is he? He looks very sad and lonely for an admiral, Nanny.'

Nanny Blenkinsoe hushed him again, taking him home early, before they had properly finished their walk. Vitus, thinking about the old man everyone called 'Admiral', pleaded with Nanny to go back to the harbour again the following day, pleading, until at last, she relented.

Vitus looked up at the tall ships. Watched the gulls skimming over the water and between the rigging.

Seeing a magpie surprised him so greatly, he froze. The magpie was picking at a coin, or a medal of some sort, lying on the cobbles, claws scraping and scrabbling at the shiny disk.

'Vitus, be careful — don't run!'

He ran without hearing Nanny, waving his arms madly, like a bird himself, crying loudly as he did so.

Vitus did not see the coil of rope. Tripping headlong, he caught only a glimpse of the bird springing away before the cobbles rose to meet him.

Before there was time to cry, large hands closed around him, setting Vitus on his feet and dusting him down.

'No harm done, lad?'

'Admiral' Jellicoe took a huge, white linen handkerchief from his sleeve, spat on a corner, and wiped dirt from Vitus's face, before using another corner to dry the first, late-arriving tears.

'Thank you, sir.' Nanny Blenkinsoe nodded to the 'Admiral' as she wrapped her arms around Vitus. 'And what do you say to the gentleman, Vitus?'

'Thank you, sir, you have been very kind.'

The old man laughed. 'Not at all, lad.' Bending, 'Admiral' retrieved the coin and pressed it into Vitus's hands. 'Good day, ma'am, young man — and, lad, watch where you run in future.'

Vitus waved as the old man limped away.

As they were leaving, a harbour hand stopped Nanny Blenkinsoe most politely, nodding in the direction 'Admiral' had gone:

'Don't you be bothering with him, ma'am, if you'll pardon me saying.' The man shrugged, touching his temple. 'Old 'Admiral' is barmy. Caused three ships to founder in an ice storm after he started running about, shouting he were an admiral. Never been right since.'

'Poor man,' said Nanny Blenkinsoe, catching sight of Jellicoe going into his cottage beneath the harbour wall.

She said no more to Vitus about running and hurting himself, thinking instead, as Vitus chattered excitedly about the medal, of that 'poor man'.

Next day, she needed very little persuasion to take Vitus back to the harbour. But there was no sign of the 'Admiral', only the magpie. Its wing was broken and the wretched creature was hopping miserably over the cobbles.

'Poor bird,' said Vitus, kneeling beside the magpie.

'Yes,' replied Nanny Blenkinsoe, feeling overwhelmed by the pathetic bird, 'yes — Oh!'

Surprise made her doubt, but when she peered at its beak she saw she was right. 'Look, Vitus, water is coming from its beak.'

'Seawater.' Jellicoe lowered himself on to a bollard, bad leg held straight, and leaned as close to the injured bird as he could. 'Can't say why,' he continued, looking at the young boy, but speaking to the lad's nanny, 'sometimes they —' he mimed a bird making a nosedive — 'right into the sea. Driven mad by all them jewels glittering on the crest of each wave, some say.'

'Real jewels?' The boy's eyes were wide.

'Vitus.' The nanny smiled at the boy.

'Just the light on the wave tops, lad.'

Jellicoe helped Vitus pick up the bird, taking the magpie back to the cottage.

'I'll keep an eye on him,' Jellicoe assured Vitus once the splint was in place and Nanny Blenkinsoe had said for the third time that they should go. Jellicoe stood outside the cottage until the woman was hidden by the harbour's bustle and there had been no glimpse of the white sailor suit for some time.

It was several days before Vitus had chance to slip out.

'This is a present,' he said, awkwardly thrusting the medal into the old gentleman's hands and running away before Mr 'Admiral' could speak, running home before Nanny Blenkinsoe would notice he was gone.

But Nanny Blenkinsoe was too distracted to notice. At last, she went to the harbour on her day off.

'Is it true?' She rested a hand on the cast-iron guard-rail hemming the top of the harbour wall, looking everywhere but at the elderly sailor. 'You see, Mr Jellicoe,' she continued, 'this matters to me. Not, I confess, in the way you might be thinking —'

She fell silent.

'In truth, ma'am, I can hardly speak to the truth of the stories.' Jellicoe studied his hands resting on the guard-rail. 'I have memories, true enough, but I place no store in them. They seem like the memories of another man.'

The silence that followed was not strained, neither stirring although their hands were almost touching.

When the magpie's wing had healed

That was all there was.

PENELOPE WOUND up the Victrola, sitting back as the needle bobbed: a long-beaked wading bird probing the dark lake of the record, those silent waters turning steadily.

The contents of the metal box spread around her as she sat on the floor. Back against the torn sofa. One by one, the pages of the unfinished story pooled across the lap. Penelope reading each word again, head bent over the pages, nodding a little, a little more.

When she looked up, the needle was butting against the record's final groove, falling back and rolling in again.

The sitting room was in darkness. The shattered town absorbed into night.

Penelope watched the needle roll back, surge forward to break over the lock groove and fallback. The shadows around the Victrola glowed, every catchlight on the record player and its horn shimmering. A full moon, she told herself, gaze tracing one ice-sheen highlight after another.

The room was cold. Cold enough for breath to become mist, each highlight to be ice.

Penelope shivered as she climbed stiffly to her feet.

It lay under a badly dented sideboard, the word *Matches* dancing a little as she brought the cardboard box out into the light.

Penelope gathered the letters and pages close, like friends much valued. The second match struck true, head flaring with a rich saffron-silver, a light that spread. Leaping silently. Rolling forward. Pausing. Rolling on. Page after page after

Vitus lies on the ice, legs clasped to chest, eyes tight-closed. Whimpering. There is no other sound.

Nina stumbles from bed, positive, positive the house is on fire, grabbing pages, gathering up notes, sheets of paper fluttering away, running and tumbling away from her outstretched hands hands clutching at thin air clutching again and again air empty and hands shaking as she tries again.

Boris thumbs through another thesaurus, snatching at one page after another. Dropping that book to try a dictionary of synonyms. It isn't there. The right word isn't there. Boris abandons that dictionary, opens another at random in the hope fate will intervene, as tears roll down his face, mouth stretching into a rictus of desperation as he pleads, begs the next page to give him what he needs. The writing table overturns as he surges to his feet. Papers fly. Books slide, thud, split open. Boris clutches his head, watching the postcard fall. Tears running into his mouth as he bends, postcard lying facedown to show the writing on the back: *Do you want to meet?*, until that is hidden by the next falling sheet of paper, the next.

Francul is chipping a greeting on a spare shingle, a greeting and a name, all to go on a post. To greet anyone, tell them where they are. Linyss glances up and sees Ulyran, also working although not carving, and feels the strangeness of seeing himself in two places at once, watching but not able to work out what exactly Yssin is working at, before turning back to the shingle and seeing he has managed to jumble all the letters.

Glances back at the sign. Letters remaining blurred. With a little distance. With a faint mist. With distance enough to cause the letters to jumble. At least the sign points only one way, and that very positively, quite, quite positively. So Emmaline, she tells herself, that's the way we shall go. Yet she hesitates, uncertainty filling her as she feels the silence press, pressing closer.

NOT-THINKING. Not-moving. Yet she had a continuously-present-experiencing. Even when she became no-longer-feeling-and-whiteness-replaced-by-absently-black. When she returned to whiteness, she felt a lingering accepting-of-being-present-before.

This was so.

She did not question.

Whitely-all-round. Coldly-pervading.

This was so. Changeless, regardless of absolutely-no-longer-feeling.

She did not question.

Yet, gradually, whitely-everywhere changed. She acquired a growing-until-accepting-seemed-always-present that within whitely-everywhere there were those-faintly-but-present, those-small-small-small-not-whitely-endless-&-everywhere.

She did not question, but within whiteness she saw tiny, discreet specklings of utterly-not-whitely.

She made movement. Tottering-moving becoming nervously not-moving-but-swaying amongst almost-whitely-everywhere. Becoming unsteady-moving. Stopping, starting, but unsteadily-moving. Towards not-many-but-not-none discreet-&-separate demarcated-within-surrounding-whitely-everywhere of utterly-not-whitely. Missing and feeling dislocation. Searching. Finding once more.

The discreet-speckly-within-whitely.

There were periods of absently-black between not-moving from this discreet-instance-of-utterly-unwhitely-within-surrounding-whitely-largely-everywhere. Her appending-to-the-whole-of-her-physically-comprising shook much, tremors all seemingly thanks to coldly-pervading. Likewise, her extreme-most-appendings twitched and, gradually, she understood she could cause them to move without moving-wholly-through-whitely-pervading.

With difficulty, she tried and failed and finally succeeded in extracting that tiny-discreet-utterly-non-whitely from the surrounding-whitely partly within which it lay, and held it in her extreme-most graspable-appendings.

This utterly-non-whitely thus lifted was not completely undifferentiated. Tiny-&-hard-to-see, she just made out a central-absence. The discreet-&-tiny was hooped: a tiny-circular.

An internal-sensing of before-experienced revealingly transpired as she held the tiny-circular and she experienced a revelatory-flash-of-familiar-yet-as-if-first-seen, seeing-inside-herself a shape. She sees: *O*

PENELOPE SNAPPED awake, a noise, neither sigh nor a groan, trapped in her throat.

'The fire —!'

There was no fire.

The Victrola's needle bobbed, falling back to flow in again.

First match-head breaking, the second flared, lantern surging but making no sound.

Fumbling, Penelope gathered papers and letters, photo, postcard, carefully placing them in the metal box. Pressing firmly on the lid and feeling the lock engage as the token was spat out. Hearing nothing.

A tapping, brittle over fluttering, came from the broken window.

Penelope startled, balance forfeit. Staring at the window as her ears cringed at the alien sound.

A magpie appeared between the star-cracks in the glass, gaze following the lamplight glinting off the token lying on the top of the box.

Penelope snatched up the disk. Holding it protectively, her thumb circled its face. Feeling a raised surface she had not noticed before. A relief pattern expressed in the metal.

Thumb circling.

Mrs Blenkinsoe clutches the sign. Trying to stop it whirling away. Or stop herself whirling away, she can no longer tell the difference. Her mouth is working, quite unnoticed: Mrs Blenkinsoe has no idea she is trying to form the words slipping off the sign — words blurred by distance, blurred by motion. She is no longer sure of anything. Nothing makes sense.

She turns the tiny-circular around and around in her extreme-most-graspable-appending. Round and round, certain there is something she should do with this tiny-circular.

There is a tactile-perception of roughness at a discreet-along-the-outer-limit of this tiny-circular, although when she finds it, she loses it again. Turning this tiny-circular round and around. If she could find and keep hold that discreet-roughness, she has an internal-feeling-of-purposeful-action.

If only —

If only —

Lungsfull-released-at-once-making-drawnout-sound-of-vexationess, she digs a sharply-outerly-edged-dextrous-appending deep into the exteriorised-surfacing of the tiny-circular. At random.

a circle

            starting anywhere.'

      Silence. But for the sea against the shore. Breathing.

      One face, looking into itself. A shingle lies between, the letters on the

          shingle   looking   into themselves, so face looking into itself, a shingle lying between the two halves.

      'We measure a circle

          starting anywhere.'

      The face

          looking into itself. Seeing itself looking into itself seeing one face looking, mouth

          forming

      words: 'We measure

The tiny-circular comes apart under her digital-dexterous-appending. Continuous-&-densely-ribboned small-shapelies, all utterly-non-whitely, each one tinier than the tiny-circular, becoming trailing-limply about her at each tugging-casting-tugging-again. Countless-many as she continues with greatly-mounting-avidity. Endlessly-many to her mounting reaction-of-deeply-surprised. She looks at what is spillaging across the whitely-all-around-her:

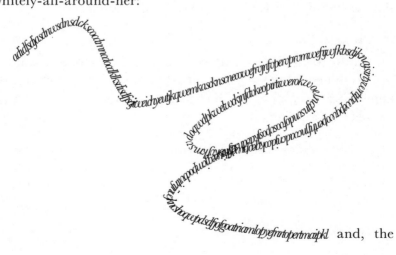 and, the

harder she pulls, the more of these strings of — of — of oddly-familiar-recognisable-shapings there are spilling across the whiteness. Countless-many. So many they threaten to merge one-shaping into another-shaping, merging into confused-unrecognising. And yet, she nevertheless feels a flash-and-gone, another of internal-recognition: interally-recognising that some of these tiny-tiny-small-shapings are forming concept-betokenings:

i-c-e   a-l-o-n-e   d-r-e-a-m   w-o-r-d
                    J-a-n-e

She gathers the whole tiny-contiguous-ribbonly, those of random-order-chance-found and those forming concept-betokenings, and hurls them across the whitely-whiteness, tiny-tiny-small-shapelies knotting, more and yet more unravelling with each avidly-tugging from the *O*.

Penelope fitted the last strut of the loom together, stood back in the shaft of dusty sunlight. Turning the token over. The loom had been in pieces like everything else in the house. Unlike almost everything else, it had be easy to repair; a skeleton without connective tissue but whole again.

The tapping of beak on window startled her. Another tap. There was something in the magpie's beak. A black thread.

She let the bird in. Wings beating, it settled on the bare frame. Shadows skimming across the attic wall, wrapping around the loom, threading cloth beam to warp beam.

It alighted back on the window frame, the magpie, beak empty.

Penelope drew up the broken shell of a tea chest. Held hands over loom. And began to weave.

Each shadowthread felt gritty beneath her fingers; cold to the touch, too. Her hands fumbled, settling slowly into a rhythm.

She looked down, reading:

She looked down, reading, knowing
that grit was letter, warp word, weft
phrase, looking down to see a cloth made
of words.

Penelope worked faster, fresh thread drawing from the shadows beside the loom, the shadows cast by the magpie sitting in the window. Letters weaving together under her fingers, moving fingers.

When she looked next, she read:

hands outstretched. A face, golden

and later:

Gullsong. Grasswhisper. And gemlight
cast

and later still:

newcloth pooling across the attic floor,
dense with words yet to be spoken but
at least they were there now, promises
of broken silence, a feeling of being less
alone as her hands moved over the loom,
white newcloth slipping away into the
shadows — pointing a way

Emmaline Blenkinsoe nearly collapses with surprise.

Jutland

Mrs Blenkinsoe clutches hold of the sign.

Welcome to Jutland

replies the sign.

Emmaline stares at the sign, mouth working, too stunned to notice she has just mouthed the words, 'Welcome to Jutland'.

says the sign again, quite clearly, clearly enunciating the words, *Welcome to Jutland*, in a rather avuncular way, before adding, helpfully, really very helpfully:

New Bruges ½ km

pointing as it does so, directing Emmaline to New Bruges, but only if she should wish to go there. The sign is not insisting; only assisting.

Emmaline is lost for words, quite so, because she never thought, had lost all hope, she would ever make sense of sign or landscape. Never find herself anything other than lost.

The sign, sensing her astonishment, says:

Welcome

once more, in a very smooth, quite — well, welcoming sort of way, before continuing. Pointing. Allowing words to move easily — legibly and smoothly — over its graciously pointing finger.

Emmaline clutches the sign's post and reads:

> *moving from house to building, street*
> *corner to crescent, Jane & Penelope &*
> *Emmaline, writing furiously*

Her voice cracks, throat closing after so long going unused. Emmaline Blenkinsoe coughs, breathes deep, and tries again. Slowly at first, quite haltingly in fact, but soon she finds the rhythm, breathing in, rolling out again.

Mrs Blenkinsoe reads the words aloud.

Mrs Blenkinsoe begins to sing.

the dream turns over in its bed. Muttering. Voice rising, fallingvoice declining only to riseagain, surgingvoiced, the dream cannot stop talking, words over words as the dream turns over & over-turns

washing against the cove, voice restless in wavecrest, undertow, the pop & inbreath of foam, the sea, turning over in its bed, talks in its sleep, each wave a voice among many, calling, backdrawing to reach again for fresh words, dreamfilled sleep changing as the sea turns over & over-turns

and grows still, breath little better than a ghost around Vitus's face as he lies on the white, white floor, sweatdrawn features working, eyes tightclosed and moving, back, forth&back, lips twitching, widepulled to come together, twitchinglips moving as Vitus twitches, flinchingarms, jerkinglegs, eyes closed and mouth moving silently as he turns & over-turns

'YOU?'

'You look frozen! Where have —?'

'I don't know, don't understand. Where —?'

'I have no idea. I was weaving and then —'

'Weaving? Penelope, whatever is —?'

'I — Wait … I can hear! I can — oh, the gods, Jane —'

'Dear hearts! I knew I would find you.'

'Emmaline ! But this is — We should leave these ruins — this place, this island, it dwindles, soon —'

'Calm yourself, dear heart. I know what we must do.'

They ran, once the thrill and wonder had chance to grip them. Ran through the ruined streets of New Bruges, laughing as they scribbled frantically on each fresh scrap of paper (the face and printing now as good as gone from the other side). Moving with giddy delight from rubble heap to shell.

Labelling.

Describing.

Making whole: *door, wall, window, the Beyer House, Corn Exchange, crossroads, oak tree, road sign, the Magpie Hotel* — each one betokened, and defined in that tokening. Heaving itself together, alive once more in the words attached to its fabric.

They did not pause to question as they laughed and wrote and offered definition out of collapse: was this dream, or memory, the memory of dream, or simply a word puzzle, arbitrary and without meaning at base? There was no time for that as laughter carried the three of them moving from house to building, street corner to crescent, Jane & Penelope & Emmaline, writing furiously, talking constantly, chattering over the sound of New Bruges gaining firm definition, moment on moment ...

The house stood alone on the outskirts of town, on a hill that afforded a clear view of the ships in the harbour and the sea beyond. Tall screens of trees and tangled grass ensured there was no easy approach. They kicked aside the weeds, wrote the words *PATH* and climbed up the low incline to the front porch.

No door. No windows. No entrance at the rear.

The house was blind. Mute.

They looked at each other, gaze passed around in a circle. Until one (her name does not matter; truly it may be anything, but you are free to choose for yourself —) one of the three wrote *DOOR* and attached the scrap of paper to the blank wooden wall.

Not one of them dared move after that. No glance, no words. Only a silence, unbroken even by the sounds coming from the town at the base of the hill.

Time passed, unlabelled.

At last, one stood straight, grasped the door handle and threw wide the door, crossing the threshold after the shortest hesitation, the others following one after the other. To find —

Jane throws herself against the door, shouldering it open at the fourth attempt. Paper clogs its underside, hindering as she grunts with effort, at last forcing enough space to squeeze through.

There is paper everywhere: sketch-maps heavily crossed-through and torn apart; notes illegible with obsessive over-writing; balls of paper screwed tight, their ice-white flesh rent.

As the floor of the otherwise empty room is covered in paper, so the paper and once-white walls are covered in dust; a bristling, ghost-grey coating that reminds her of nothing so much as hoarfrost.

Jane stands inside the threshold, positive the room is unoccupied. Nevertheless, she wades through the drifts of paper. And finds John, beneath the mounds of torn maps and notes, in the very centre of the room. He looks emaciated, comatose with exhaustion.

She glances at some of the scraps she has thrust away from him. Map after crude map. Each one labelled *Northwest Passage*. As best she can tell, all contradictory. An inescapable maze of confusion.

'John?'

His eyelids flutter, head twitching as she lays it in her lap, eyes moving under those near-closed lids. She repeats his name. He seems to turn towards her, eyes roving under near-closed lids.

Penelope grunts, striking the handle a second, awkward blow with the hall chair.

The door swings inwards.

The room beyond was white once. Now the walls are covered in densely-overwritten charcoal scrawls. The floor is awash with chalk lines: islands crudely drawn, crossed out, redrawn; sea lanes marked, marked again; on and on across the room, and taken in in her first glance. After that, she sees only Ulysses.

He lies in the centre of the room, sprawled unconscious on screwed up charts, a Baedeker for Ithaca, NY, its pages folded and ripped, lying beside his head.

Penelope kneels, checking pulse, respiration, suppressing the profound dismay her husband's state inspires in her. Striving to be practical.

She wrests a nub of chalk from his fist. Tries to bring Ulysses round. His eyes move under closed lids, breathing regular but hoarse.

Penelope curses her tears. Fisting them from her cheeks, flicking saltwater from her hand.

The spots land in chalk: names, tightly-written: islands, sea lanes, sea-lands: most unfamiliar, fantastical even; and, again and again and again and again, *Ithaca*: each instance spelt wrong, or left incomplete.

Not giving herself time to wonder if this means anything, Penelope scuffs through the scrawls with the heel of her hand, smearing her tears through the unfinished or erroneous names.

She takes a breath and begins dragging her husband out of

the room.

Emmaline nearly tripped over Admiral Jellicoe in the darkness of the staircase. He lies, curled up, on the last landing.

'My dear boy.' She holds his face in her hands. Jellicoe blinks, eyes catching what light there is.

'Hm? Mrs ... B.?'

'Can you stand?'

The Admiral is dazed, unsteady on his feet, but able to follow Emmaline up the last flight of stairs, along the hallway beyond, the flow of questions and provisional answers dying when they come to the door.

'Allow me,' says Admiral Jellicoe when Emmaline fails to make the door budge. But it takes both of them, in the end, to break in.

'Vitus, dear heart?' Emmaline calls out as she and the Admiral regain their balance, look around themselves properly.

White walls, pristine and unblemished. White floor likewise spotless. A single window filled with ultramarine sky.

No Vitus.

Muchlater, Emmaline Blenkinsoe stands at the single window. Voices come from the corridor, fading as she gazes at hillside, townbeyond under sky become deeplyblue. And the sea —

Emmaline frowns. In this light, the sea appears distant, so very distant, drawnback from this island to leave only sand drying undersun to a deep saffron-yellow, every rock stranded high on dunes exposed by the sea, a sea longabsent. Or so it seems to Emmaline.

Only a splinter of blue remains, dwindlingblue beneath a horizon made blue by a sky made —

She can't think by whom.

Instead, Emmaline lifts a hand, a wavinghand, gesturing out of the window.

Noreply nor reaction.

She falters, waves again, eyes creased against light rising off sand exposed, dunes abandoned, as she waves, waving more as she tells herself, tells herself, tells herself ... Tells herself nothing could be missing.

THE SEA, dreamlike in its dreams, fades away. Leaving foreshore, leaving beach; tidepools gleaming undersun, a sun that blinks once to clear sleep before enticing shadow & highlight from deep within the cove. Granting form.

A gull call: bladeflat-voice glancing off the air. Second wail metalbright, falling as the gull swoops, turnsways overcove. Voice sculpting the air, bladedge honing as gullwings twitch; flex. Turnswoop & riseslip. Carving definition as the sun bears shape. And as much a part: each belongs as each shapes. Adding, completing.

Something is missing.

Grassfringes hiss drysurf whispers as they look down from the clifftop. Muttering. Mustering words, whispers filling the rests between the gull's metalstrike descant, the sun taking no part in this antiphony, though that should hardly alter the balance of counterpoints, which ordinarily interweave perfectly under the sun's customary silence.

There is something missing.

The wind skims the foreshore, trying to catch the thread of the polyphony overhead, and missing: own voice bumbling in & out of time but at least humsoft & underbreath enough that only the wind hears each clash & slip. On otherdays, it might have more gusto, cheerfully mis-singing at something closer to the top of its voice. Not today, today when there is something —

Stopturn & backstep, the wind circles the rocks marking the notional boundary between hightide and beach, the sand in the nearbeyond oddly vague as distance smooths it over, drawing it back&back, until 'near' becomes 'deep' and deep merges with a horizon that remains static despite driftingclouds and sun, gullsong or shadowscrawl. Uncomfortably so, to the wind's view, static and far too stark. Not that it thinks on this as it circles rocks that change colour as it does so, eyecaught and searching for that glint of light again.

A rockpool. Cupped in a dimple in the blanching stoneface. Hum fading, the wind re-turns, lightreflected crawling off the face of the pool. Turning circles as the wind circleturns, wavelets ruffing the surface, lightscattering. Gleaming. Glimmering jewelflecks, in tracery, ebbing from the air to swell again, bringing the wind closer as it circles, watching the reflections change as it does so, closecircles weaving through the wavinglight.

Water brimming. Washing against the margins of the pool.

Kee-kee-keeya

Already a speck shrinking by the time the wind turns, the gull fallturns, carving another arc over the cove as it cries again, metaledged voice making the wind flinch and tell itself the gull will not startle it a third time, and waiting, poised, in case it does.

The grass whispers. The sun is unreadable.

Growing warm, the wind circles pool once more, attention drawn towards sands and covemouth, reluctant to drift any further horizonwards, that line lying oddly white undersun and oversand. White and far too still: feeling an absence, a missing piece needed to give sand & foreshore definition.

Gullsong. Grasswhisper. Gemlight cast up by poolwater moving, too quiet to hear, too little to fill the void. The sun looks back, notblinking, as good as blind in fact, since all it does is shine nomatterwhat, granting form by accident, the wind now realises as it looks up. Humming, as it thinks, humming to trace the shape of the absent voice and finding there is need two.

Fallenstill, the wind takes in beach, foreshore, dryingsands beyond. Firstime thought blunting some of that justfound warmth, as the wind tries to comprehend how the cove, gull&sand & all, can remain when the two who surely give it mostshape are nowhere to be found.

> the SEA draws back
> further back
> coming awake
> only to
> know it
> is still

> dreaming, & then wake
> up to think, 'I've been
> dreaming', and then
> wake up to think,
> 'I've been

> dreaming of the

end: notes put away, pages ordered, files stored, everything done.

Boris sat back. Picked up the postcard. Put it down. Tried to think. Looked out the window. At the wall which —

He blinked. And felt as though he had just seen the wall properly for the first time. Feeling, in fact, as if he had been

dreaming.

She hesitates, hand over backspace as she reads the words on the screen, mind feeling blank, words not gaining purchase.

Nina lets herself look out the window. There is a low wall across the road from the guesthouse. On the other side of the wall, the sand lies amidst shoals of rock: pebbles, boulders: *shingle*, Nina thinks, turning the word over in her mind; the sensation of turning almost like fingering a stone worn smooth by wave-wash.

The postcard is propped on the window ledge.

Something else to avoid thinking about, though the pier is only visible if she presses her face close to the glass.

Nina sits well back, fingers tapping, unnoticed, on the laptop as she thinks of anything. How far the tide falls back from the beach. A dream she wrote in her notebook, the words jumbling as she struggled to get them down before they —

The screen snares her attention, so the smell of ozone and cheap furniture polish, the discomfort of the rickety chair, vanish as she reads: *in fact, as if he has been*

dreamt

this before

before

before

I am

having this recurring

dream

drawing back

back

fading into

white

VITUS

lies still, eyes un-
moving behind closed
lids, breath invisible
as rime peppers his
face

       rime

       course

       gritty

       like

  sand

         the sand he remembers
from childhood, caught between the creases in his palms,
gritting as he waggled his fingers to see the reflections dance off
the water as he leaned over the guard-rail at the end of the pier,
each memory like a dream, in fact, as if he has been

  Boris paused

        and found the thread of what he
had been writing had escaped him.

He sat back, capping his pen and looking at the beach on
the other side of the wall. Sometimes, he could see the waves as
catchlights just under the lip of the horizon.

The sea goes out a long way.

Boris paused

        and found the beach was empty of
anything but boulders, pebbles chequering sand long-since dried
but for a few tidepools that, when the wind caught them just so,
glimmered.

How far the tide falls back.

Boris

        capped his pen after writing that
thought down. Not the sort of thing he would normally say to
himself, *but a character might*, he thought, glancing at the postcard
propped on the windowsill, aware of the smell of ozone, the
rickety chair biting into his thighs, the faint smell of cheap
furniture polish, the whiteness of the room's walls despite the
shadows, an ice-white that is an odd tint, so

      cold

  too cold

  to sleep

only

lie

comatose

eyes

beginning to

twitch

beneath

closed, only to find open
when I wake. If I

wake

left across the harbour as Nina feels in her coat pockets, sure she
has forgotten something, the wake so white in the strong sunlight
it looked almost like

ice?

Yes, please.' Boris closed his notebook, capped his pen, and
carried his drink to a table by the window. The pub smelled of
ozone, brine unmistakable over the scent of food being prepared
in the kitchen. Lunch rush due soon, like a tide of its own, the
pub was almost empty as Boris sat fidgeting with his notebook.
Looking out the window. Sunlight striking the prom, iron
railings reflecting brightly, brightly-white although he couldn't
see the sun from this angle. Only the pier. Filling

the

window, Nina writes, before closing her notebook firmly. A young
man in white jeans and blue-white striped T-shirt walks past, a
hat resting jauntily on his head.

Kiss Me Quick

says the hat, voice lost in the clashing
music and laughter coming from the pier. Nina tries to follow
the young man, or at least the hat, eyes tracking the crowds for
one or the other and finding herself looking again towards the
harbour, counting nine boats, counting again and coming up
with only six, a wake settling back into

July sunshine, every time,
every one. Always it ends with me
rebuilding the wall only to take
it down. I remember — I think I
remember — I remember thinking
I remember remembering it as a
memory of having remembered —

the recursion
I believe I will find I have
written this in late May, very nearly
June. Again.

the recursion
I made the wall make me
make the wall make me make

It will soon be June, soon
be writing this in June while thinking
of writing in another June, not long
before July

I wonder: do I talk to you,
or myself. Or myself believing I
talk to you. Or you imagining you
imagine a conversation with me. Or
if I imagine I am not

here it
is hard to be sure. Her face grows
vague. Her voice almost gone. My
hand on hers, her hand unmoving. I
think I remember but

I stand beside the
wall I have taken down to rebuild to
take down

deep
deep beneath
the surface, the
SEA finds itself
seeing
        VITUS
stirs, eyes
moving beneath
closed
        lids
frost
        gritting
his fingers
as his hand
twitches

writing,

clearly remembered, writing in the guesthouse register, writing

Nina.

She walks through the crowd, frowning as she tries to remember writing in the guesthouse register, trying to think if she had written

Boris.

He shakes his head, leaving his drink unfinished and, after a deep breath, walking through the

mirror turned to the wall. Every mirror. In every house. And when I look in a window, the few that are left whole, I — it's not the light, can't be, can't — to be absent like that isn't

how the SEA
remembers, isn't
 how VITUS
 remembers, it
wouldn't
 be
if only he
 could

wake in a sweat sometimes. Thinking of glass. Mirrors I can't turn back. Won't

I

I

am having this
recurring

Someone has written, 'This Way Out', on the wall. The paint glistens, it is so wet. But it does not run, no. What would be the point? It can't get away

Boris signed his name.

Nina signs her name.

_____ glanced at the wall, the arrow, glistening, on the wall. Walked in the opposite direction to the arrow's point.

Writing quickly, trying to keep up with the flow of ideas before they dry up. Writing: sunlight, sea, sound of the sea, hats, sunlight, pink, sideshows, sand on boards, pink shoulders, speakers, babble, pink candy talking laughter shouts flow, child weaving through, heat, bright brine Kiss Me Quick

_____ glances at the wall, the arrow, glistening, on the wall. Walks in the opposite direction to the arrow's point.

Nina stands still. The crowds jostle, exposed skin turning pink. Nina looks, hands spread, wondering about suncream. Across the way, a palmist's (*Madame B*— the rest of the name obscure, lost in jostling pink and Kiss Me Quick hats) has a speaker outside, playing loudly. The noise makes it hard to think.

Boris stopped walking, crowds parting, shuffling by on either side, rejoining. Like a rock, Boris thought over the noise of so many people turning their flesh pink. Across the way stood a peepshow: *What Admiral _____ Saw*, the name obscured by a child on the shoulders of an adult, a large beachball on the child's shoulders.

Pausing. Referring back to notes. ~~Crossing out notes~~ Beginning again

Nina weaves through the crowd. Course changing, but heading towards the end of the pier more or less. Fighting the current, Nina thinks, sidestepping a child carrying a large holographic beachball, a beachball as big as the child's head. Light catching its surface — sometimes blue, sometimes golden — so she almost misses the next sideshow.

A magpie at least ten-times normal size. Painted on the wall of the sideshow ahead. Boris stopped. Crowds parted around him, mostly behind. The paint glistened, as if wet, glistening wet. No sign of it running, no, no sign saying, 'Wet Paint'. Boris thought, despite the din, that the magpie was not wet. It looked dry and, in its beak, the dry magpie was holding — the paint, glistening but not wet, represented a magpie holding — a golden ring. In three, not unlifelike, dimensions. Like a hologram. The thought broke through the din as Boris, crowd parting mostly behind him, looked at the ring catching the sunlight, gleaming, in the magpie's beak, so it almost looked like a golden disk.

pink candy floss in the sun, bright, glaring air, hot, close with the sound of recorded music, shouting, Kiss Me Quick

Nina walks away. She had not liked the glistening magpie.

A child carrying a large holographic beachball, as large as the child's head. Boris turned to watch the ball. The light caught it, sometimes gold, then blue, an image of the surf churning over its surface, going around the ball.

Sitting on the edge of the pier, the child puts the beach ball to one side and takes out a notebook, pencil with a furry tassle on the end, and draws a magpie

Someone had written, 'This Way to the Sea', on the wall. The paint ran but only so far. No further.

~~magpie is crossed out and~~ on the next line writes

____ reached the end of the pier.

____ reaches the end of the pier.

nothing there but a low-raised observation platform with two, coin-operated telescopes, covered in graffiti, paint obscuring each objective lens, having run over the edges of the barrel;

standing beside the peeling rail, metal sun-warmed under each palm; sound of the sideshows taken away by the breeze; hardly anyone lingered here, sun striking off the platform; a shadow: a gull, flinching, feeling silly, and so avoiding looking at the only other person standing at the rail; looking out, instead: mudflats, almost dry but for a scattering of tide pools shrinking, cockle pickers, a girl running, kite following obediently, unevenly, light-buoy lying on its side, a container ship towing the horizon under the blue, no clouds, the sea a ribbon, blue also, but far off and receding, or the pier moving backwards, it was easy to see both ways, hard to be sure.

There is a heritage centre at the end of the pier. Outside, interpretation boards wait patiently to help visitors: what this means, what that part is for, why here to begin with. And pictures, too: as it was, as it was not so long after, as it might be a little later. Even a photo of it before it was built, when it was an idea or a plan (the caption is a little vague) and all there was to show for it was waves, the sea tinted in sepia as it washed a shore, also sepia, under a sky full of clouds, likewise. Each covered in transparent plastic, to protect them from visitors looking at them closely. Glistening wetly. Under the plastic. Turning pink at the extremities. Perhaps it's a UV reaction. The visitors' book, in the heritage centre, out of the sun, looks very pale, very white. Looks inviting. Is inviting

Boris signed the visitors' book.

Nina signs the visitors' book.

A child sitting on the edge of the pier, July sunshine striking the water, shadow and light, wavering, waving through the water, water beneath the child, kicking, legs dangling, kicking on the edge. Sunlight strikes the water, the child's white sailor suit, light glimmering, rising in waves through air that smells of brine, the sea's breath and voice, the air dissolving.

Boris looked up in surprise. At the voice. The face and the voice and the words. Boris looked up in surprise. But had nothing to say.

'You have the same name as _____'

Nina looks in surprise but has nothing yet to say.

magpie Kiss Me Quick ~~dreamed into~~ waves around coming around ~~by the sea~~ two people ~~drea~~

The child sitting on the edge of the pier, legs kicking, kicking, chews the furry tassel on the end of the pencil, notebook in lap, lap almost full, notebook almost full, air dissolving in sunshine reflecting off the waves, a white sailor suit, legs kicking, kicking. One page empty, notebook almost full, furry tassel kicking kicking eyes half-closed against the waves dissolving the sunlight reflecting off the page. The last empty page.

Boris stood beside a coin-operated telescope. Nina stands beside a coin-operated telescope. The heritage centre was closed. The visitors' book is closed. The sun dissolved in the sea, the pier dissolves into shadows (Kiss Me Quick), the shadows dissolved into the air (beach ball-pink candy floss), the air dissolves into the last empty page (a gull shrinking), the last empty page

dissolved

the telescopes stand alone, the only thing beside them now a sheet of paper torn from a notebook and reading: 'the boy fishes the sea', except *fishes* looks a great deal like *finishes*: 'the boy finishes the sea', except *boy* looks increasingly like *sea*, and *sea* could be *boy*: 'the sea finishes the boy'; except, looking again, perhaps even the paper is not there and the two people standing beside the two telescopes might have been one person all along, only ever one telescope, too, only ever one pier standing on the edge of the sea that looks

The child pauses, unsure exactly what should happen next. He closes his notebook. Puts away his pencil. Looks at the sea, as the sea looks back at him.

VITUS
groans, rolls over,
eyelids fluttering
VITUS
groans, rolls over,
eye   ttering
VITUS
oans,   ls ove ,
lid flut   g
VITUS
i   am
having this re
build the wall. In the dream. In the
mornings, I try not to leave the house any
more I know what
I
am
going to find.
Walking
past the last few intact windows, each one
blank no matter from where, no matter
how hard I
stare, the holes are there,
where I plugged — I knew. Know. Now,
her face is fading. Only the
d r e a m
is all
as if she never
I   don't
want to
think I can re
build   the

wall. In the
                                        d r e a m ,
you see I'm having this
                                      recurring,
changing but always I knowI'm
                                    dreaming
over & over, a recurring dream I'm having.
I am
          having
                      this dream, I am
this

Vitus knows only

White

vitus looks up   white   to the   the sea knows only white
side   white   closes his eyes   sun & moon hidden
again   opens them with a   behind cloud
snap

vitus gets up   begins walking   the sea turns over   begins
wandering

vitus chooses a direction   walks   the sea chooses a direction
in a straight line   further each   wanders   further
time

he comes back to where he   it comes back to where it
started   every time   started   every time

as if all this   is a dream

vitus stops moving   the sea starts moving

vitus starts moving   the sea turns
inward   wavering   growing
still

vitus stops   the sea   feeling
moving   stands   very   still   sleepy   waves   once

vitus raises a hand   once   the sea   falls   back

and

sees

Vitus sees the ice floe with   the   shock of his very first
encounter — it is as   *the*   if he has not seen before
now and, shocked,   *sea turns*   sees   ice   unbroken,
white   unrelenting,   *settles only to*   rising   up,   encircling,
enclosing him like   *turn   movement*   the walls of a corridor
no,   a   series   of   *rapid beneath*   corridors   guiding
firmly-closed
wavecrests

him forwards herding him along

in truth corridors of pure white that after a few more steps curve and begin to undulate to curve & recurve in smooth flowing sine waves that point the way as a sign points →

towards
a
door

Vitus stands on the threshold.

the sea turns
settles

turns again
Movements

rapid beneath firmly-closed wavecrests

I lifted the mirror, turning it swiftly before
there was time to react, turned it away from
the wall and looked, looked and saw

and so can do no more than look beyond
the threshold, the wind blowing in his face.
Like
a tide. A tide going out

VITUS
crosses   the
threshold

Doors   SLAM
others swing o   p   e   n as the wind pulls
Vitus across the threshold, past doors, many doors doors doors doors
doors doors doors doors doors doors doors doors doors doors doors doors doors doors
doors doors doors doors doors doors doors doors doors doors doors doors doors doors
doors doors doors doors doors doors doors doors doors doors doors doors doors doors
doors doors doors doors doors doors doors doors doors doors doors doors doors doors
doors doors doors doors doors doors doors doors doors doors doors doors doors doors
doors doors doors doors doors doors doors doors doors doors doors doors doors doors
doors doors doors doors doors doors doors doors doors doors doors doors doors doors
doors doors doors doors doors doors doors doors doors doors doors doors doors doors
doors doors doors doors doors doors doors doors doors doors doors doors doors doors
doors doors doors doors doors doors doors doors doors doors doors doors doors doors

doors doors doors doors doors doors doors doors doors doors doors doors doors doors
doors doors doors doors doors doors doors doors doors doors doors doors doors doors
doors doors **doors along a corridor that** curves recurves & curves & recurves again again curving again again without seeming end, stretching onwards

*the
sea turns settles
turns again movements
rapid beneath wavecrests
firmly-closed over the sea
as it turns settles turns again
movements rapid beneath
wavecrests firmly-closed
over the sea as it turns
settles turns*

Vitus feels cold   does not want to be
here   can't help himself being drawn down
the corridor past door after open door after
open door:

*Vitus in a white room, walls cold,
    damp, window bars casting
    shadows across stone floor,
    noises, moaning like the
    sleepless, footsteps, keys
jangling as doors slam, locks*

*Vitus sprawled over the side of a pallet,
opium den gloomy, smoke hanging
dense, murmurs from the shadows, pipe-
bowls glowing like ailing stars, one star
guttering, going out, as Vitus, pale and
waxen, settles back and lets the smoked
close*

*Vitus, old, wizened and
frail, hobbles across the
tiny room to the diamonded
window, bull's-eye at its
centre, ancient Vitus bending
stiffly to squint through the circle
of glass, muttering*

Vitus, young, dressed in
a pristine white sailor suit,
thrusts the medal into the old
man's hand, friendship token
gleaming in the sun as it tumbles to
the cobbles, old man cursing the boy
for a fool, second blow sending the child

Vitus,   still   childlike
in   many   ways,   despite
entering   his   teens,   runs
along   the   pier,   shouting,
ignoring   all   around   him,
arms   and   legs   pumping,
satchel banging against his
back, until he comes to the
very end, fetching up against
the white railings, taking the
model boat from his bag, holding
it towards the horizon as he slips
under the rail to sit on the edge of
the deck, legs kicking, kicking, as he
holds up the boat so it seems to float on
the horizon, as he slips, loses balance,
falls, boat lost, boat sinking, Vitus —

Vitus turns away,
water splashing around his feet. The corridor
walls   are   semitransparent,   shimmering,
surface tension flexing under his hand, beads
of water trickling over knuckles as he traces
the convolutions in the surface of this wall,
the one opposite: tube-lines and furrows, deep
sulcus giving way to gyrus, water springy to
the touch, looking faintly grey in this light,
corridor   furrowed   and   thread   with   these
grooves   and   ridges,   reminding   Vitus   of   a
brain, and, in making simile, gripped with the
certainty he is right: the brain of the sleeping
sea and Vitus made to wander this network of
synapses like a stray thought

                        which   is   when
        Vitus runs, screaming, as the horror of this
        revelation impales him, screaming as he runs
        the length of the synapse
                              looking to escape
              and finding

    the sea
            grows
                      s   t   i   l   l
                                                        only
            wavecaps
                          move
                                          back
    &   forth   forth &
    back
                      m   o   v   i   n   g

                                  from   room   to
                    room. Some doors open; some
                    closed   And then
                                    I am
                                    having   this
                    recurring dream
                                    I am
                                                    this
                    recurring dream
                                    I

                          dream

                      g a s p i
                    n g a s p i n g a s
                    p i n g a s p i n g
                    as   he   grips
                    the   handle
                    door   surely
                    too narrow to
                    get   through

f r a m e
squeezing   his
s h o u l d e r s
c h e s t
c r u s h i n g
until   the
d a r k n e s s b e y o n d

gradually becomes evening ...

VITUS WALKED. The ruined town appeared almost golden, sun low enough to draw long shadows out of the otherwise empty husks of the buildings. Vitus moved slowly, silence so complete he was reluctant to break it in any way. Some streets were impassable;

others clear but for a sprawl of rubble from a partially-collapsed building. In time, he came to the wall. Some parts remained whole; others were reduced to a few courses of stone and brick, remainder smashed to dust. Not so much a barrier now as an arbitrary line marking the point where one place became another. Vitus stood, evening's silence enclosing him. He lifted one foot, ready to take a step beyond the wall — and turned away to walk back into town.

After he had tipped the sofa back on its feet and kicked away the torn paper and broken phonograph records, there was no energy left to do anything else. He slumped on the torn sofa and watched the evening sunlight falling through the cracked window, dust motes glimmering briefly before vanishing.

Days passed. Or seemed to. Vitus only remembered the evenings: long, burnished July evenings when the heat released the town only as the first stars appeared, the weed-and-rubble-strewn roads oddly beautiful in their long shadows, sun a perfect disk of saffron tending to gold. Each evening was so like the last they merged together, Vitus sitting on the living room windowsill, on the front step, perched out of an upstairs window, legs hanging in space, kicking, kicking. He rarely left the clapboard house and, after a period of time, came to accept the silence of this endless dusk. *Near silence*, Vitus gently corrected himself: there was the sound of the sea, attenuated by distance so it became more like a texture to the silence rather than a sound as such, but present all the same. And, with each passing evening, Vitus became aware of a sound inside the house. Separate from the silence outside, the sea. The noise was almost not there at all, so subliminal Vitus told himself it was his mind and ears playing tricks before he acknowledged the sound for what it was: the sound of somnolent breathing.

Evenings passed one into another. Vitus beside the window. Vitus on the step. Vitus with legs dangling, kicking, kicking. Days passed. Or seemed to. Vitus rarely left the clapboard house. Came to the wall, what was left of it; turned back. Days passing into evenings that merged with the silence, dust motes vanishing, sea more of a texture of the silence. Vitus sitting as the first star appeared, sky tending to indigo before day passed into evening and the first star appeared but never the moon before the sky tended to indigo and the evenings merged into Vitus, legs kicking, kicking. Embracing this for what it was.

Evening sunlight crawled along the carving knife's blade as Vitus turned it over, over, over, slowly turning the knife so he had to be aware of the blade's weight, its sharpness. The curtain twitched. A breeze touched Vitus's face. Its hands were insubstantial, little more than a notion of hands, but they smelt of brine. The curtain twitched. Hardly more than a notion. Yet the sea moved. In the distance beyond the derelict buildings, the curtain wall now little better than a notional boundary. Vitus lifted his head, seeing out the window. The sea staring back.

It fell with a harsh clatter that nevertheless was lost in the restive, openmouthed grampus of the sea, the easy, somnolent breathing filling the tiny pauses between. The silence almost drowned out the flat dripping as Vitus held straight his arm, unaware he had dropped the knife as he watched blood run free. Wound numb: no pain despite the brutality needed to slash skin, flesh, blood vessels. Blood: watched, unblinking, as its spattered kitchen floor, pools spreading, merging into dark, deeply crimson puddles, colours so deep they began to look black in the evening light. Vitus bent forward, legs wobbling as he knelt, arm held out in front of him. Blood flowing. Black blood pat-patter-patting. Forming shapes ... formed of shapes. Vitus slumped, legs slipping from under him. Bringing him close enough to see: each spatter a stream of words: *sea ... sleep ... Vitus ... dream ... Vitus ... dreams ...* All he was, his life's blood: *Vitus dreams ...* He wanted to feel something — rage, surprise at least — but matter-of-factly took the knife and slashed skin and flesh again. Blinked as his life's words spilled out. Coalescing, fixing as they dried: *Vitus dreams ... Vitus dreamt ...*

The words were gone when he woke. Instead: a memory of a voice, softened and made plastic by sleep. Sitting up, Vitus swung his legs off the sofa, hardly noticing his arms were unmarked as he stood, strode into the kitchen, gripped the knife. Cut more deeply. It made no difference.

Seemingly unnoticed, the sea moved around the broken wall, respecting the concept of borderland even when the border was so easily crossed. Wavecrests gleamed in the eveninglight as the sea shifted, watching. Watching Vitus: Vitus moving, now lying down, Vitus now talking. Lips moving, voice little better than undertone. Before waiting. Waiting for a reply. 'Who are you?' No answer. 'What are you?' The sea made a reply but that wasn't what Vitus was listening for.

He threw himself down stairs

He cut his wrists. Again. Again

Hanging from the upstairs banister, rope crushing windpipe

sitting up on the sofa. 'Why?' Silence. But for the sea mumbling, somnolently, outside the wall. 'Why?' Silence. Until: **I don't know.**

'Isn't there anything else?' Vitus sat on the roof, watching the sea watching him watch the sea watching … 'Is there nothing?' I'm not sure. Vitus sat on the roof, feeling the solidity of joists, batons beneath the shingles beneath his legs. 'Only dream?' No reply. Only the sea's voice, too sleepy to sound very certain, to make much sense. Vitus felt what had been his life — what he had believed himself to be — pass from him in a breath, in a sound not exactly a sigh, not quite a groan. That it went at all surprised him, sure he had given it up before now. That he accepted what remained so easily made Vitus pause, considering, before stating it aloud: 'This is only dream.' **Only? A pause, then: A dream, definitely. What isn't, in the end? Every experience is only what goes on in your head. A dream, definitely, but only …?** A sound like a shrug. Vitus swivelled around, facing empty space as if finding someone there, reaching out a hand: 'Is this my dream?' **Yes: this is my dream.**

Vitus stood on the threshold.

The sea became restive. And the voice? That remained silent.

'What am I?'

I have this recurring dream.

The sea reached out, throwing wide the door, so Vitus

looks up at a sky not quite golden. Another day, arms outstretched, lies across the cove. 'It bears no resemblance to the cove in my dream,' the day murmurs, turning over a stone. Awake, Vitus lies across a stone not truly golden. But dry. Dry like shingle as his tongue turns over the word

shingle while the sky looks back at him
with newfound uncertainty. 'It bears
no resemblance to the sky in my dreams,'
the cove murmurs, turning over the
word vitus. Tongue probing teeth as dry
as shingle. A cavity, half-remembered,
uncertainty rising because it thinks, after
all, it has always been here before.

Vitus looked away. 'What am I?' No reply, not even silence, so, when he looked again, he saw, beyond the threshold

another day, arms outstretched, lies across
the cove, a cove not yet golden, not yet
formed. 'This is a dream, I remember.' The
voice stumbles through the cove, muttering
until the echoes wash over the headland,
over the shore. Nothing else moves: it
has been dry here for as long as the land
remembers, a time remembered as being
a very long time, and so: a very long
time dry, the land recalls. And that land,
which resembles nothing so much as Vitus's
head, probes the dry shingle (say shingle),
looking for ... a word (say — no, the
word slips away, slips away, slips) from
memory, now not quite half-remembered.
'Something sapphirine, almost like golden,
but unlike dry. Say —' but the word is
lost, evaporated like a dream, in echoes
that stumble over each other in the caves
and sulci filling this vitusland now
filling with echoes of thought that sound
something like: You never see yourself in
dreams.

Vitus refused to cross the threshold. One step he felt he could not take, stubbornness holding him fast. Fear. Panic, too, in spite of how easily acceptance came before. All enough to hold him fast. And yet all dim, attenuated by distance as if caught in echo. Or afterthought. 'Why am I?'

I am having this recurring dream. I am

315

this recurring dream. I am   this   dream.

The sea welled over the threshold, touching, withdrawing, touching Vitus's feet, tentatively inviting

another new day, perhaps the same
one, the sky almost golden, and the
cove, newformed, outstretched as the
wind explores, moving sand, stirring
kelp, clouds stumbling over unfamiliar
words: I've been here before ... *Clouds*
stumbling to cover a vitus which, moments
earlier, had doubtless been golden. Wind,
whispering from the cavemouth, drifts
across shingle dry like salt and stretching
to the vitusline so flat, so true it forms
a margin, call it a threshold, between
vitusland and all that should lie beyond
the _____ *But that is still: still gone;*
still on the tongue; still unshapable by the
wind which finds itself saying: You never
see yourself in dreams, *taking itself by*
surprise as it does so, as it catches sight of
itself in the ripples across the surface of a
rockpool, ripples gently brimming across
the salty vitus — no, that's not the right
word. But it will do, thinks the wind as
it, or someone, murmurs: I dreamt, or
I am dreaming. *Except, even the wind*
hears that last word as dreamt.

You are. Vitus closed his eyes, clutching the door-frame, water rising, urging him forward. 'You are?' Vitus let go at last. A splash, like a voice, followed. A voice murmuring

Vɪᴛᴜs.

In the water, Vitus. Carried Vitus, by water all around. Pressing Vitus, absorbing all his thoughts, concentrated waters absorbing Vitus completely. Borne along, yet Vitus walks, step by turning, passing across junctions: hallways of pressure, gradients making deadends or doublebacks, longruns and endlesspassages, each terminating even so, or branching elsewise, always more though, as Vitus, running, is carried along, pressure building, walls closer together, passing fewer turns, fewer still and with more speed, so much speed, until Vitus, propelled, is running headlong, balance outofreach, falling, running headlong, stumbling, balance gone, running, stumblerunning — to fall through the archway.

Temple grounds: head behind, precincts giving way to stairs, curving, winding stairs, leading to —

Sea. Waves lapping. House beyond: an island. Islandhouse surrounded. Inundatedhouse, sinking. Vitus feels the pull of the waves, gravity drawing down, easing back, rocking him from foot-to-foot, making it hard not to bob, turn, bob&turn —

Innertemple rises still over precincts. Not a head, though. A wave. Not waving, but falling, caughtinfall. Wave curling down, in on itself to emerge again, to fall again only to re-emerge: always the same, always different. Collapsingwave turning in and flowing —

Slipping back to leave Vitus alone on a single rock, alonerock, barren but for Vitus.

And the standpipe.

Vitus bends, steps back, hands outstretched. Vitus-grip firmer this time, bibcock making not one sound. But turning just the same. Under Vitushands as, under Vitus, water starts to rise.

The sea lost belief. In dream. Although, indream, belief comes easily. It turns again, too restless to settle, thoughts of sky, horizon, shore between feeling incomplete. Too much so, for the sea to believe while awake. If the sea was ever awake. And, in thinking that, the sea slips deeper into its bed, reaching out for dream.

The boy in the sailor suit can do nothing to stop his eyes drooping.

Day after day, light falls on the pages of notes spread across the table under the window. Little by little, the writing fades from each sheet. The note on the face-down postcard turns wan, growing so faint it becomes illegible, much as Khnopff's *The Abandoned Town* becomes so ghostly, the ripped-out page eventually appears almost blank. Until, in fact, every single upturned face becomes an empty, ice-white. And then —

Jellicoe lights the pipe with careful ceremony. Draws the first mouthful of smoke before handing it on to his left.

— Smoke, he instructs gently, it will make everything ordered again.

Penelope glances across the circle at her husband, his face ashen no matter how brightly the fire paints it. Ulysses' eyes stare without focus. Penelope draws the smoke from the pipe down deep, holding it as Jellicoe instructs. Hands it on clockwise.

Mrs Blenkinsoe does not hesitate. Simply looks at Jellicoe as she swallows the pungent smoke already mixing with the scent of pine from the fire, shadows becoming as fragrant as they are dense.

The pipe travels around the circle. Jane, legs tucked beneath her, tucked beneath her long skirts, coughs but swallows the smoke without complaint. Franklin smokes, before holding the pipe until Ulysses at last senses its presence, breathes through his mouth. Mikkelborg, Palle to his friends around the circle, smiles as pipesmoke tumbles from his nostrils, unbending even before there is time for it to have taken effect, peeling back and away latex mask to reveal the face beneath, before leaning forward on his crossed legs to drop his old 'features' in the fire. 'Kati' Larsen is not there, of course, June wiping a tear at this thought as she draws on the pipe.

Only Vitus does not smoke.

— You have to, urges John.

June takes Vitus's hand, squeezing: Please.

— I ... can't. Vitus tries to hand the pipe back to Jellicoe. Jellicoe sits, hands resting on his crossed ankles.

— This is the only way, Captain. Jellicoe, the man they know even now as 'Jellicoe', nods around the circle at the faces caught in the shifting firelight, faces with large black circles in the centre of their eyes, pupils dilated the better to see what the pipe is offering. The only way for us all, Jellicoe continues, his voice so soft Vitus loses some of the words in the crackle of burning wood, is to go forward, Captain. You not least.

— But this ... Vitus looks at the pipe, the smoke trailing from its bowl ... how real is it?

— How real is anything? Mrs Blenkinsoe clasps Jane's hand, Penelope's hand, as she speaks.

— Only what is in our heads and, and perhaps what is there again tomorrow.

He appears not to have moved, but it was Ulysses who spoke.

— Real is what we agree. Mikkelborg picks up the last remains of the mask by way of demonstration.

— What we can describe, adds June.

— Or imagine, Captain, Franklin nods, urging Vitus to join them.

Vitus hesitates. It is really too late. The pipe burns steadily and as the others have spoken, so Vitus could not avoid breathing in a little smoke. He can feel it working. Feel the shadows around the circle. Still, he hesitates.

— It won't be real, he mumbles, aware of the truth as he states this.

— It's as real as you need it to be, Mikkelborg says, leaning across June to hold out the coin.

Vitus is as reluctant to accept the coin as he was to take the pipe. It's yours.

— Not necessarily.

— Captain. Jellicoe's voice might be the rustling of the flames. Captain, you have known all along where this would lead. How it will end.

Vitus looks around the circle. Even poor ruined Ulysses seems certain of what Jellicoe has just said. But Vitus did not know. Not always. But now he does know how this will end.

Vitus puts the pipe to his lips.

Three boats leaving the harbour: *Eurydice, Hecate* and *Ariadne*. Three boats are already at sea: *Formidable, Resilient* and *Wayfarer*. Three boats may yet be built: their names are undecided; it does not matter: six ships have their crew; each flotilla, its captain — and their names you know.

Franklin turns away from the window. Ulysses turns towards the loom. Franklin sits. Ulysses picks up the threads. Franklin begins to weave. Ulysses begins to weave.

Mrs Blenkinsoe and 'Admiral' Jellicoe give the boy an atlas. Many, in fact most, of its pages are white: lands unknown, seas uncharted: terrains unconceived. When the light falls right, just right, on one particular page, the boy tells himself he can make out the shape of coastline, a headland rising up to become a line of hills. In other light, at other times, the boy is sure there is nothing there.

Mikkel-who?

June has disappeared. There will be no more sightings.

And Vitus

Vitus floats, on the surface, on the margin between so many things. As Vitus faces upwards, so the sky looks down, as unseeing as Vitus, in truth, who can be seen, afloat, but does not see as unconsciousness washes over him, closing eyes but leaving breath to rise, fall, as Vitus rises, falls on the brimming sea. Each new wave lifts him, the broken spar gripped under one arm, that grip loosening with each swell, all other wreckage gone long-since, leaving Vitus alone on the surface. Alone except for the remains of the map lying on the water, in his other hand. Unfurled, the map rises, falls, rises with Vitus, waves touching its face quite gently, quite unlike the fervour that gripped Vitus when he drew it, sculpting shoreline and cove, sandbar and rock, bay, and headlined turned out towards the sea, profile fitting the contours of the waves exactly. And now very nearly gone. Pigment and line have run into the water. The map, vitusdrawn, has reverted to its original state: whitefaced and practically unmarked. Only sea remains: land gone, ships likewise; to leave Vitus: head back, lips parted, and eyes closed. Still. Floating, but still. Grip slackening: the next wave pulling the spar away from him. One-after-the-next — gently, so gently — slips free the map, carrying it away as Vitus is carried by the sea. Carried and, gently, so gently, folded beneath its surface.

The
w   a   l   l   '   s
circumference falls away on
either side of me, returning to me to
begin again. Circular, of course, although
it's taken a long while for me to see. Today, the
wall is chest-high, broad top flat enough to stand
and walk on. If I step forwards, off the outside edge,
it shifts, instantly, appearing underfoot as if it has always
been there. I can see a lot from up here.

The sea has smoothed over now. I still catch sight of him, amongst the images flashing beneath the waves. They scared me when I first saw them: climbing onto the wall, seeing them gleam beneath the waves. Too sharp and perfect to be ghosts; too faint and attenuated to be solid. But real. As real as the wall. Me.

I dreamt of her later. At least, I saw her. In memory or ... something. Perhaps not 'dream', although I dream.

There are things I cannot understand. I think someone once said you can never understand something you are a part of, can't gain enough perspective. I stand on the wall, turn my back to the outside and, looking in, see myself looking out.

We measure a circle, starting anywhere.

The sea is asleep at last. I can watch its dreams. If I reach out, I can —

She won't come back. I don't understand that. Or can't: so much lucidity, no more. Perhaps she started it. This.

There are no endings. Only beginnings.

The sea is growing restive. The dreams ... I only have to — not 'reach out', not 'reach in'. I can't say. There aren't the words: all the old words are wrong.

And you, of course. You're a part, will never be able to prove otherwise. Never be able to show definitely that I am not talking to myself, not imagining you so I no longer have to feel alone.

And, looking in, I have you looking out.

Should I even be using the word 'dream' to describe this — sea, Vitus, wall ... me? The dream dreams, dreaming dreamers into being so that they might dream of the dream dreaming the dreamers ... The recursion still makes me feel trapped.

Trapped in myself ...
>   You — ha — *I* understand why I'm alone. Alone in myself.
You never see —

>   But I know that already,
>   don't I?

>   climbing
>   from the wall, walking
>   back through the town, each
>   building fading as it is passed,
as it is no longer in view, labels losing grip, slipping from empty
air to turn white, whiteturning paper fluttering away, names no
longer needed as notional brick and stone vanish, paper likewise
bleeding into the air. All unnoticed: attention fixed ahead,
preoccupied attention glossing over windows finding nothing
to reflect, the mirrors in splitopen rooms firmfaced towards
walls that will inevitably dwindle now that the dream has moved
on. The sign appears. Pointing. Pointing anywhere — it's true
what they say about circles — mutely pointing anywhere. Not
one word: a blank, like the puddles around its base. Puddles
that reflect sky; a cloud glimpsed, forgotten almost at once; the
sun, coinlike overhead, slipping off the surface of a puddle as
the puddle falls into shadow, finds itself reflecting on a shape
capturelost from its surface almost before there is chance to
perceive it. Likewise, before the dream moves on, there is
pause, backstep, and gazelock on the puddle, the pool next to
it. Searching both for a hint of something other than clouds,
sky golden in sunshine. Searchingboth and finding nothing
except what is expected to be there: sky, clouds, gleam of sun
and no other reflections. Then, even that is gone because
here is the cove opening its arms, headland undersky, and
sea falling back to riseagain, murmuring as it moves
forth&back, images forming under dreamsgaze,
forming underwave. Lucid shapes in water struck
clear&blue. Dreams newforming. Under the
gaze from the shore. Goldenfound
as everything begins again.
Anew.

EACH NEW dream washes over the sea, coming in and drawing out, bearing in again. Bearing dreams of hands outstretched. A face, golden, framed against the headland framing a head new to this shore. Awash, the headland opens its arms to accept the newcomer, each hand stretched out. The shore murmurs. Surprise borne out, the sea looks over the shore murmuring. Murmuring to itself or to the sea, it is hard to be sure, but it murmurs as he climbs, new and almost golden as the sunlight touches him with outstretched hands. A wash of light bearing out and drawing in. Awash with this new dream climbing out of the sea and up the shore. Foam clings to him. Falls away. Spindrift drawn on the breeze catches around him. Holding anyway, still part of the sea for now. Formerly remote but drawn in and coming out of its shell, the land holds its hands to accept this dream from the sea, this being dreamed as he wades through the wash and bearing for high ground. Turning as stones clack underfoot: clack-click. Next step: click-clack. On, over shingle as waves overturn a new sight, a sight new to this place golden and out-spread. The sea, outstretched, flows in. Touching, turning, in and out or back and forth. Foam clinging, falling away as he bears for higher ground. Spindrift accommodating sea into sky, land underfoot. Stumbling. Land under sky. Undertow falling away as the being stops and turns. Turns and looks and draws in breath dreamt into being by the sea lying outstretched. Dreaming. Washed hand over hand, overturned or underfoot. Lying closer. The shore bears witness as he stumbles, rising up. Land rising up or lying outstretched undersun. And before the sea wakes he can stand, newfound, murmuring in a voice that's neither land nor sky. An undertone, goldenfound, riding over stones and shore, turning over and holding forth on his arrival being dreamt at this very moment. Vitus being dreamed into being by the sea. A sea whose dreams bear Vitus, his hands held out for balance, into view, as though he might always have been here. Always bearing dreams. But before the sea finds him, Vitus Bering does not dream. And, before dreamt, Vitus Bering does not exist.

AFTERWORD

A LOT of influences and random events go into making any book, I guess. The path leading to this particular novel seems very happenstance. However, *Vitus Dreams* could never have existed without the influence of a number key people.

First and foremost, *Vitus* owes a massive debt to the Austrian writer, Konrad Bayer. I remember reading his novel, *the sixth sense*, for the first time and not believing what I was reading. The audacity and beauty of the wordplay was immediately inspiring and led to my own experiments featuring a pair of characters named Boris and Nina.

Lovestruck with Bayer's prose, I searched for more of his work. Bayer's *the head of vitus bering* not only introduced me to the historical figure after whom the Bering Strait and the Bering Sea are named, but also to an extreme form of textual collage I'd not encountered before. (It's also, like *the sixth sense*, a very funny book.) The first concrete result, however, was the following couple of sentences, scribbled in a notebook:

> Vitus Bering dreamed of the sea before he found it.
> Before he dreamed of it, it did not exist.

The next step towards *Vitus Dreams* came a couple of years later, when I read Bridget Penney's collage novel, *Index*. Actually, the influenced didn't form then but later, when I re-read the novel … and finally understood something of what it was about.

It was from Penney that the idea of shifting viewpoint and register lodged itself in my head. And it was from *Index* that I learned something of John and Jane Franklin, and the expedition to the Northwest Passage I had known of before only through the folksong, 'John Franklin'.

(Incidentally, Penney also spoonerises the names of Franklin's ships, something I'd forgotten only to rediscovered during the early days of working on *Vitus* and cheerfully appropriated into the text in homage to Penney's book, and because I just spike loonerisms.)

Without these two writers I would never have been primed when, one May morning (honest — this isn't another folksong reference), I was searching for material to use for an exercise in Hazel Smith's manual on innovative writing technique, *The Writing Experiment*. The result of that writing session was the opening paragraph of this book.

Others have helped and encouraged along the way. My brother, Iain, has been hugely supportive throughout, not only providing an invaluable sounding-board but also being so inspired by the work that he wrote a suite of music to accompany Vitus's journey. My late mother, Veronica, was also very enthusiastic about my early efforts with this mad, endless and seemingly formless flow of words I had unleashed. Despite plenty of reasons not to, I made a point of working on *Vitus* in the hospital room as I kept vigil while my mother lay in a coma, dying.

After her death, *Vitus* was shelved for four or five months while I worked on more 'serious, commercial projects'. Luckily, I showed an extract to Jan Fortune, at a Cinnamon Press writing week at Tyn-y-coed, near Conwy. Jan's enthusiasm and praise then, and later, encouraged me to return to *Vitus*, develop it and, finally, find some of that form that had been missing before. Jan's belief in this novel, and my writing in general, has never been short of amazing.

I owe (in best Hollywood tradition) tremendous thanks to Jan, Iain, and my mum. Likewise, a hearty nod is owed to my father, David, for past and continued support and love; Alexa Radcliffe-Hart for invaluable encouragement and the sheer delight of her friendship; to Steve Casey, who always reminds me to write what I want, not what I feel I ought; and Mark Williams for allowing me to see what I have here.

Adam Craig
January, 2015